Also By Cathryn Grant

Cathryn Grant

THE WOMAN IN THE DARK

An Alexandra Mallory Novel

D2C
D2C Perspectives

Visit Cathryn online at CathrynGrant.com

Cover design by Lydia Mullins Copyright © 2017

ISBN: 978-1-943142-40-8

1

I woke in utter darkness. Wide awake, unsure what had startled me out of a deep, dreamless sleep.

Despite the confidence that my sleep had been dreamless, I searched my mind for scraps of a dream that I'd forgotten after all. Was something swimming through my subconscious, startling me awake? Finding nothing, I felt around on the nightstand for my phone. Three-twenty-six. The rhythm of my pulse and the activity in my nervous system seemed to believe it was ten o'clock in the morning.

After trying for quite a while to ease myself back to sleep, I got up and put on a long, loose T-shirt. I dug around in my bag for my cigarettes and lighter, filled a glass with a few inches of water, and went out onto the balcony. The air was deadly still. The palm fronds that tapped in the softest breeze were silent. It was too early even for the kookaburras and their deep-throated hooting that sounded as if they were laughing at the human race.

Those birds seem prehistoric to me. Their laughter is almost human. At the same time, there's a predatory undertone. They're meat-eaters and scavengers, so possibly they're constantly eyeing us as an emergency food supply. Still, I love the sound of their calls for that very human quality mixed with something out of the rain forest. They remind me the earth is alive with so many creatures, one person can't possibly know and name every species and breed.

I put the glass on the ground and lit a cigarette. I inhaled and blew out a pencil-thin stream of smoke. The smoke hung in the air a few feet beyond the edge of the balcony. It dissolved slowly, overpowered by the greater force of oxygen, I suppose.

My body remained hyper-alert, yet my mind drifted with a pleasant emptiness, giving itself over to the soft comfort of the motionless air on my skin.

The darkness was complete. None of the surrounding houses had lights on. The moon was headed toward the horizon, an eighth moon that was crisp in the cloudless sky, but not giving off much light. Stars glittered and I tried to make out which one was Jupiter, which was Saturn. After a few minutes, I realized those planets weren't visible at this hour of the morning. In early June, they appeared before midnight. Within a few hours of their appearance, the part of the earth where I sat began turning away from them as it faced toward daylight.

I couldn't figure out why I was so wide awake. I rarely wake at night and this didn't feel like night at all.

Maybe it was the black bottom swimming pool sitting below my balcony, its dark water always threatening. It was silent now, not even a whisper of water lapping against tile, and yet I felt it there, disturbing my peace of mind. Always. I tried to think back over my time in Australia. Had my sleep been disturbed in some way every night, feeling that pool of water in my bones, in the spider sense that crawls through my nerve endings and prickles my skin? That sense all of us have that makes us know there's a threat whispering behind us? The voice of death deep inside our ears, always reminding us it will win in the end? It's made worse in the dark.

I dropped my cigarette into the glass of water and went back inside. I picked up the small dish with a six-inch white pillar candle, now burned down to four inches, and carried it outside. I set it on the table and touched the wick with my lighter. The flame stood straight and unwavering. I stood by the railing and lit another cigarette, wondering whether sleep was gone for the rest of the night.

Shifting my body to the left, I took another drag.

With a flap of wings but no sound, a large bird, unidentifiable in the darkness, swooped down into the yard, flew low over the swimming pool, and rose sharply. I startled at its sudden appearance, closing my eyes for a moment. I opened them and inhaled more smoke.

Its passage had activated the motion sensor lights surrounding the pool and garden.

I leaned forward. Something was floating in the pool. Not something, someone. A woman. It was a woman floating there. Her skin was milky white and her legs and arms drifted just below the surface of the water like something malleable, no bones or muscles giving them mobility, only the water holding them in place.

In the darkness, against the black plaster of the swimming pool, I couldn't make out her head. Was her hair short and black, indistinguishable in the water, or was her head missing? A chill ran through me.

2

A moment before I saw the woman's body floating in the pool, I briefly considered whether it was my agenda for the day that had woken me much too early. Later that day, Tess was flying to San Francisco. Superficially to get her cockatoo ready for his trip to Australia, which is quite funny when you think about readying a native Australian bird for a trip to Australia. But like me, she had an agenda. Her trip home would give her a chance to ask for a face-to-face meeting with Detective Gorman, grilling him further on the circumstances of her ex-lover's death.

I'd never seen a woman so enthralled with her ex, when the breakup was her choice, rather than one thrust upon her, driving her to despair. Her fixation on proving Steve hadn't died of an accidental overdose made no sense. But there it was, staring me in the face every single day since I'd arrived in Australia. Part of the reason for accepting her job offer was so I could distract her and lead her to the belief that his death was an accident, covering up my involvement without a backward look. It hadn't worked. The more I tried to re-direct her thoughts, the more tenaciously she returned to her suspicions.

She was convinced the detective would be more forthcoming if he met her in person. She was convinced she'd be able to persuade him to see that something wasn't right, that he would eagerly re-open the case and begin the hunt for a person or persons who had forced heroin into Steve's body to the point where he'd stopped breathing.

While she was enduring her thirteen-hour flight, I would be on the phone, making contact with the detective before she had a chance to meet with him. Since I couldn't turn her mind in the direction I wanted, I'd have to do some minor manipulation of his. I didn't think it would be difficult.

His sharp tone when I'd questioned him about the overdose suggested he didn't have a lot of patience for wild theories. Every piece of evidence pointed to careless misuse of drugs. I would tell him in a soft, caring tone that Tess was fragile. I had all the words worked out in my head already —

She loved him. It's that simple. She kept those feelings to herself because they worked together, but she did love him, and she's absolutely devastated. Hiding their relationship from their peers caused the loss to hit her even harder. She's looking for something that makes sense in her shattered world. Please be gentle with her.

I was confident the soft touch would lead him easily into taking me at my word. I wouldn't seem interfering, nervous, or overly interested. I was a caring friend, worried about Tess's fragile condition. And the word fragile was perfect. It implied slightly off balance, her mind on the verge of cracking, her theories and concerns nothing but fantasy.

3

Bluebeard and his decapitated wives was my first thought as I observed the body in the swimming pool. I squinted at the water to see if there was blood swirling around, liquid thicker than the water, suggesting something so brutal as decapitation. The body turned slightly and one of the garden lights touched the upper portion and I saw a wisp of dark hair across a cheek.

I gasped as my mind raced to Tess. But it was only the confused flow of thoughts trying to process something so horrid. The woman's body, the red lace underpants, nothing else, was not the shape of Tess. I dropped my cigarette in the glass of water and went inside. I pulled on a pair of leggings and picked up the key to my room. I went out, locked the door, and stood for a moment in the hallway.

Because the house belonged to Sean, it was logical to wake him and tell him what I'd seen. But Sean would not take this well. He was very concerned about karma. He was emotional about maintaining the aura of perfection for the incubator he'd created for his optimistic start-up inside his ultra modern luxury home. He was already beside himself over the negative energy resulting from two murders and a suicide in the neighborhood. I could imagine how he'd react to a corpse in his own swimming pool. That pool symbolized what he wanted for our little four-person company and our world-changing app — the pool was a place for camaraderie and play.

I walked to Gavin's door and knocked softly. I needed his cool, logical presence first. Maybe she wasn't really dead. Of course I knew that wasn't true, but it's good to verify what you see from a distance under a dark sky.

I knocked again. The sound of rough murmuring came from inside, but the words were shaped into the nonsense of a dream. I gave one short rap, much harder this time. The mattress and bed frame creaked, followed by the thud of feet on the floor.

A moment later, the door opened. Gavin smiled at me with a twist of uncertainty and hope.

I slipped past him into his room. He put his arm around my waist. I pulled back and spoke in a low voice. "There's something in the pool. A body. Can you come take a look?"

He frowned. I walked to the armchair and picked up a pair of jeans. I held them out to him.

He followed me out of his room and down the stairs. We went through the billiards room out to the pool. The garden lights had gone out, but the minute we stepped away from the covered patio, they flicked on. He walked to the edge of the pool and stared down at the body. It floated lazily, coming close to the steps leading into the shallow end of the pool.

"I wonder who she is." He didn't turn to look at me, staring hard at her skin, blindingly white up close.

"I thought you might know."

"She doesn't seem familiar" he said. "We'd have to turn her over."

"I don't think we should."

"No, probably not." He continued staring into the water.

He shifted his feet slightly and for a moment I thought he might reach his leg out over the edge and nudge her with his toe, trying to turn her onto her back despite our agreement it wasn't a good idea.

"We should call the police," he said.

"After we tell Sean."

"Yes. Sean." He knelt down as if it would bring him closer to her side, give him a better view, that he would somehow be able to observe her face.

"Do you want to wake him up?" I said.

He stood and wiped his hands on his jeans, removing grit from the concrete, possibly, or the touch of death from his thoughts. "And Tess."

"Why don't we let her sleep a bit?" I said. "Let Sean digest it first."

He shoved his hands in his pockets. "I'll get Sean and we can phone it in." He coughed. "He won't like this."

I shook my head.

He went into the house and I turned toward the patio. A lounge chair was pulled up near the shallow end of the pool, out of place from the others. I settled down on it and watched her body drifting in the water, shifting slightly every few seconds, moved by an unseen current.

4

It seemed as if barely half a minute passed before Sean flung open one of the great room sliding glass door panels. He crossed the patio, stopping a few feet from the edge of the pool. He didn't seem to notice me sitting there. I swung my legs over the side of the lounge chair. As I turned, I saw a bottle sitting on the ground beside the back legs.

"This is terrible!" Sean pressed his hands against the sides of his head, his elbows extended. "How could this happen?"

Gavin moved over beside him.

I picked up the bottle and held it closer to the light. It was Macallan's scotch. A few inches of shimmering gold liquid sloshed inside. I put it down, realizing my mistake in touching it. Now, I'd be required to give fingerprints. I'd managed my whole life not to give fingerprints to anyone. I didn't want them lingering in some database where I had no control over them, where they'd follow me forever. Of course, it was unlikely that countries shared fingerprints, it would only be a problem as long as I remained in Australia. I took a deep breath, putting the thought to the side.

I set the bottle on the ground, near the back of the chair, farther out of sight. Maybe I'd get a chance to wipe it clean before the police arrived. Although being in a house where a dead body was discovered might require me to give fingerprints anyway. Wiping it clean would raise more questions. I stood and walked to where they stood. They stared into the water as if they expected her to begin swimming, and they could heave sighs of relief and return to their beds, hoping for one more hour of sleep.

I moved around to Sean's opposite side. He glanced at me, his face empty of recognition, then back at the water.

"I don't understand. I don't…" he said.

"We should call the police," Gavin said.

Sean nodded.

"Did you bring your mobile?" Gavin said.

"No."

Gavin pulled his phone out of his pocket.

"Not yet," Sean said.

"Why? We need her out of there, right?"

"How did she get there? Maybe there's a serial killer. John…and now her."

"I doubt that," I said.

"We don't have any information, so it's possible. If there is, the police will take over the house. We can't have that. Why did she have to end up in my pool?"

"It could be an accident," I said.

He turned toward me. He folded his arms. "What kind of accident?" He swept his arm out to the side. "She just tripped and fell in the water and drowned? I don't think so."

We stood in silence for a few minutes.

"This can't be happening," Sean said. "It can't."

"Let's just call and get it over with," I said. "They'll take her away and everything will be fine."

"Not if she was murdered."

"I really don't think…" I said.

"You can't possibly know."

"Maybe she wanted to drown herself," I said.

"How would she do that?"

"Maybe she jumped into the deep end," I said. "Maybe she couldn't swim."

"That's not as common as you might think." Sean scowled, still not making eye contact. "Just because you can't swim…it's very unusual. I think it's a serial murder. First, John, now her."

"You should let the police decide," Gavin said.

"If they want to take over the house…I can't have that."

"There's nothing we can do," I said. "I'll go tell Tess. She should know, before they get here."

Gavin nodded.

Sean grabbed his head again, his fingers disappearing among the long tangled curls. "This is so, so terrible. This is not what we need. How can this be happening?"

He wasn't building my confidence in his leadership ability. I got that he didn't want our start-up interfered with by a murder investigation, but he didn't even know that's what it was. It seemed more likely it was an accident, or suicide. There was no blood, which was made more clear as the sky was growing light. It made no sense that two people would have come into his yard, one to murder a woman and dump her in his pool. Unless Sean had violent friends he hadn't mentioned.

Once again it struck me how little we knew about each other. We were a foursome of strangers.

5

Sean stood on the front patio waiting for the police. He felt he should have placed the call himself instead of yielding that responsibility to Gavin. Taking charge of this, being the primary contact for whatever investigation ensued should be his role, not Gavin's. He hadn't heard whatever the police said to Gavin, and now he couldn't establish a foothold of authority up front, making sure he was aware of all their questions. He would not have his home turned into an office for a criminal investigation.

Alex had seemed quite certain there was nothing criminal about it, but she was sticking her head in the ground. Wishful thinking. John had turned up murdered and there were still cops popping around to the house next door nearly two weeks after the event. Yellow tape still hung like party streamers across John's front door. Alex liked to think she knew everything. She was quite certain in the way she spoke, but she didn't know about this.

The warble of a siren penetrated his ears.

Less than a minute later, a sedan and a white van rounded the corner. The sedan pulled into his driveway. He didn't like that, making themselves at home. He sighed and pushed his hair away from his face. He should have cleaned up a bit instead of standing out here waiting, but it was a choice between looking decent and making sure he took charge.

A man and woman got out of either side of the sedan. They walked along the fence that surrounded his front yard, out to the sidewalk, and turned onto the walkway leading to where he stood. They stopped several yards away from him. Both wore black pants, white shirts, and black jackets.

The female constable spoke. "Sean Farmer?"

"Yes."

She held open her badge. "I'm Detective Constable Martin and this is Detective Constable Bender."

Sean walked toward them and extended his hand. She shook it firmly and briefly. Bender did the same.

"You called about a woman's body in your swimming pool?"

A faint smile brushed across his lips, knowing he would be viewed as the main point of contact after all. He tried to adjust his lips back to something more solemn. Detective Martin seemed to note the smile and raised her eyebrows very slightly. He swallowed the smile quickly but it was too late.

"Don't worry about it," she said. "It happens."

"That's a rather casual approach," he said. "Maybe you find dead women in swimming pools regularly, but it's a first for me."

"I meant your inappropriate smile. It's inadvertent. Nerves. Speaking to the police."

He was not a nervous guy and he didn't like her attitude. She was treating him as if he were an anxious child. She knew nothing about him. What right did she have to comment on his facial expression, *inadvertent* as it was? He glanced at Bender, who returned a smirk of his own. In the space of a minute and a half, he had a read on both of them — pompous female and junior male partner laughing at the stick up her bum. He was tempted to smile again. Thankfully this time, he held it inside.

"Will you show us in?"

"Through the side gate is best," he said.

She shrugged. They followed him down the path that meandered along the front of the house, passing several feet in front of the offices, looping out to circle around a cluster of shrubs filled with white flowers, and then straight back to the side gate. He unlatched the gate, pushed it open, and stepped to the side for the detectives to go ahead of him.

"Any reason you didn't take us through the house?" Detective Martin said.

"We don't know who she is, so I'm assuming...I thought you'd take her body away and that would be the end of it. No need to go inside."

"We'll decide that," Martin said.

Sean swallowed. He pressed his shoulders and back against the gate, making sure there was adequate room for them to pass by.

He followed them around the side of the house to the edge of the pool. Bender turned to him. "Prop open the gate, will you? So the ME can get back here without a problem."

Sean nodded. He didn't want to miss the conversation. He hesitated, watching them study the swimming pool, taking in the position of the body.

"Now, please," Martin said.

He jogged to the side of the house, picked up a rock from the strip along the fence and pushed it against the gate to hold it in place. He hurried back to the pool. Neither detective had moved. It wasn't clear whether they'd been talking. Martin was tapping a stylus on her electronic notepad.

A moment later, another young woman appeared carrying a large camera. She took off the lens cap, stuffed it in her pocket, and began taking photographs of everything — the lounge chair, the silent waterfall, the edges of the pool. Slowly she moved closer to the spot where the woman's body floated near the center of the shallow end. The camera clicked loudly in the silence.

It was getting light and the birds were starting their chatter, but none of the officials let out a peep, not even a clearing of their throats. They were obviously intent on keeping all thoughts to themselves.

A few cops and workers arrived and then he was pushed to the far corner of the patio. He didn't turn to look, but he could feel Gav and Alex just inside the great room doors, watching as silently as the police were working.

He'd thought someone might get into the water to bring her body to the side, but they used ropes to pull her close to the edge, then two men rolled her up over the lip and onto a sheet of plastic spread across the pavement. Her flesh hitting the concrete landed with an awful smack.

The bad energy that was going to flow from this situation stirred up a rage that he could barely control. He had no idea where to direct it. Some of it seemed to be pouring out onto Detective Martin, some brushing past Gavin and Alex, although he couldn't understand why.

Tess was upstairs, finishing her packing. He was due to drive her to the airport in a few hours. If the police were still lingering at that time, he would ask her to call a taxi. He couldn't possibly leave while this was going on.

As if to argue with him, insisting there were things he couldn't avoid, his stomach rumbled, suddenly waking up along with the rest of his body. He hadn't had a coffee or even a few bites of an apple.

They'd covered the woman's body quickly, before he could really get a look, but what he'd seen would stay with him for a while. Her breasts had looked like poorly shaped pancakes, seeming to slide over her ribs as she lay splayed on the ground, her feet flopped to the side. Even her head collapsed, falling to the left, as if she were looking away from him.

He'd never seen a dead person before. Thirty-five years old and he'd never encountered death face-to-face. He'd been to memorial services, and buried his fair share of pets, weeping over their empty bodies. But this was something very different.

The detectives murmured to each other, still careful of being overheard.

After her body was encased in a heavy plastic thing that looked a lot like a garment bag and wheeled away on a cart, the detectives approached him. "How many people live here with you?" Detective Martin said.

"Three others."

"We'll need to talk to all of you. One at a time."

Sean glanced toward the pool. One of the men who had helped remove her body from the pool was kneeling beside the lounge chair holding what looked like a scotch bottle. As Sean watched, the man held the bottle up slightly then deposited it into a large plastic bag.

"One of my housemates is leaving for America today."

"Then let's get this moving," Martin said. "Where can we speak privately?"

"I guess one of the offices."

She smiled at him. "Lead the way. First, we'll talk to the person who found the body."

"That would be Alex."

"And his last name?" Martin said.

"She. Short for Alexandra...last name Mallory."

It gave him a sick feeling to think of Alex talking to the police without him present.

6

The female detective was waiting for me in the office I shared with Tess. She sat at the small conference table, her arms folded across her perfectly ironed white shirt. It looked like a heavy cotton and despite the coolish weather, it was still muggy, which usually turns cotton into a dishrag. Hers was crisp, as if by a force of her will to keep it looking professional and under control. She had fine blonde hair with bangs across her forehead, wispy and a little too short so that her eyebrows, darker than her hair, jumped out from her face. Both feet were flat on the floor as if she was prepared to bolt. More likely, I guessed that she considered crossed legs an act of friendliness, or maybe even weakness — her pose interpreted as trying too hard to project a mood of calmness.

"This will be quick, I think." She gestured toward the chair nearest the door.

I sat down.

"Your name is Alexandra Mallory, is that correct?"

"Yes."

"How long are you visiting Australia for?"

"I'm on a work visa."

She nodded. "Employer?"

"Sean."

The eyebrows rose and remained there, searching for the edges of her bangs.

"I work for his start-up. The name of the company is TruthTeller."

A tiny smirk flitted across her face. She removed it quickly.

"What time did you find the body?"

"I woke up early and…"

"What time?"

"I'm not sure. It was dark. I went out on the balcony for a smoke and…"

"You didn't check the time?"

"No."

"That's odd."

"Is it?"

She glared at me but said nothing.

"I was having a smoke. A bird flew across the yard and set off the sensor lights. I saw the body in the pool."

"And then what did you do?"

"I woke Gavin."

"Why not Mr. Farmer?"

I shrugged.

"Wouldn't it be natural to wake your employer? The man who owns the house?"

"No."

Now the brows crouched lower.

"Gavin and I went down there and talked about what to do."

"Why did you need to talk about it? Wasn't the logical action to call the police?"

"We were shocked, I think."

"Shocked?"

"Wouldn't you be? Finding a body in your pool?"

"Do you know her?"

"Not that I'm aware of. I didn't see her face."

The detective nodded.

"Any idea why a woman you don't know was in the backyard at night?"

"No."

"Any idea why…"

"All I know is I woke up and she was floating there. I've never seen her, don't know why she was naked or how she got in there."

"Did you hear a splash?"

"No."

"Any other sounds?"

"No."

"What do you think woke you, while it was *dark*?"

She emphasized dark, as if to chastise me again for failing to check the time. I had checked the time, but I didn't think they needed to know how long it had taken us to finally place the call. It wasn't important. "I don't know. But I didn't hear anything."

"Did you touch the body?"

"No."

"Did you find any clothes, or other belongings?"

She must know if there were other belongings in the yard, but she didn't let on to me. Maybe this was a trick. But then, how would she know if I'd seen anything else? There had been a few minutes after Sean went to wait for the police and Gavin had gone inside to make espresso that I was alone. I managed to wrap the hem of my T-shirt around the bottle and do a quick polish. I'd decided that no prints were better than mine. And I'd only held it near the label. If I was lucky, there might be prints around the neck where I hadn't wiped. I hoped they figured out suicide as fast as possible. Or a drunken splash into the deep end, and there would be no discussion of fingerprints. "It was dark, but I wasn't looking around, so maybe I missed it. If there were clothes, or other belongings, I didn't see them."

She tapped her stylus on the table as if she was getting ready to conduct an orchestra, raising the tiny wand like a baton. Instead, she placed it beside her tablet. "Thank you. We'll be in touch if we have more questions."

"Sure." I stood and walked out of the room, suddenly aware of the condition of my skin, still un-showered. I desperately needed one, right that minute.

I didn't see the point of questioning all of us separately. None of us looked like killers. Although I know better than anyone — looks are deceiving. Still, it was so obviously not a murder. I suppose I know what murders look like more than most, and I'd certainly faked a few accidental deaths. Maybe they were just meticulous detectives. I hoped they weren't too good, the type that strays afield from their assignment, poking into John North's recent death, joining with the detective looking into that, which was considered a murder, no question.

I took the stairs slowly, then stopped halfway up to see who went into the interrogation room next. It was Sean. He didn't look up, didn't seem to notice me standing there. His posture and the scrunched up expression on his face were a weird blend of worry and combativeness. He clearly was not pleased with what had happened. From his perspective, the timing couldn't be worse. He'd just given the team a pep talk to get us functioning better together, brainstorming and playing games and bonding as he'd originally envisioned. Now his plans were disrupted by Tess's trip to the US and a dead woman in his swimming pool.

Standing under the pounding water of the shower, alone with my thoughts for the first time in a few hours, I realized I was not in a good position. If the police became bothered by so many dead people turning up in three houses right beside each other, they might put more effort into tying them together. There was no obvious connection between Lisa's death, her husband's suicide, and their neighbor's murder, but it's the digging that I don't like. It doesn't matter whether the reasons are good ones or not.

I dressed in a navy blue skirt and white T-shirt and navy blue sandals. I put on a white cardigan and admired the results in the mirror. I looked as innocent and pure as they come. I brushed my hair back and wove it into a single braid. The only thing missing was a hair ribbon. I put on a bit of mascara and nude lip gloss to complete the picture.

I went downstairs, hoping to hear whether they'd connected the scotch bottle to the dead woman. It bothered me that Detective Martin hadn't asked me about it.

7

Detective Martin had run through all the checklist questions about Sean's ownership of the home and basic information about his housemates. Now she shifted in her chair and folded her arms, giving prominence to her very nice tits. Sean looked away, focusing on the photographs of New Zealand on the wall behind the couch. After her comment on his inadvertent smile, he didn't need her catching him staring at her tits. Women like her were very tuned in to that sort of thing. They were never flattered by it.

Sean waited for her to speak, but she let the silence linger. Did that mean she was certain this was a murder? If it was a simple accident, wouldn't she ask perfunctory questions and be done with it? If she thought it was murder, she would be scrutinizing all of them. He forced himself to sit still, to avoid the desire to cross his legs or stretch them out in front of him. He had no reason to be nervous. The dead woman had nothing to do with him. The only reason for his anxiety was this intrusion into his home, the dragging out of the sickening details involved in taking care of the body. He wanted it removed, the police gone. He wanted to focus on starting over yet again. Would there be no end to the starting over, some new horror thrown into his path every week?

"Do you know who the deceased woman is?" The detective kept her arms crossed instead of preparing to take notes. Her body language said they were having a simple chat while her tone said something different.

"No."

"You're sure?"

"Yes."

"Have you seen her before?"

"I didn't get a good look."

"Why would a woman be in your pool?"

"I have no idea."

"You don't keep the gate locked?"

"No."

"It's the homeowner's responsibility to safeguard swimming pools. Did you know that? Children might wander in. Aren't you aware that's in the code?"

"Are you saying it's my fault she drowned? That's nuts."

"Is that what I said?"

He crossed his arms, mirroring her posture, not caring if it made him look belligerent. He felt belligerent. He wanted her to ask her questions and leave. This had nothing to do with him or anyone living here. If it was murder, a serial killer as he'd initially suspected, his house was chosen at random. It had absolutely nothing to do with him. More likely, it was some sort of freak accident.

"Do you think someone is trying to send you a message?"

"Are you joking?"

"Nothing about this is a joke."

"Why would someone do that?"

"You tell me."

"No. Of course not. I don't associate with that sort of people."

"What sort?"

"Killers. Criminals. Drug dealers."

"So you believe she was murdered?"

"How would I know? Isn't that your job to figure out?" The room was stuffy with the door closed. He wanted to open the window. He wanted to stretch his legs. He wanted to go back to the previous day and have events unfold differently — a scenario where there wasn't a dead woman in his swimming pool.

"Did you find any of her belongings in the patio or pool area?"

"No."

"There wasn't any clothing?"

"I don't think so," he said.

"The only thing we've located was a nearly empty bottle of alcohol. Did you leave a bottle out there?"

"What kind?"

"Macallan's scotch."

"I have some of that, but I don't normally take it outside."

"We'll need you to check to see whether the bottle is missing. You only have one, I presume?"

He nodded. "Should I check now?"

"When we're finished."

He waited for her to say more. The questions seemed to be made up on the fly. He'd said he didn't know the woman, why were they still sitting here? The detective had no idea what to do, no idea how to figure out why the woman was in his swimming pool. Because the pool belonged to him, Martin's only plan seemed to be asking senseless questions to make it look as though she was doing her job.

She studied him, her lips a thin line, her face slightly

flushed. It was so easy for people with that shade of washed out blonde hair to turn red, as if their skin were thinner than normal, as insubstantial as their hair. He couldn't tell whether she was also feeling the close, warmth of the room or if she was tense because she realized he saw through her flimsy questions. He felt another inappropriate smile rising to the surface as he realized her questions and skin and hair all had the same flimsy quality.

"Anything else?" he said.

"I'll decide when we're finished talking."

"I'm just not sure what you're looking for. No one here knew her."

"Are you sure?"

Well, no. He wasn't sure.

"What else can you tell me about your housemates?" she said.

"What do you mean?"

"Do any of them have relationships that are concerning to you?"

"No. What are you trying to say?"

"There's a reason this woman's body was found on your property — whether she died in your pool, or somewhere else and was deposited here — it's not a coincidence. There's a reason."

"Not everything happens for a reason," he said.

"There are hundreds of homes in this neighborhood. Why yours? That's the question I'm asking myself."

Again, he wanted to laugh — inappropriately. It was the same question he was asking himself.

When Sean emerged from the office, cool air circulating

through the house from the open patio doors washed over him. He walked through the foyer and into the great room, seeking more fresh air. Detective Bender sat at the bar in the kitchen drinking an espresso. None of Sean's housemates, rather his employees, were anywhere in sight. Nice that Bender felt he could make himself at home.

Sean went to the fridge and pulled out a jug of orange juice. He poured a glassful and took a long swallow. He turned toward Bender. "Enjoying the espresso?"

"It's very good."

"Gav made that for you?"

Bender nodded.

"Where is he?"

"Went to shoot some pool," he said, "Until Martin calls him in."

"Can I be straight with you?" Sean said.

Bender nodded.

"This seems like overkill. No one here knew that woman."

"It has to be done."

"I suppose."

"We need to talk to everyone, make sure there's not some seemingly insignificant thread that can point us in the right direction."

Sean took another sip of juice. He walked to the bar and set his glass on the granite. The sound of glass hitting the stone was sharp and loud, like a gunshot, he imagined. Not that he'd ever heard one.

"Don't let her get under your skin," Bender said.

"What?"

"She's a ball buster. Needs to prove herself as a crack

investigator. Stand up to the guys, you know the type."

Sean didn't nod or change his expression. The detective was baiting him, trying to get him to think they were buddies so he would talk freely, give up information they suspected he had about why a woman died in his backyard. Or was dumped there. Whichever it was. It gave him a headache. "How long do you think this will take?"

"No way to know. It takes what it takes."

"I'm trying to run a business here. We can't afford the disruption."

"Dead body turns up in your pool, there's bound to be disruption," Bender said.

Sean sighed.

"Look, it's an obvious suicide to me...Like I said, Martin needs to prove she's something. Women in men's jobs, you know how it is. Trying too hard. Looking for murder under every rock. Don't take it personally if she holds your feet to the fire."

"Maybe it's a serial killer."

Bender laughed. "It's a suicide. The faster someone fesses up to who this woman was trying to punish, getting half naked and killing herself in your pool, the quicker we'll be done."

"How do you know it's suicide?"

"Naked. No obvious signs of violence. Empty bottle of booze. The autopsy will probably turn up pills of some sort. I could be wrong, I've been wrong before. But in this case, I don't think I am."

"Thanks," Sean said.

"Thanks?" Bender tipped the cup and poured the rest of the espresso into his mouth.

"For giving me your opinion. And just to be clear, none of us had anything to do with her. She wasn't getting back at anyone."

Bender nodded, but it was obvious from his smirk that he didn't agree.

8

When I came downstairs, Detective Martin was still in the office, talking to Gavin now. Sean was sprawled on the great room couch and the other detective was sitting at the bar eating nuts out of a plastic package. An empty espresso cup sat on the counter in front of him.

I smiled at the detective. He nodded at me and poured nuts out of the bag into his open mouth. He looked like a fish swallowing pellets, too lazy to chase his own food. He was a skinny guy, only a few inches taller than me. He was cute in a boyish way. I went to the couch and sat beside Sean. He was holding a glass of juice that was almost empty.

I spoke softly so the detective couldn't hear me. "When do you think they'll be done?"

Sean drank the rest of the juice and shrugged his shoulders. He got up and went into the kitchen, put the glass in the dishwasher, and walked out of the room. At the same time, the detective finished his nuts and went to the sink. He pulled open the cabinet door beneath the sink and peered inside. He glanced toward me. "Where's the trash?"

"It's in the drawer to the right. Recycling in the front section," I said.

He pulled the handle and dropped his plastic in the container. He left the room without saying anything more.

I went outside and looked at the pool. The water was still,

not even a strand of hair or a damp mark remained on the pavement to show what had been there a few hours earlier. The scotch bottle was gone and someone had pulled the lounge chair back under the patio roof where it belonged.

I settled in the chair and crossed my ankles. The dead woman had been the last person to occupy the chair. I closed my eyes and tried to think about whether that made it feel any different. Who was she? From what I'd seen, she looked about forty, maybe a little older. Of course they tried to keep us from looking at her, so I only caught a few glimpses, but you can tell a lot in a flash of a second, even with a dead woman.

There had to be a reason she was in Sean's yard. Sean seemed more upset about the location of her body than that she was dead to begin with. As if she were out to sabotage him. Maybe she was.

I wanted to know if the others had been asked the same questions. I wanted to know what Tess was thinking, but she'd closed her door, saying she was almost out of time to pack and would have to discuss it another time.

The cushions of the lounge chair were strong and comforting around me. Sean's lounge chairs were the nicest I'd ever sat in. They were comfortable enough that it would be entirely possible to get a good night's sleep. Was that what the dead woman had done? Fallen asleep, woken and stumbled into the pool? But the lounge chair was near the shallow end, so if she'd simply walked down the steps, she wouldn't have immediately drowned, even if she didn't know how to swim.

I let my mind drift, thinking about wanting a more substantial breakfast than two slices of buttered toast and an espresso. No one wanted to cook a full meal with the detectives lingering in the house, watching everything, reading into every gesture.

Finally, they left. I heard the front door close, more loudly than it needed to. A moment later, Sean and Gavin were in the great room. I got up and went inside.

"I'll make breakfast," Gavin said. He got busy pulling things out of the fridge.

Sean turned to me. "Will you ask Tess to come down so we can strategize on this situation?"

Strategize? I wanted to laugh. We didn't have any control over it. Strategizing was pointless. "She's very focused on her packing," I said.

"How much does she need to pack for a seven-day trip? Tell her we have to talk. We have two hours before we need to leave for the airport."

Tess didn't resist my invitation to breakfast and a strategy session. She followed me down the stairs without talking. Gavin was halfway through frying a pan full of hash browns and another with sausages and tomatoes. Tess suggested mimosas would be nice, a necessary relief after what we'd been through. Sean overruled that idea. "We need to have clear heads."

"I'm not sure what there is to talk about," Tess said.

"First, we'll share the contents of our interviews. To be sure we're on the same page."

"What for?" Tess said. "You're acting as if one of us is guilty of something."

"They seem to want to involve us in this, and I don't like it," Sean said. "We need to stay aligned."

Gavin said nothing. I was sure there were all sorts of

comments he was keeping to himself. Clearly he liked being occupied with cooking, removed from the conversation and the intense glare of Sean's eyes.

We ate in the dining room, talking in circles about nothing. All the questions had been essentially the same. It seemed like the detective had gotten wound up with each interview, asking more with each successive interviewee, fishing around for some sort of connection that eluded her. She couldn't believe none of us knew why the woman was there. She couldn't believe we didn't know who she was. But it wasn't as if they'd asked us to look at her face. How would we know for sure? Had she considered that? It's not as if we recognize neighbors or acquaintances by their underwear.

She'd asked everyone but me about the scotch bottle, and instructed Sean to check whether it had been taken from his liquor supply. It hadn't. When he told her that, she'd looked doubtful, as if he had two of the same brand and was hiding that fact from her.

"But we can't let this distract us from our mission. Keeping to our timeline is critical," Sean said.

We assured him it wouldn't distract us — an empty promise.

"Besides, Detective Martin might just be using us to further her own career," he said.

"What does that mean?" Tess picked up her phone, checking the time.

"Detective Bender said something about it."

We waited.

"He said she wanted to prove herself as a top investigator, prove that a woman could be better than a guy in that role. He said it was clearly a suicide and she wanted to make it into something more. Turn it into a murder investigation."

Tess laughed. "It's not 1970. He was baiting you."

Sean nodded. "I thought of that."

I really could not understand the point of our conversation. He was acting guilty, and maybe the detective picked up on that. Maybe he did know the drowned woman.

"But I don't think he was," Sean said. "I didn't react, and he still went on with similar comments."

"She's just doing her job." I was shocked at the sound of my own voice, defending a cop. But he was painting a woman as a freak for wanting to do what she was paid to do. It was her job to find out who the dead woman was, how she died, and whether anyone else had a hand in it. The process was really quite simple and I experienced an odd and unusual sense of camaraderie with a police officer. She could easily start looking into other unexplained deaths and end up causing me problems, but Detective Bender was a jerk, bad mouthing his colleague and making it about her being a woman. Maybe she had instincts he lacked.

They stared at me, expressions of agreement on Gavin's and Tess's faces, disbelief on Sean's.

"It made sense to me," he said. "She's making it into a big deal, questioning all of us alone. It was a terrible tragedy but it has nothing to do with us. I want it wrapped up fast. If they ask more questions, don't stall or play games. Got it?" He looked at me.

9

Tess had a very clear agenda for her trip to San Francisco. She would meet with Ted and they would join forces to persuade Detective Gorman it was his duty to look more closely at the circumstances of Steve's death. She felt as if this was her purpose in life right now — fixing Steve's reputation, no matter how undeserving he was. It was something that needed to be done. Working overtime to improve his memory was repugnant, but she was not one to shirk unpleasant tasks. It was similar to an open item on a product launch plan, something requiring completion and she couldn't rest until it was ticked off the list. It had taken on a life of its own.

After the events of the past few weeks and that horror show a few hours before leaving Sydney, she felt surrounded by death. Untimely death. Suicide. Murder. Drowning. It was horrible what had happened recently — Lisa punched in the stomach after an abortion and left to bleed to death on her own front lawn. Her husband hanging himself for whatever reason — it wasn't completely clear. Guilt. Shame. Rage. Maybe all three. The man next door suffocated in his own bed, not unlike Steve. Now the dead woman in the swimming pool.

Most people went their entire lives without encountering such horrific and tragic death.

She settled back in the cab, eager to see her condo, but especially Damien after so many months away. Isaiah and Jen were ready for her arrival. According to Jen's text message two days ago, they'd prepared breakfast for her. Meaning, Isaiah had planned and executed the meal, meaning it would be a gourmet feast. She didn't really care. She'd be happy with a turkey sandwich, hanging out talking to Damien and watching him revel in a plate of fresh mango. Besides, after the long flight, it felt more like lunchtime even though the clock said nine-thirty in the morning.

The bird seemed to know her the minute she walked into his room. He chortled *Chardonnay time* — his favorite phrase, one that he associated with her. He bobbed excitedly and let her stroke his back. When she leaned in close, he rested his head against her cheek. She laughed. She couldn't wait to get him crated up for his trip around the world. It would be tough on him, but worth it in the end. He was a wonderful companion. She'd missed him.

Isaiah had anticipated her desire for lunch after all. He served homemade linguini with clams in a cream sauce so light it rested on her tongue like champagne. It was accompanied by an endive salad. Tess gave Jen and Isaiah superficial information about the start-up. She told them a bit about Australia. Then she steered the conversation to their careers and reveled in the food while they talked and she simply listened.

She and Ted had arranged to meet for dinner at a Chinese restaurant. They were scheduled for seven o'clock and she wasn't sure how to fill the hours until then. A bit of shopping would keep her on her feet and awake. It was the wise thing to do, but her body craved sleep as if she'd been deprived for weeks.

In the end, she succumbed to her king-sized bed with its crisp white sheets and the silence of being so far above the city, behind tightly-sealed windows. The absence of laughing, cawing kookaburras and magpies to wake her before the sun rose above the horizon was heavenly. And now, even at mid-day, the utter darkness of well-fitted window shades drew her toward sleep. Just the knowledge that she was in her home was soothing — a place where she set the rules, where she didn't feel a gentle pressure to socialize. She hadn't realized how the social requirements weighed on her, and hadn't realized how tired it made her. Sean's idea was a good one, she fully supported it, but she craved her independence and solitude.

She'd be jet-lagged for two days. Five days after that, she'd fly back to Sydney, kicking off another few days of the same. It didn't matter. She wanted to sleep. She longed for it as if she hadn't slept since her first day in Australia.

When she arrived at the restaurant, Ted was waiting. He sat in the lobby, looking like he had all the time in the world. She loved that about him. A man who ran a global company worth just over a billion dollars, and he sat there like a guy who had enough free time to arrive early for the simple pleasure of people-watching.

He shook her hand then gave her a brief, one-armed hug. "How is it to be back on your home turf?" he said.

"Like I never left."

The hostess picked up two enormous leather-bound

menus. She wove quickly through several rooms, ending up in one that featured floor-to-ceiling windows, looking out on a long narrow pool of water filled with Koi. The pond was surrounded by papyrus and other water-loving greenery. A small bridge arched over the center. Tess wondered whether anyone but the gardener ever went out there. Had a single human foot ever stepped onto the bridge's back?

They ordered soup and appetizers, chicken salad, and three main courses. It was far too much food, but she was ravenous. Her sleep was so long and deep, Isaiah's linguini and clams seemed like a meal eaten the previous day.

Ted ordered a bottle of Zinfandel. She found herself looking forward to it more than she should. The Australian wines had lighter body. California wine was one of only a handful of things she missed.

It was a lie to say she felt as if she'd never left. Everything felt slightly strange, foreign. She missed the tropical air and the less frantic pace, the musical accents. Everyone here sounded mildly angry.

"You look refreshed," Ted said.

"I took a four-hour nap."

He laughed with a teasing sinister undertone.

"I know. Big mistake, but I was exhausted."

"At least you won't fall asleep with your cheek in the hot and sour soup."

"Definitely not."

The wine arrived and they were silent while the bottle was opened and the glasses filled. "Welcome home." Ted clicked his glass against hers. "To a fresh start."

She took a sip. "A fresh start?"

"We're discussing your return to CoastalCreative, right?"

He put down his glass and plunged an egg roll into a perfect circle of dark yellow hot mustard.

She was stunned by the amount of the spicy stuff he could consume in a single bite. Did it say something about his fortitude? She dipped her own egg roll in the tiny dish of soy sauce. After she chewed and took a few more sips of wine, she explained that she was supremely happy at the start-up and loved Australia. He finished his egg roll with even more mustard slathered on it, and told her he was disappointed, of course. She said she'd turned a corner in her life, moved on from her career at CC, except for one thing. She believed it was her charter to ensure proper closure to Steve's death.

"You're not serious," he said.

"Very."

"I told you that matter was finalized."

"And I thought his life was worthy of a face-to-face conversation."

"The police are satisfied. There's no conversation to be had," he said.

"Are *you* satisfied?"

"My opinion doesn't matter. Only the truth brought out by the facts of the situation."

"Is that the truth? It seems sloppy to me. It seems as though they saw heroin on the nightstand…"

"Dresser. It was quite a lot, on the dresser. He snorted it and then went to lie down."

"Fine. The dresser. They found heroin and decided it was an overdose and they didn't look any further."

"They did."

"In what way?"

"There was no evidence of anyone else in the apartment."

"None?"

"That's right."

"Well wouldn't there be some fingerprints and hairs and fibers from the course of normal living? Occasional guests? He wasn't a monk. No fingerprints at all suggests…"

"The point is, there's nothing else to look at. There aren't any leads from the neighbors."

"What about the woman the guy at the front desk mentioned?"

"They had no way of identifying her or locating her."

"But it means there must have been some fingerprints from her, and if there weren't, doesn't that seem strange? They should at least call it possible homicide with no suspects, not an overdose."

"If there's no evidence, no witnesses with usable information…if there are no leads, there are no leads. And it points to overdose."

"Did they check his phone records?"

"Not that I'm aware of."

"Well why not?"

He sighed, making the exhalation of air louder than necessary. She wasn't going to be cowed by that.

"It's not like you to be so emotional," he said.

She was not emotional. She was being factual and straightforward. His comment suggested she was a *difficult* female. It wasn't true. Rather, Ted was shirking his responsibility to Steve.

He picked up his wine glass and took several sips. "If you want to push this, you should talk to Detective Gorman, not me."

"I thought we could approach him together."

"No."

"That's it, just *no*?"

"That's correct. I'm satisfied. You should be too. You're being foolish."

She resented his attitude. And she was disappointed. Persuading Detective Gorman without Ted's help would be more challenging. Maybe Ted wasn't the leader, the man of integrity she'd thought he was.

10

Portland, Oregon

Tony Marks wasn't my first boyfriend, but neither was he technically a boyfriend. However, he believed I was his girlfriend because we sat beside each other during church services and at youth group meetings. He stuffed greeting cards into the side pocket of my purse every time we had a church event. The cards contained hand-written poems. The poetry wasn't half bad, although my judgment may have been clouded by the rhyming flattery.

Of course I wasn't allowed to go out with boys or attend dances at my Junior High school. But how were my parents to know that a boy was following me around at every youth group event? During church, my parents sat close to the front of the auditorium while my brothers and I were allowed to sit with the other teenagers. My parents didn't seem to notice that the same boy angled to find a spot beside me every single week for nearly three months.

Tony was cute. He had dark hair and big brown eyes. He hadn't hit his growth spurt yet, but he still had an inch or two on me. I liked looking at him and I liked reading his poems which made me out to be a goddess. He rolled his eyes at some of the things our youth group leaders said, making me smile. I was glad to have someone else who didn't swallow all of the biblical stories and their purported hidden messages. Occasionally, one of the poems stuffed in my purse addressed his view of the things we were taught.

The other boys at church didn't like him much and I wasn't quite sure why. It might have been his looks — he was almost pretty with those thick curls and soft, very red lips. I didn't know for a fact they were soft, but they looked soft, despite the intensity of their color. The only slightly off-putting aspect of Tony's very nice appearance was his fingernails. They were long. Not freakish long like those people who grow their nails for twenty years and wind up with curved claws. But they were long and delicate, about a quarter of an inch, his thumbnails longer.

The kids at Pure Truth Tabernacle were indoctrinated multiple times a week, and I do mean indoctrinated. Critical questions were not permitted. They didn't allow expressions of doubt or the introduction of ambiguity into any conversation about whether something written by a guy nearly two thousand years ago was the absolute truth inspired by god. The indoctrination took place overtly during Sunday services and Sunday school, at Wednesday night Bible study, and even at social events. We prayed before everything, even softball games or trips to the beach. The prayers were often long and instructive, providing another opportunity for delivering not-so-subtle indoctrination.

Among many other things, we were taught to be kind, to treat others better than ourselves, to avoid gossip, to keep our thoughts pure, to only talk about worthwhile subjects. All lofty goals.

But kids are kids, and kids are vicious. Maybe it's the animal nature not yet socialized out. There's a kind of survival mentality that recognizes there's a top dog, followed by a pack that turns on the weak creatures in its midst, terrified the weakness will touch them or put the pack in danger. Tony was called a fag for no reason whatsoever. He wasn't gay. It was the generalized use of that word among homophobic males to anyone whose behavior didn't fit their definition of male. Maybe it was the fingernails.

I thought Tony was okay. I liked being around him. I think he liked me in part because the other boys left him alone when he was walking with me or sitting beside me.

About seven poems into our *relationship*, there was a Friday-night song festival. We sat on the grass surrounding a huge fire built in a concrete ring near the back of the church property. We roasted marshmallows, drank soda, and channeled our sugar high into singing religious soft rock songs.

The fire was at its height, blazing hot, sending sparks into the moderately dark sky, bleached by streetlights from surrounding neighborhoods. I was sitting beside Tony on a blanket. Boys and girls were required to have at least eight inches of space between them at casual functions like this. The leader carried a ruler to make sure that guideline was adhered to.

Of course my brothers were at the song-fest and of course they left me alone, despite instructions from my parents that they keep their eyes on me. They had no interest in watching over me. They always reported back to my parents that I behaved myself, that I was a godly girl.

Tony took off his hoodie and dropped it into the vast open space between the kneecaps of our crossed legs. A few minutes later, I felt the tentative touch of his finger on the edge of my hand. I kept my hand still, my arms turned so that my thumb extended toward him and the heel pressed hard against the ground. His fingers crept farther, now touching the webbing between my thumb and index finger. They rested there for a minute and then moved again, his index finger now caressing my knuckle. Still I didn't move.

It seemed like an hour, possibly only ten or fifteen minutes, but finally, his hand was resting fully over mine, his fingers curled around and tucked underneath. We remained like that, singing our sugared brains out, not moving, not looking at each other or in any way acknowledging what was happening.

As the flames lost their intensity and the area around the fire grew darker, and the songs became less rousing, he pulled his hand away from mine. He picked up his hoodie, balled it up, and stuffed it into the opening made by his crossed legs.

The next day, even though he went to a different school, there was a card in my locker. He was a very resourceful kid. On the front of the card was a sketch of a girl wearing a dress spattered with daisies. She was holding a long-stemmed rose. Inside the card was a poem about the softness of my skin — like a rose petal — and the smell of his fingers after touching mine — like a cupcake.

11

Sydney

The day after I found the woman floating in Sean's swimming pool, the doorbell rang at nine-thirty. I knew, we all knew, it was the detectives. There was something about the tone — forceful and piercing — that suggested who was on the other side of the door.

Sean insisted we wait on the patio while he went to let them in. We complied, but my curiosity was eating at my stomach. I didn't want to miss a word they said. It was a welcome change to observe the aftermath of an unexplained death that I didn't cause and didn't have to work overtime to conceal. I was curious to know whether she'd killed herself or drowned, preferably not murder, so the whole thing could be wrapped up without unnecessary poking around to find out why there had been three homicides in three neighboring houses in the space of three weeks.

Gavin and I sat across from each other at the patio table, not talking. I think both of us were concentrating, hoping that through some miracle of acoustics we'd be able to hear what Detective Martin had to say. It was as if we expected her voice to travel through the vast foyer with a ceiling that rose to the second floor, past the glass-enclosed pond with its turtles and plants, into the great room, and out to the patio.

An impossibility, but still we remained silent, not wanting to speak over the slightest echo that might come our way.

Several minutes went by without a sound from the foyer. We looked at each other. After a few seconds of gazing into each other's eyes, the connection began to veer toward the erotic, our bodies suddenly aware we couldn't touch. Our facial expressions remained steady, while our eyes bled with desire.

People make a big deal out of eyes — windows to the soul and all of that. I wonder why that is? We imagine we can see thoughts seeping out of the brain into pupils and irises. It's the shimmering nature of the eyeball, the liquid quality. We're awed by the amazing feats performed by our eyes, transforming the world into images our brains can interpret. It's the fact that when someone's eyes are looking at you, there's a sensation that you are actually seeing inside of their head, because those white and colored balls jitter and move, the pupils expanding and contracting, the eyelids snapping down and up every few seconds of their own volition. You know those eyes are taking in things about you and so you imagine they're also giving out information. But really, they aren't. They're just little cameras, not something with consciousness of their own.

When I saw Sean out of the corner of my eye, I didn't want to stop looking at Gavin, but slowly, I released the hold of his eyes. I turned my gaze toward Sean. Detective Martin was a few steps behind him. I hadn't expected her to come inside. I'd expected information about the death, maybe the woman's identity, and that was it.

"The detective has a few questions," Sean said.

Of course we couldn't ask any of our own. His eyes said

it all, he wanted her to go away and leave us alone to transform the world with our app.

"As I told Mr. Farmer," she said, "we've identified the body." She pushed her filmy hair away from the side of her face where the ceiling fan insisted on pushing it back across her cheek, a strand floating across her eyelashes. She stabbed her middle finger at the corner of her eye, trying to lift the hair out of the way. "Her name is Karen North."

That wasn't good. I swallowed and moved my lips slightly.

"She was the former wife of the man at number twenty-six. The murder victim." I suppose she added that last part in case we didn't know the order of the house numbers and confused John North with someone on the opposite side of us, someone not murdered.

"She lives in America — Chicago, Illinois. She arrived in Australia yesterday. She was here to see to the details of her former husband's estate."

No one said anything.

"Now that you're aware of her identity, I need to ask you again, have any of you met her?"

We shook our heads.

"Were you aware she was staying in the house?"

Each of us said no, in a string of staccato sounds.

"You weren't aware of any activity next door?"

"The police have been in and out," Sean said.

"I've spoken to some of your neighbors," Detective Martin said. "Several of them noticed her on the front patio."

"Well we didn't see her," Sean said.

"Did you?" She looked at me and then Gavin.

We shook our heads.

"One of your neighbors, Elizabeth Strand at number

twenty-seven, saw Ms. North arrive early yesterday. She spoke to her briefly."

No one responded.

"So you're saying that for the entire day, *none* of you had any idea this woman was in the house? You didn't catch even a glimpse of her?"

"We're pretty busy," Sean said. "I told you, we're running a business here. We work long hours."

"Your offices are at the front of the house. You never look out the window? You never leave the house for a walk or an errand?"

"I think we've been clear," Gavin said. "No one saw her. It's a coincidence that others did. It happens."

She gave him a stiff smile.

"What kind of interaction did you have with Mr. North?"

"Alexandra did more than Gav and I."

The detective looked at me. "What kind of interaction?"

"He showed me the stars through his telescope. Twice. All of us went over the second time."

"What else?" She pulled out her tablet and stylus, tapping at the screen so fast she looked like she was stabbing a small animal to death.

"That's all," I said. John's comments about his wife flitted through my mind — *She can't swim. She doesn't like the water. She doesn't even own a bathing suit.* A deep pool of water seemed like a strange choice for late night solitary drinking, or for suicide.

"Did he ever mention his wife?" Detective Martin said.

"Actually, he told me she was visiting their children in the US. Sean told me later he was divorced and they didn't have any children."

She turned to Sean, still looking at her screen and tapping.

"Mr. North told you this?"

"We already gave this information to the detective looking into his murder," Sean said.

"I'd like to hear it myself."

"She committed suicide?" I said.

"We don't know that. We avoid assumptions until we get a clear picture of the whole situation. So, Mr. North lied to you about his wife?"

It wasn't clear who she was talking to, but I nodded.

Still looking at her device, she managed to absorb the nod anyway. "What else can you tell me?"

"Nothing," I said.

"Mr. Farmer, how did you know they were divorced?"

"The guy across the street told me."

"What guy?"

"Jeff. Jeff…I guess I don't know his last name."

"Not a lot of interaction in this neighborhood, is there?"

No one answered.

Detective Martin tucked the stylus in her pocket. "Detective Bender and I will be back with more questions. Probably tomorrow, but I'll ring you first to let you know we're coming."

"Why?" Sean said.

She stared at him. Those dark, commanding eyebrows ticked up ever so slightly. "Because, Mr. Farmer. We investigate unexplained deaths, that's what detectives do. We need to understand what happened and we need to determine whether a crime has been committed."

"It seems pretty obvious she was upset, divorce or not. She drank too much, and drowned."

"It's not obvious at all." Detective Martin smiled. "I can

find my way out." She turned and walked into the great room and disappeared into the foyer. We didn't hear the front door close.

"Aw, shit." Sean collapsed in the dead woman's lounge chair.

"No worries," Gavin said.

"We're losing focus."

"We don't have to," Gavin said. "We'll put this out of our heads and get to work."

Sean closed his eyes. "It's bad energy. A dead body in our pool. Murder. All these questions. It has nothing to do with us and I don't understand why she won't leave us alone."

"She can't know it has nothing to do with us," Gavin said. "Let her do her job and she'll be done. Let things unfold. The only bad energy is in your head. Why don't I get busy draining the pool and you can get some work done."

Sean opened his eyes and gave him a look that was quite similar to the detective's — not quite trusting that anything could be taken at face value.

12

Flight #209 — Los Angeles to Sydney

Karen Ellison North sat in first class sipping a glass of champagne. She hated that she was flying with the last name North, but that's what her passport said and she was stuck with it. She wasn't sure the celebratory reputation of champagne was the right way to travel to Australia to deal with the things her dead, possibly murdered, husband had left behind, but it was offered and she liked champagne.

Walking away from John had been the easiest decision of her life. When she discovered how he'd been spending his evening hours, not observing the constellations at all, she'd run to the bathroom and thrown up the entire meal of beef stroganoff, two glasses of red wine, and salad with shredded carrots, tomatoes, and radishes. Her heart vomited him out as quickly as the rest of her body had. Two days later, she was on a flight — coach, that time — back to LA and then home to Chicago where she filed for divorce. He was nice enough about the settlement, she should be thankful for that. She'd never had to worry about money.

Learning of his death had elicited a shocking response from her body. The moment the police detective spoke the words that John had been found dead, tears began pouring down her cheeks.

It confused her.

She hated him. She was repulsed by the things he'd done, the one thing. But apparently, she still loved him. Her body didn't lie. Had she been in denial the entire time? Did his watching naked women in their bedrooms while he pretended his telescope was pointed at something millions of miles away hurt after all? She'd thought her body's response was disgust. Rage. Her actions had been threaded with rage. She booked her flight and packed her suitcase in a fit of rage. The three months since the divorce had been finalized, she'd assumed the thunderous energy she felt was fueled by rage.

Then why the tears? And it wasn't just a few dribbles, generic sadness at an untimely death. It was a flood of grief that shocked her as it convulsed her body. She'd spent an entire day in bed, sobbing, feeling as if her heart had been torn out of her chest. How could she hate him and love him with all of her soul?

She settled back in the seat, teary even now. She took a long swallow of champagne, letting it bite at her tongue and throat, moving her attention away from her trembling upper lip and blurred eyes.

John had been unusual from the moment she met him, and she wondered, quite often, if she should have seen there was something wrong. Why hadn't she noticed his quirks were more than that until after she'd married him? Long after... There were hundreds of men she could have fallen for. Why him? Why did he have to rob her of everything she'd ever wanted? She was a simple girl, born in a suburb of Chicago. She didn't have big dreams. She wanted a happy marriage, a man to cook for, a man who loved her. She wanted a man who took care of her so she didn't have to be one of those women who went mental trying to contribute to the support of a family, manage a career, and raise children at the same time.

Do one thing well. That's what her father always said. Her mother echoed him.

Karen had wanted two children, a boy and a girl. Maybe three if they didn't get one of each on the first try. She wanted a nice house she could decorate, friends to shop and play tennis with. She wanted a man who made her feel safe. Not one of those men with a secret life that you heard about much too often.

She'd been certain John was that man. He was building a lucrative career working for an oil company. He was good looking and attentive. He was intelligent and interested in the things she had to say, or so it had seemed. Their courtship was relatively short, their wedding large and lavish. Their home only eight miles from where she was born, was over six thousand square feet. It had a white picket fence, heart-melting when it was draped with evergreen garlands and a backdrop of snow drifts at Christmastime.

They'd been married seventeen romantic months when she first hinted to John that the time seemed right for a child. They'd never talked about children. She wasn't sure now if she'd been stupid and naive about what went into a marriage, or if he'd somehow misled her. She searched her memory for negative comments about children, for little things he'd said that painted a picture of their future without children. She couldn't think of a single thing.

Had he misled her?

When they'd talked about the future he mentioned wanting a large house with lots of bedrooms. She'd assumed this was for children. When they talked about traveling to Europe, he'd said that would be better when they were a bit older, and again, she'd *assumed*, he meant once their children were old enough to appreciate the history.

She had been naïve.

She held out her glass to the flight attendant. He was a slim man with thick blonde hair, beautiful eyes, and no smile. He looked right past her as he filled her glass with champagne. He asked if she wanted anything to eat. She declined.

It was satisfying, letting your thoughts run back through time, recalling your life as if it had some shape or meaning when looked at as a single unfolding bolt of fabric. She tried not to let her thoughts center on John's occasional odd behavior, the things that should have made her run as far and as fast as she could from him, but to step back and look at the whole landscape.

She'd been so caught up in the glamor. Even as a senior manager, John made a very good salary, and as he climbed higher up the ranks, the money flowed faster and thicker. They belonged to a tennis club where they played with other couples several evenings a week during the summer. After a match, they ate late dinners of elegantly plated prawns or crab or delicate strips of chicken drizzled with delicious sauces. They enjoyed exotic vegetables and rich chocolate desserts — all perfectly sized portions so she never felt stuffed or worried she was putting on weight.

They took small trips — to New York City and Los Angeles, visiting art galleries and museums and eating out. They drove to the Grand Canyon and flew to Vegas two or three times.

When she'd asked about having a child, John didn't equivocate. He didn't suggest the timing wasn't right or that they should enjoy a few more years as a couple. *No.* That's all he said. When she pressed, his answer didn't provide any further explanation. *No, I don't want children.*

It felt like a punch in the face. She was so shocked the first time, she didn't even ask why, and didn't point out that he'd known she wanted them. Surely he'd known? She'd assumed from the time she was a little girl she would be a mother someday. How could he not have known? And how could he not want them? He didn't have to be concerned with the drudgery of raising them. She would discipline them well, they wouldn't be rambunctious or defiant.

He peered at her over the tops of his reading glasses as if it were the most stupid comment a woman had ever made.

13

Sydney

The police hadn't said anything about not draining the pool, so after the crime technicians left, Gavin rented a pump. He set about connecting hoses that would carry the water into the sewer. I sat on what I now called the dead woman's lounge chair, watching him work.

Gavin wore board shorts and a sleeveless T-shirt, despite the cloudy sky and cool breeze. He looked excellent and I enjoyed watching him work. I wore leggings and a sweater, but my feet were bare. I wiggled my toes and admired the fresh coat of lavender nail color. I'd had a pedicure the previous afternoon, calling an Uber to get me away from the house and Sean's anxiety over his inability to control the police.

It was fantastic, spending a few hours without someone looking over my shoulder, suggesting how I should utilize my time, knocking on my bedroom door, demanding I join the others for lunch. After the manicure I went to a Tapas bar and had pulled pork street tacos and a glass of Pinot Noir.

Sean liked putting on an easy-going air, but burning not very far below the surface of his skin was a strong desire to control everyone and all situations. It was becoming more obvious as he scowled at the detectives and complained about the impact of this woman's death on the company. Of course a death like that is disconcerting. If it were my luxury home, my swimming pool, I wouldn't like it either. I didn't like it. I didn't want detectives showing up every day with all kinds of questions. You never knew where the questions were leading, but the smell of them leading somewhere was pervasive. They loved asking questions without explaining the reason for their interest in that particular point, working hard to keep you slightly off balance at all times.

What Sean didn't seem to realize was that his prickly attitude was piquing their curiosity about him and about our shared living arrangement. Police officers in Australia probably didn't have a lot of experience with the Silicon Valley mentality on the other side of the world. Encountering a house inhabited by a handful of slick people who were running a company out of their bedrooms was foreign to them. That alone stirred their interest.

Of course they weren't going to let go of the suspicion that one of us must have known Karen. Why else would she be in our swimming pool? It wasn't as if the house next door had a balcony that hung over Sean's yard and she'd simply jumped off. The presence of the nearly empty bottle suggested she'd spent quite a bit of time lying around in his backyard. And without her clothes? It wasn't mid summer, the evenings were cold.

I would never defend cops, but I could see their point of view. Sean would be better served if he could bring himself to see that as well.

I got up and walked in a wide arc around the pool, over to the grass beyond the opposite edge. Gavin was standing by the hose, staring at it as if he had x-ray vision and could see the water flowing through it, down beneath the city, and wherever it went after that.

"That was a good idea to empty the pool," I said. "It will make Sean feel better."

He nodded.

I moved my hand up under his shirt and stroked his back. He smiled, then took a step away from me, forcing my hand to slide away from his skin.

"Do you think he knew her?" Gavin said.

"Karen?"

"Yes."

"He said he didn't."

"So? People say a lot of things. He seems very anxious to be rid of the detectives, to have this finished."

"We all want them to go away," I said.

"Sure. But he's more wound up. Frantic."

"He thinks it will distract. And it is."

"It's more than that," Gavin said.

"Why would he lie about it, if he did know her?"

He shrugged. "Not sure. It's just odd."

"It's the energy thing. He doesn't like bad energy, you know that."

"Absolutely."

"He has a utopian vision. A dead body in the swimming pool doesn't fit that."

He laughed.

I laughed with him.

"I'm just wondering. He lived here before any of us. She's only been gone a few months, I think. Well, maybe almost a year, but he must have met her," he said.

"When did he buy the house?"

"I don't know. He never said."

I considered this. I walked over toward one of the queen palm trees and leaned against it. The bark was smooth. The solid, straight shape of the trunk felt good on my back. I pressed my spine against it, trying to ease the tight muscles between my shoulder blades. "He seemed shocked she was dead."

"Maybe," Gavin said. "Maybe not."

"We should try to find out," I said.

"I don't want to cause trouble. It's just a bit senseless, trying to think about why she would come over here and drink, go for a swim, if she didn't know him."

"It would be good to find out, but I hope you didn't tell the detectives you think this."

"No. I suppose I won't. I'm not sure."

"If he lied, if he has anything to do with it, telling them would spoil everything. The company might fall apart. Even if it's just that he lied and he knew she killed herself, or knew she tripped and fell. Or anything like that."

"There are other jobs."

"Not for me. My visa says Sean is my employer. I'd have to leave Australia. I'm not ready to do that yet."

He smiled. "I'm not calling him a murderer."

"But if he lied for a reason and you call him out to the detectives, it will absolutely spoil things."

He walked to the edge of the pool and looked at the water. It had only gone down a few inches. There was a lot of water to be drained. It would take all night. "We should get stoned later," he said. "If we all get high, maybe we can get him to talk."

14

The water in the swimming pool had gone down several feet by dinner time. It was fascinating to watch the water become less threatening while not having any sense of its actual departure. It was silently sucked out of the plaster and concrete pit, flowing through tightly sealed rubber tubes, disappearing into the pipes that ran beneath the streets and houses and gardens. By the next morning, I'd stand at the railing on my balcony and look into a dark hole with only a few puddles in the bottom.

Of course, it would be scrubbed and re-filled immediately.

I was still entertaining thoughts of asking Gavin to teach me to swim, but I wanted to make sure I was ready. Every single day since Sean had tossed me into the pool, I'd looked out at the water and imagined no longer being cowed by it. Every day I wondered how it is that most people on earth have come to terms with water, able to navigate it without slipping beneath the surface, free from the ever-present thought that it could easily take their lives.

Gavin had proposed a nice dinner, suggesting he and I cook together in preparation for luring Sean into answering our questions about Karen North. A nice dinner with a bottle of wine, followed by a neatly rolled joint, or two.

I'm not a great cook. I only prepare the easiest meals and

only when absolutely necessary. Eating out is preferable. Most of my life I've managed to shirk off cooking to others. My mother liked to cook and never asked me to do more than help out. As a kid, helping out meant taking an extraordinary amount of time with every task she assigned, effectively reducing the number of assignments. I could turn the act of grating cheese into a half-hour dance with a block of cheese sliding ever-so-slowly over the metal teeth of the grater. I'd pause every few strokes to change the position of the cheese, ensuring the block was shredded evenly.

If she noticed my lethargic pace, she never commented on it.

Once I began sharing an apartment in college, and after, I usually managed to persuade roommates to cook for me. It was fairly simple because unlike most people, I love to clean. Others were happy to trade cooking for cleaning. No one but me wanted to scour and polish sinks, making the faucets and stoppers shine. I was alone in my desire to mop a floor, easing the sturdy sponge into corners to remove every last piece of grit. When the mop failed, I was happy to get on my hands and knees with a sponge and a toothpick.

I figured cooking with Gavin meant he would provide the creative vision and do all the heavy lifting, while I fluttered around him looking busy, *helping*. If I cleaned as he went, he wouldn't really notice the help was minimal.

He was planning a vegetarian meal — soup made with vegetable stock, small white beans, farro, and Parmesan cheese, along with a whole grain bread baguette served with unsalted butter, and a beetroot salad. I wasn't sure how the lack of meat would sit with me, but I was willing to try, and the farro sounded interesting. I'd never had it, never even heard of it. Some sort of grain in a world that seems to produce more varieties every year. Maybe it's that I grew up in a narrow world where you basically had white rice. Now there's basmati and jasmine, short and long grain brown, and Arborio and regular white. There's quinoa and farro and buckwheat...

Maybe being a vegetarian could be more interesting than it sounded. Gavin wasn't one, but he was intrigued by the lifestyle and liked to try veggie-only meals whenever he got a chance. He said he often ordered the vegetarian choice in restaurants. He wasn't crazy about meat, so why bother, was his view. I could not see myself ever in a thousand years going without a nice rare steak or crispy bacon. But his soup sounded good, and I like beets. And of course, any kind of bread smeared with soft butter gets my tongue salivating.

He served the meal in the dining room, placing the large pale gray soup bowls on turquoise linen place mats that he'd asked me to set out, paired with yellow napkins. Rather springlike colors for nearing the dead of winter, but maybe that was the point.

The soup was fantastic. I ate two bowlfuls and could have gone for a third, but the grated Parmesan cheese was gone, so I satisfied myself with two more slices of bread with a generous layer of butter.

Sean was agreeable to smoking a joint. I thought about running upstairs to get my cigarettes. It would be easy to slip one in while we were passing a joint, but at the last minute, just as I closed the dishwasher door, I decided the focus needed to be on finding out whether he knew Karen. Pulling out a tobacco cigarette might spin his attention in the wrong direction.

We turned on the gas fire pit and pulled three heavy wood patio chairs up close.

Gavin lit the first joint and inhaled slowly.

We passed it in silence for ten or fifteen minutes, simply enjoying the bite of smoke in our lungs, the anticipation of changes coming to our brains, and the laughing, goofy conversation that would follow.

"Thanks, guys," Sean said. "Good call. This is exactly what we needed."

Gavin nodded and put the joint to his lips.

"What a week," Sean said. "And it's not over. They're going to pester us until they get what they want. And if they never get it, which they won't, since they're barking up the wrong tree…" He sighed and took the joint from Gavin. He touched it to his lips, his eyes half closed as the dope made its way through his nervous system.

"Are they?" Gavin said softly.

Sean passed the joint to me. "Are they what?"

"Are they barking up the wrong tree?"

"Of course they are. What kind of question is that?"

"No one wants detectives digging into their life," I said. "They always ask more than necessary." I made a mental note to slow down on the pot. It wasn't something I should have said.

"Always?" Gavin laughed. He glanced at me and laughed again. "You have lots of experience with detectives asking you questions?"

"No. Just a general statement. From what you see on TV…if you get stopped for a traffic violation. It seems like they always want to know more than they need to."

Gavin stood. "I'm going to open a bottle of red. He

stood. "Or should I get a few beers?"

"Beer," Sean said. "I'm thirsty."

I gave Gavin a thumbs up.

When he returned to the patio he was carrying a small cooler filled with beer and a bag of pork belly crisps. The things sound nasty, but I'd grown quite fond of them — a chip flavor well-stocked in the few Australian grocery stores I'd visited. I'd never heard of them in the U.S., but maybe that was a Silicon Valley oversight, not an American issue.

We munched and opened our beers.

"So you never even saw her?" I said.

Sean looked at me hard for several seconds. "That's what I told the detective."

I put my beer bottle to my lips and took a small sip. "Is it true?"

He leaned his head back, staring at the patio roof, his eyes glazed and drifting, as if he expected to peer through it to the stars.

After several minutes, I spoke again. "Is it true, Sean?"

Without moving his head, he spoke in a low, sloppy voice. "I agree with you. They dig for information they don't need. What difference does it make whether I ever met her? We didn't have a relationship and there was no reason whatsoever for her to drown in my pool. She was trespassing. If I told them I met her, there would be more questions, more digging into my life in a way that does not matter at all for their investigation."

"It's not a good idea to lie to them," Gavin said. "If they find out later…"

"How would they find out? I met her one time, we exchanged ten or twelve words. End of story. If they grab onto that, it becomes the easy line of thought to pursue and this whole thing will take longer to wrap up. They need to decide suicide or accident, and finish without involving us, because it doesn't. If they decide murder, they need to look somewhere else. As I've mentioned quite a few times, it has nothing to do with us."

"It could backfire," Gavin said.

"It won't. I want to pretend this never happened and move on."

"You can't pretend it never happened," I said.

"We absolutely can. We can erase that negative energy. Already the pool is almost empty, thanks to Gav. Now I just need to dump these lounge chairs, buy some new ones, and scrub down the patio to be absolutely sure all the bad shit is washed away."

I didn't like the thought of him dumping the lounge chairs. I wanted to lie on the chair Karen had used, stare up at the sky, and try to imagine her last thoughts. I wondered whether thoughts had a physical presence. If they did, could those thoughts linger in the fabric and stuffing, then slowly seep into my brain?

After two beers, and half of the second joint, Sean stood abruptly. "No more for me. Off to sleep." He walked smoothly, as if in a trance, into the great room and disappeared into the entryway.

"What else is he lying about?" I said.

"Exactly," Gavin said. He handed me the joint.

We finished the joint and cleaned up. We went up to my room and slowly took off our clothes, kissing and gently touching each other's skin. I thought about the promised return of the detectives. Did they already doubt whether Sean was telling the truth? Police can be clever that way. They have a lot more experience reading expressions and body language and tone of voice than the average person.

15

The darkness was fading when I woke on Saturday. A moment later, my phone chimed, set to get me up for my run.

I went out onto the balcony and looked down at the pool. It was empty, a few puddles glimmering in the dark gray light. Despite hating the water, and hating its proximity to my room, the pool was beautiful, especially when the waterfall was flowing. Seeing it empty made me think of a forest ravaged from strip mining. The hole was meant to hold water, meant to look refreshing and inviting, meant to create that tranquil atmosphere that most people find around water.

I got dressed. Downstairs, I stood by the kitchen sink and drank a glass of water. I stepped onto the front porch as the kookaburras were waking up. I did my usual stretches and started my run. I'd missed the past few days, for obvious reasons, so I planned on six miles.

Within five blocks, I was feeling good, my body warming up, my heart thumping at a faster rate, the effects of pot and one and a half beers and a glass of wine with dinner easing out through my skin in a sheen of sweat.

When I arrived back at the house after five and three quarters of a mile, the sun was fully up, the sky pale blue. There were a few dark clouds, but nothing guaranteeing rain.

I made espresso and two slices of toast. I took that and a cup of peach yogurt up to my room. The guys seemed to be sleeping still, unless Gavin was awake and working on the app, even on a Saturday, which wouldn't be surprising.

The house felt oddly empty without Tess, unbalanced. It was quieter, somehow, although I guess that was my imagination. It lacked a certain friendliness. Or maybe it was the dead woman. It was hard to tell. Still, I missed Tess's steadying presence, left alone with Gavin's minimalist approach to speaking and Sean's unpredictable moods.

I ate at my desk, trolling through Twitter — liking and re-tweeting and firing off a few tweets of my own under the name of TruthT. So far, I'd managed to gather seven-hundred-twenty-four followers. Whether any of them were remotely interested in the app remained to be seen, but quite a few of them liked my tweets, which were mostly about the value of truth. What's not to like? No one wants to admit they aren't on the side of truth.

I showered and put on jeans and a black T-shirt and black ankle boots.

Two days earlier, just after Tess left for the airport, I'd called and made an appointment to speak with Detective Gorman today. It was four p.m. on Friday in California. Our appointment wasn't until five, so I had time to fill. I tweeted a bit more then took my dishes downstairs. I went into the billiards room and started playing, waiting for the hour to pass.

Getting all the striped balls in the pockets first was my initial goal, followed by a game that began with all solids eliminated first. I didn't win my next game, trying to sink the balls in numerical order, but it distracted my brain very effectively. I returned to the kitchen and cut an apple into eighths and shaved off a few slices of cheddar cheese.

Back in my room, I nibbled on apple and cheese and watched the clock move slowly toward ten. I thought again about what I planned to say. I didn't want to make it too scripted, I needed to be equally prepared for something unexpected.

Finally, my phone ticked over to ten. I dialed the detective's direct line and waited.

I started by telling him I totally understood the situation with Steve Montgomery, that no one wants to accept a sudden, shocking death without blaming it on some sort of villain.

The change in his mood, the subtle openness to anything else I had to say, was tangible.

"I wanted to talk to you about Tess Turner," I said.

He waited.

"I don't know if she gave you a heads up, but she's in San Francisco. She's planning to schedule a meeting with you. She wants to talk more about her belief that Steve didn't overdose."

"She flew all the way to San Francisco for this? I have nothing to tell her. She's going to be very disappointed."

"I wanted to give you a little bit of background on her."

"What's that?"

"She was very much in love with Steve."

"Tell me something I don't know," he said.

"Steve broke it off, just a month or so before he died."

"I see."

"You need to understand…she's…fragile. She used to be a senior vice president at the same company Steve worked for. She had huge responsibilities, tremendous respect from everyone. She did very well financially," I said.

"I can imagine."

"She threw all of that away to move to Australia. Now she's running around in bare feet. She's living in a house with these two guys who are developing an app that's going to change the world." I laughed softly, tenderly, I hoped. I wanted my laugh to sound like a friend who forgives anything but is more than a little bit worried. It's a lot to pull off in a simple chuckle over a cell network carrying my voice thousands of miles.

"An app?" he said.

"For mobile phones."

"I know what an app is."

I waited.

"This is very unusual," he said.

"What is?"

"Your call. But I understand your concern, and the situation. She did strike me as somewhat frantic. If I'm not reading in too much, she sounded like she was looking for something that really had nothing to do with the man's overdose."

"She's extremely fragile, I can't emphasize that enough."

"We're not looking into this any further. It was a very cut and dry case."

"I just hope you can be gentle with her. Gentle but firm."

"Iron fist in a velvet glove?"

"Exactly." I smiled. Even though he couldn't see, smiling communicates a tone.

"I might not have agreed to meet with her, if you hadn't called. Thank you for letting me know and for explaining the situation," he said.

"Thanks for your hard work. I'm sure your job isn't easy."

He laughed.

We ended the call. I felt I'd had a very productive day already. I was confident the Steve issue would be put to rest, once and for all. I trusted the detective would say something that gave Tess no choice but to move on. No one would look hard enough to become curious about my relationship with Steve.

16

San Francisco

Standing in the closet in the bedroom of her high-rise condo felt like stepping back into her previous life. Tess hadn't realized how extreme the change had been until she turned slowly, studying her skirts and jackets, silk blouses and high heels. Why had she felt she needed six pairs of black leather high heels? No wonder men mocked women for their shoe fetishes. Looking at the black heels with a cold eye, she was hard-pressed to distinguish three of them. It would feel strange, putting on a suit, but she wanted to make sure Detective Gorman took her seriously, and there was nothing like a dark skirt and jacket and serious high heels, not too flashy or *too* high, to make people take you seriously.

She was a little surprised the detective had agreed so readily to meet with her. It was the reason for her trip and she would have been both furious and despairing if he'd refused, but his immediate, easy reply caught her off guard. *Sure. I'm available on Monday morning. You can stop by at nine-thirty.* His tone suggested he was doing her a favor.

The more she thought about it, the more she realized that technically, the police force worked for her. They were public servants, she was a taxpayer, and he owed her clear answers regarding Steve's death. The man's work had been sloppy, althoughsheneededtofindabetterwaytophrasethat.She'd thought of, and discarded, several descriptors — *sloppy, incomplete, lacking in thoroughness, easy answers, leaping to a conclusion...*

She chose a short navy blue jacket and pencil skirt, a pale yellow blouse, and three-inch navy heels.

After a long shower, she dried her hair and put on makeup. She dressed and picked up her phone. She called Alex.

Before it rang on Tess's end, Alex answered. "Hi. What's up?"

Tess gripped the phone, trying to focus on her hand so she didn't clench her jaw instead. She hated asking again, but she had to know before she met with Gorman. It was critical to have every available fact, to make sure there wasn't anything Gorman knew that Tess didn't. She couldn't let Alex dodge the question again. "Did you ever sleep with Steve?"

Alex laughed.

"Is that funny?"

"It's funny that you want to know."

"Why?"

"You care so much. A bit of jealousy?" Alex laughed softly. "Anyway, no. I didn't sleep with him."

"I want the truth. I need to know before I meet with Gorman."

"I didn't sleep with him."

Tess sighed. She believed Alex, but there was a whisper at the back of her mind — *You wish you believed her, but do you?* "I'm not jealous. I don't care. I just need to know the truth."

"I didn't."

"Okay, thanks." She ended the call. That had

74

accomplished nothing.

She walked down the hall to the kitchen. There were no sounds coming from Damien's room. It was possible he'd adjusted to Jen's schedule. Jen had said Damien seemed to get unsettled when she and Isaiah had taken turns caring for him, so Jen had taken over all the bird care — *Isaiah feeds me, I feed Damien.*

Tess decided not to spoil the pristine look of the counters and sink. She'd have breakfast out and be early to the police station for her nine-thirty meeting. Instead of her usual latte, she'd have a chai tea to enhance her calm mood.

Even though she was four minutes early, she was shown into a small conference room as soon as she signed in.

Less than two minutes later, Detective Gorman appeared in the doorway holding two coffees in Styrofoam cups. She gave him a polite smile and stood. "I'm Tess Turner."

He set the coffees on the table and shook her hand. His skin was cool, despite the coffee cups.

He was about her height and younger than she'd guessed, talking to him on the phone. She'd imagined him as a man with twenty or thirty years of experience. He appeared to be a few years younger than her. Did that give her an advantage? He had blond hair and brown eyes, partially obscured by the glare of the fluorescent light that bounced off the lenses of his black wireframe glasses.

"Detective Gorman," he said.

So, he wasn't going to reveal a first name. Setting the boundaries already. She took her seat and crossed her legs.

He moved one of the cups of coffee toward her.

"No thanks."

He didn't seem fazed. He picked up the other cup and

took a sip. "What can I do for you, Ms. Turner?"

"I thought an in-person meeting would be beneficial. I didn't get the sense you understood my concerns when we spoke on the phone."

"I understood your concerns."

"Steve did not die of a heroin overdose."

Gorman said nothing. He moved the cup toward his mouth and took another quiet sip.

She softened her tone. "To be honest, I'm a little confused. I don't understand why there wasn't a more thorough investigation."

"There was nothing to investigate."

"Nothing to investigate, or no obvious leads?" She smiled, hoping her words didn't sound overly critical. It was such a fine line — needing to be firm, to make this guy do his damn job, while not antagonizing him so much that he shut her down completely.

"Nothing to investigate."

"I was told a woman went into his apartment with him the night he died. No one could identify her," she said. "Doesn't that make you a little curious?"

"Probably a hooker."

"Probably?"

"I'm not going to say definitively because we never located her, but that's the best explanation."

"Did you try to locate her?"

"Yes."

"Why did you stop?"

He put down the coffee cup. "I know it's very difficult when someone dies and leaves behind unexplained pieces of their lives. It can torment those who are left, and…"

"I'm not tormented."

"Let me finish," he said. "It's very difficult, it can torment, or whatever term you want to use to describe those feelings. They can be devastating. I see it all the time. But there was absolutely no evidence in Mr. Montgomery's condo suggesting that a crime had been committed. None. If there was, yes, we would have continued to pursue her."

"Did you look at his phone records?"

"There was no reason. Perhaps I haven't explained evidence clearly. It's…"

"I know what evidence is. And per*haps* there's some in his phone records. They might name the woman who was at his apartment."

"We have no reason to believe that woman is implicated in his death. There was no physical evidence of her even being in the condo. But for the sake of argument, let's say I check his records. A dealer or a hooker is going to have a burner phone."

"What if it was someone he knew?"

"Without physical evidence…"

She sighed. "Doesn't a man's reputation deserve more?"

"That's not my job. My job is to investigate crimes, and in this case, there is no suggestion of a crime."

"Selling heroin is a crime."

"It's good you brought that up." He gave her a kind smile, as if he was trying to project a father image. "Heroin gets ahold of people. It changes them."

"But he wouldn't use it willingly, he's never…"

"It's enthralling, seductive."

"You make it sound like a woman."

"For many, that's an appropriate analogy. At first, using

becomes the other woman, or the other man, in any relationship where heroin comes into the picture. Eventually, the need to recapture that euphoria replaces all relationships."

"Steve would never try it at all, so how would he get seduced?"

"You can't know that." He shrugged. "I don't mean to sound cold. I know this is hard, that you...Well the death of someone so close is life-altering. You're never the same. But there's nothing here to suggest he was murdered. I'm sorry." He gave her another almost-kindly smile.

He thought she was a love-sick girl with no self regard, no sense of self beyond her lover, filled with regrets and grief and *might-have-beens*. Alex had laughed at her. She thought Tess was obsessed and weak. The detective made it sound like all sorts of normal people were using heroin. Maybe Steve was into it after all. He'd seemed rather celibate after she'd broken up with him. Maybe heroin had been her replacement.

As she walked out of the building, after Detective Gorman ushered her out of his office, her train of thought shifted. What was she doing? In fighting so hard for Steve's reputation, what was she doing to her own?

17

Sydney

Sean settled back in the leather chair facing his nude statue, expertly carved and polished into something that had an essence beyond the wood. He understood Alex's fixation with it, even if he didn't understand her lack of consideration for his privacy. Twice, that he knew of, she'd crept into his room to admire it. She'd asked him to move it down to the living room so everyone could enjoy it, suggesting there was something perverted about his private admiration of it. She made his attachment to it into something ugly. That statue had a purpose in his room, and it wasn't going anywhere, and it wasn't perversion.

After the last time she'd simply walked into his room, he'd considered following Gavin's lead — locking the bedroom door. With someone like Alex, locking the door was for the best. The negative energy created by her invasion of his personal space, looking with cold eyes on one of the most beautiful things he owned, was worse than setting up the barrier of a locked door. But locking interior doors was counter to the atmosphere he wanted to foster and he hadn't been able to bring himself to actually turn the lock. Maybe deep inside, he wanted to trust her, even now.

The statue's back was arched, her arms lifted over her

head. Something about her reminded him of Terri. He'd seen the resemblance the first time he saw the statue, and he hadn't been able to stop thinking about the similarity, even if it was obscure and something he couldn't really explain. Now, he spent time every single day gazing at it, admiring the shape of her body, thinking about the things he'd done. There were some very good things he'd done in his life, but there were others… He closed his eyes and forced his thoughts to something else — plans for a vacation, once the app was launched. An extended diving trip would be good.

The pool was refilling with fresh, pure water. New lounge chairs for the patio were on the way. He was ready to pretend the drowning had never happened. Alex was quick to call him out on his desire to pretend, but you absolutely *could* pretend. People were too dismissive of the value of pretense. In many ways, you created your own reality. If they put Karen's death out of their heads, cleaned away the things that had touched the physical event, they could pretend and it would become real.

He laughed. If he said these things out loud, people would think he was mad.

Now Alex and Gavin were stirring it up, clucking over his white lie to the detective. They were wrong to make something of it. Encountering Karen that one time was not important to their inquiry. If the detectives stuck to relevant questions, they might be more effective at their jobs.

It had been a ten-word conversation. Insignificant.

With his eyes closed, he could see Karen now. She was very attractive, with long thick hair and a nice body. He'd noticed that from the start. He'd never seen her naked, nothing like that. But he could tell with a glimpse that she had a nice body. Seeing her body in his pool confirmed it. She'd chopped off her hair into something supposedly stylish. Why did women do that? Why did they imagine hair sliced over their ear on one side, hanging to their jaw on the other, looked good? Why did some of them think a haircut that looked like a man's hairstyle was the way to deliver vengeance on an ex? As if the guy who dumped you cared about your hair any more.

She'd given the impression her marriage to John wasn't going well. When she left him, Sean had assumed it was her doing. So why the need to chop off her hair to punish him? Unless it was some chick-style declaration of freedom?

He'd first seen her almost a year ago, standing in her front yard, head tipped back so all that dark hair hung almost to her waist. The edge of her right hand was pressed over her brow, shielding her eyes from the sun. She'd stood that way for several minutes. Finally, she'd lowered her hand and walked to her front patio. He'd thought she was too good looking for that guy who appeared to be her husband.

The only time he'd spoken to her was early one morning as he was leaving for the airport. He'd backed quickly down the driveway, not expecting cars or pedestrians at four-thirty in the morning.

When something flashed at the corner of his vision, he'd stepped on the brake and jerked his head to the side. She was standing right there, almost touching his car. She wore a beige jacket with a hood and looked to be returning from a walk. He lowered the window.

She smiled. "You're up early."

He was confused. They'd never spoken. He was pretty sure she hadn't even seen him when she was standing in her front yard looking up at the sky. Her words sounded like something you'd say to a roommate or someone you saw every day.

"Headed to the airport. Are you okay?"

"Of course. Aren't you sweet for asking." Her eyes grew glassy, shining out from a face that was mostly obscured by darkness, only a single streetlight casting a faint triangle of light. She blinked a few times. "I wish I could take a trip." She sighed.

He glanced at the house next door. All the homes on this street cost millions to purchase and thousands to maintain every month. Surely they weren't strapped for cash. Besides, hadn't that guy…John…retired early? You didn't do that if money was tight.

"I reckon you can any time." He laughed.

"You're right." She glanced at her home, then back at him. She reached her hand into the car and ran one finger down the side of his hair. "I love long hair on a man."

He gave her a smile without putting effort into the act, leaving it small and, he hoped, polite but uninterested.

She tilted her head to the left. "You should invite me over for a drink sometime."

"I…maybe." He couldn't tell her about his vow. She was a stranger. It was private. Besides, that would be assuming he'd read her signals accurately, and with someone he didn't know, the odds of that were slim.

"I'll ask my girlfriend about setting a date, with you and your husband." He hadn't realized he was searching so hard to send the correct message, he'd blurted out the most obvious lie in the book.

"Oh." She smiled and her eyes watered again.

"I need to get to the airport," he said.

She touched his hair again, stroking it softly. Finally she pulled her arm out of the window and took a few steps away from the car. He backed into the street.

The lights of planes taking off were in the near distance when it finally struck him — he didn't know her name. He doubted she knew his.

Not knowing her name at the time proved none of it mattered. The cops would get no useful information out of the encounter. If, by some wild stretch of the imagination, Karen drowned herself in his pool because of his rejection, nearly a year after the fact, that didn't matter to the police anyway. They needed to determine suicide or accident, neither of which had anything to do with him. If they decided murder…he didn't want to think about that. Then, they'd linger for days, possibly weeks.

18

The sub-detective, or whatever he was called, let Sean know there would be three detectives showing up Tuesday at eleven in the morning. The pool was filled and the new patio furniture was in place. I wondered whether they'd notice the furniture had been replaced, and if they did, whether the quick replacement of lounge chairs that were clearly not cheap might raise their curiosity even further.

When they arrived, Bender said he would be questioning me this time. The third detective was a female named Axton. It appeared as if they had a plan for mixing up the genders. Maybe they thought we'd be more charming to the opposite sex. Maybe they didn't truly plan it, maybe Martin wanted Sean and the rest was the luck of the draw. Who knows how they decide these things.

Sean and Gavin and their curious detectives took the offices.

"Where's a good place for us to talk?" Bender said.

"Anywhere."

"Someplace private."

"If the others are busy, everywhere is private."

"They might finish before us, then it won't be so private." He gave me a look with narrowed eyes and although I was pretty sure it was threatening, it felt like a slight come-on at the same time.

"We can go out on the patio and close the doors," I said.

"There's no sitting area upstairs?"

I didn't think Sean would like me taking him upstairs, but saying so would put Sean in a bad light. "The patio's nice. I'll get us some drinks. What would you like?"

"A glass of water is fine."

I led the way to the kitchen and filled two glasses with filtered water. I carried them to the patio doors and waited while Bender pulled one open and stood to the side for me to go through first.

When we were seated at the table, he pushed the glass away from him, as if all that effort had been simply to watch me juggle.

"Tell me more about your background," he said.

"Why is that important?"

"Because you're not an Australian citizen."

That didn't seem right, but it also didn't really matter what he asked. I could find an answer to anything, some truth, some diversion, some redirecting it back to him. "What would you like to know? My life story could take some time."

"Why are you here, really?"

"For a job. I told the detective that."

"I'm the detective now."

"I thought…"

He smiled. "You should be glad you got me. I'm just going through the paces here. *Miz* Martin wants to turn this into a murder case. Whatever theory we work from, that's the frame we use when we talk to witnesses. She's all over the murder track. Needs to prove she can do the same job as the boys."

When I didn't answer, he smirked. "Kind of a cozy set-up

here. Two couples?"

"Colleagues, no couples."

"Really? I find that hard to believe. Two good looking gals like you and the other one. Very hard to believe. Very, very hard…"

I smiled.

He looked unnerved. He'd expected me to cringe, to blush, to fluster.

"Any idea why Mrs. North ended up in your employer's pool." He put air quotes around the word employer.

"I told Detective Martin — I have no idea."

"Miz Martin is considering the angle of Mrs. North killing Mr. North."

"I don't think she was in the country when he died."

"Doesn't really matter. A tiny girl like Karen? She wouldn't be able to kill anyone. Ninety-nine-point-nine percent of women aren't capable of killing a man. Aside from their physical inability, they don't have it in them. That cold-blooded streak. The warrior."

I nodded.

He was quiet for a moment. "You look like you're here for more than a BS job creating an app. I think you're here to sweep up a good-looking Aussie. Take one of our men from a nice Australian girl. There are too many Americans here, girls fishing for husbands."

"Is that right?"

"They're fucking up Australian culture. There's stronger will now to make visas more difficult, to reduce the number, to keep our culture intact."

I spread my lips in a straight line and said nothing.

"Now that's out of the way, I think you know it might not

be a good idea for you to be uncooperative." He waved his fingers at me, "Or bye-bye."

"I wasn't aware I was uncooperative."

"Good, then tell me about these two guys you're shacking up with. Everything you know, everything that doesn't sit right with you."

"First, I'm not shacking up. Second, I thought only Detective Martin believed this was a murder."

"And I'm doing as I'm told, like a good little lad. Asking about the prime suspects."

"Why are they suspects?"

"Tell me what you know. Anything odd they've done? Any weirdo comments?"

"No."

"This seems like a set-up ripe for jealousy."

"That doesn't even make sense," I said.

"Something strange is going on here. I can smell it." He wrinkled his nose. "Like fish."

I laughed.

"This isn't a game. You absolutely could be sent back to the good ole' USA if we find you holding out on us. It's a crime, ya know."

"I'm not holding out. I never met Karen, never even saw her. Gavin and Sean didn't know her…"

"So they say."

"We have no idea why she walked into his yard in the middle of the night. I'm sorry she died, but I don't see how, or why, someone would kill her. A stranger wouldn't even have known she was back here. She came in for a few shots, had a bit more than planned, got wasted, fell in the pool."

"Nice theory."

"The simplest answer is usually the right one."

"I don't think that applies to murder," he said.

"Untimely death," I said.

He grimaced. He folded his arms across his chest and stared at me. "Well?"

"You haven't really even asked a question," I said. "Gavin and Sean are nice, smart, hardworking guys."

"Which one are you fucking?"

I smiled.

"So it's both." He nodded as if he'd hit on the right answer without my help. "Definitely both." He grinned.

I stared back at him.

It took him almost a full minute to figure out what to say next. The rest of the questions were the same as the previous ones, a few variations, and a few irrelevant ones thrown in just to show he wasn't backing down.

The detectives didn't leave until one-thirty. The moment the door closed, I began making martinis. Neither Sean nor Gavin looked thrilled with the idea of a martini so early in the day, but apparently they decided to humor me, because they silently joined my toast and took hesitant, exploratory sips before placing their glasses on the dining room table. Sean gazed into his glass for a moment as if it contained something nauseating — uncooked egg or spoiled meat.

We sat there, no one saying much beyond an occasional comment on the cheeses and crackers Gavin had spread out on a wood plank. It would do for a late lunch — the comfort of cheese, no preparation, and no cleanup.

After we'd said all we could about the varieties of cheese, silence fell over us and we ate methodically, sipping our drinks faster than is wise with a martini.

I finally asked them how it had gone. Sean informed us he was treated like a suspect. The questions were clearly focused on the assumption Karen had been murdered, although there was no autopsy report yet.

Sean began twisting himself in knots, considering and tossing aside ideas for getting the detectives to stop asking questions, to stop assuming proximity meant guilt.

"You haven't said what they asked you." He turned on Gavin as if he was preparing to punch him in the face.

"Same old...They asked a bit about you. How long you'd owned the house, how long I'd known you, whether you had a girlfriend, that sort of thing."

Sean gritted his teeth, pulling his lips back so we could see the full effect of his clenched jaw.

"They asked me some of the same questions again," Gavin said. "Couldn't believe I'd never seen Karen. *Never?* She kept saying that over and over. She asked if we were hermits. She also wanted to know if I trusted you. I said yes. She wanted to know if you tended to lie, and I said how would I know? She pushed that point a bit — had I caught you adjusting the truth, telling white lies etcetera. I dodged it, for now."

Sean took a sip of his martini and ate two of the three olives.

"I'm telling you," Gavin said, "I'm not gonna lie for you. So you better figure out what you're planning to tell them, if you're planning to correct your misleading answer."

"I didn't ask you to lie for me, and that's not what you're doing."

"I might be put in that position."

"I met her once. It's not important."

"It's still a lie."

Sean turned toward me, waiting for me to say something. I remained still. Our eyes met and we locked onto each other for several seconds. For once, we appeared to agree. It made no sense for Gavin to make a point of lying versus truth. It absolutely didn't matter. Getting the police out of the house should be a shared goal, a team effort. No one wanted to keep answering questions, watching them meander this way and that, hoping to catch us in a lie. We needed to give simple answers, have each other's backs, and appear cooperative. That was the fastest way out. It seemed as if the detectives enjoyed messing with our heads as much as they wanted to find out what happened to Karen.

I smiled. Sean returned the smile, but our agreed thoughts wouldn't accomplish anything, Gavin's tone made it clear that if he was asked, he would tell them Sean had lied. I could imagine how things would spin out of control if that happened.

19

Karen had drunk three glasses of champagne and eaten a so-so pasta dinner. Everyone around her was asleep. TV screens flickered with abandoned movies. The cabin's primary lights were turned off. There was an eerie half darkness because there were so many safety lights — lights on the floor running the length of the aisle, overhead, and glowing out from the bathroom area behind her.

Her eyes wouldn't even close when she tried. Usually champagne put her to sleep within two hours. At weddings, she had to limit herself to tiny sips and then leave it to get warm in the glass, no matter how good it was. Sometimes, she'd ask a server to stash a bottle and she'd drink some with the cake, knowing they'd be leaving before she was overcome by sleepiness.

Something about John's death...that's what she'd been thinking about. Maybe his spirit floating up here in the heavens...she giggled...maybe more champagne. She pushed the attendant call button. Maybe...what had she been thinking about? Oh, John. Dying. His spirit out there in the darkness was resurrecting her entire life with him. She'd just as soon forget, but colorful, detailed memories kept flooding her thoughts, uninvited.

One red flag, were she to think of so-called red flags, was John's behavior before they were married. It hadn't been nineteen-sixty-one for God's sake. They'd met in nineteen-ninety-three. Everyone had sex before they were married. Most people had sex before they'd been together three months. Besides, it had always been that way, just badly concealed by women who gave birth quite soon in their first year of marriage.

The flight attendant put a fresh glass on her table and poured it two thirds full of champagne.

"Thank you," Karen whispered.

"No worries."

She drank in the music of his accent and took a small taste. Nicely chilled. The attendant slipped away into the semi-darkness.

John returned immediately to her thoughts as if he'd been waiting for the flight attendant to leave them alone. As if he had things to say to her. But what? He didn't even care about her. Well he did in that he wanted a woman in his house to make his life legitimate, to cook for him, to ensure he wasn't stalked as an eligible bachelor every time he went out for dinner or a drink.

John hadn't wanted to have sex before they were married. He never even tried. She'd assumed he was extremely old fashioned, a rarity in any generation. Or maybe he was more religious than he'd let on. She was okay with that, she didn't mind attending church services. They gave you time every week to sort through your thoughts without interruptions.

Later, though, his lack of interest took on a different color. He didn't even enjoy sex, not really. Not like other men. When he did condescend to it, he treated her like a contaminated object. Yet, he loved looking at her, loved even choosing clothes to show off her body. He loved watching her undress. He loved giving her surprise gift cards to shop for lingerie and cosmetics, to get a makeover, to change her hair color or style.

She couldn't have seen any of that before they were married, but she should have dug in deeper, asking him why he was so chaste. But her belief that the man should take the lead stopped her. His disinterest made her feel slightly unwanted and that wasn't something she wanted to say out loud. She'd let him control every conversation and she'd never said anything that might cause an uncomfortable exchange. She was still that way, more than she should be.

Of course, she couldn't say it was a red flag she'd only missed before marriage. The flag kept waving, and still she stayed with him, years after, even when she knew. She'd stayed with him for over two decades. And she couldn't say why. After they were divorced, she still found him at the center of her thoughts. It seemed as though he'd taken over her life, become part of her, and ultimately swallowed her. She hardly existed without him.

Then there was the other red flag, an after-the-fact flag, a flag for a normal woman, not Karen Ellison North who would put up with utter degradation for all those years. The other red flag made her feel even more deeply that there was something wrong with *her*. And it filled her with rage to think she'd believed such lies, that a tiny part of her still believed it. She took a long swallow of champagne. She let the carbonation dissolve in her throat and took another sip.

She raised the window shade and looked out. Nothing. No stars. It must be cloudy, but no light was available to allow her to see the clouds. John hated nights like that, when he couldn't study his beloved planets, investigate the solar system, although what was left to investigate after years of looking through his telescope wasn't clear. Surely others, experts, scientists, had that covered completely.

When they did have sex...

She took a long, steady sip of champagne.

When they did have sex, he wouldn't look at her, keeping his eyes closed the entire time. He didn't speak or touch her in a way to make her more aroused. He performed the technical functions and that was it. Then, he insisted she get up and shower rather than enjoying a nice drifting into sleep. Many nights, most, if she really thought about it, he left their bed and slept in one of the spare rooms. He didn't want to see her again until she was showered, her legs shaved, her body creamy with expensive lotion, her hair clean and silky.

Often she fought with herself, trying to decide whether her desire for him was stronger than the resulting shame.

When the shame prevailed, he didn't seem to notice if weeks or months passed without sex. Then she had to ask for his attention. There was no end to the barely perceptible, but enormous ways he made her feel undesirable. Unloved.

20

Sydney

After the martinis and cheese cleared out of their system, Gavin and Sean did what seemed to be their instinctive reaction to anything — they put on swimsuits and flung themselves into the pool. I wasn't thrilled with the idea of sitting near the patio getting splashed, but the thought of hanging out in my room and giving attention to the lagging social media accounts I was supposed to be feeding every few hours felt too claustrophobic. The sky was cloudless and the temperature creeping into the seventies, warmer than I like for running.

I decided to go for a walk. I changed into a skirt and T-shirt, flat sandals and sunglasses, and headed out the front door.

I walked down the gentle slope of Sean's magnificent stone walkway, past the lush greenery toward the street. It was deserted. All the front yards were empty. The houses appeared unoccupied, although surely there were people inside those enormous structures living out their lives, as we did inside ours. John's house to my right had an air of desertion about it, but I suppose it was my knowledge of the murdered owner and his drowned ex-wife that pushed my thoughts in that direction.

I crossed the street to get a look at John's place from a different angle, to see whether the sense of emptiness was real or imagined. In all the weeks I'd lived there, I'd never been on that side of the street. The road was wide and no one parked near the curb, so it felt farther away than it really was. I turned and studied John's house.

It wasn't clear what would happen to the house now that the owner and his most logical beneficiary were both dead. There were no children. I suppose a man like that would have had a detailed distribution of his estate, so there must be other relatives who would receive windfalls. He didn't strike me as a guy who would give all his wealth to charity, but maybe he'd donated to an astronomy foundation.

The house definitely had an unused quality about it. The lawn and shrubs were still being cared for by the gardening service, but even they gave off a sterile quality. All the blinds and drapes were closed.

I shifted my attention to Lisa's house on the opposite side of John's. It had the same deserted feeling. Maybe people coming and going, breathing and eating and sleeping, fucking and talking and thinking inside a building give it some sort of intangible energy that's taken for granted until it's not there.

"Such a shame, isn't it."

I turned. A woman about my height stood beside me. Her gaze was also fixed on the houses across the street. Her gray- and brown-streaked hair hung past her shoulders. She was older — easily seventy, but she held herself erect and her body seemed to hum with life, resting easily but solidly on her feet, her right hip cocked slightly. Her stance made me think of a dancer, and her clothes fit that image — a tight black short-sleeved T-shirt of thick cotton, a black skirt that hugged her narrow waist and flared to mid-calf, and bare feet with a ring on the second toe of each foot.

"Did you know all of them?" I said.

"Yes, somewhat. I knew John the best. He used to carry in my groceries for me. Not that I needed help, but he couldn't seem to grasp the fact that I can manage my own life."

I turned slightly and she did the same so we were partially facing each other.

"You look like you can manage your life perfectly well," I said.

"Thank you. I hope we have some happier people purchase both properties."

I nodded.

"You're Sean's girlfriend?" she said.

I laughed. Sean didn't appear to have a girlfriend, not one that he'd mentioned. Thinking about it made me curious why the detective had asked about that. I suppose the lack of a girlfriend implied something about his relationship with Karen. There was a definite sexual message in her near nudity. Maybe she was out there trying to get his attention, but she got drunk and drowned before she succeeded.

The woman beside me smiled knowingly. "I'm Elizabeth."

"Alexandra," I said. "And I'm not his girlfriend. Sean's running a company out of his house, a small company, just four of us."

"Like Silicon Valley."

I wasn't sure whether she was referring to the TV show or the actual place, but it didn't really matter. She was obviously younger than her years, not only in her appearance, but in her attention to what was happening in the world.

"Did you ever meet Karen?" I said.

"A few times. She was a very unhappy woman. Not the bitter, angry type. More, sad or…confused might be a better way to describe her. As if there was something she didn't quite understand about life."

"Do you think she killed herself?"

Elizabeth obviously knew the details of the death. Everyone on the street did, I assumed. Despite the deserted yards, surely some kind of connection ran through the neighborhood, stories and gossip shared, even if all of that took place on secluded backyard patios or in online communities. When Lisa's body was found and the police and paramedics came, a few neighbors on this side of the street had come out to gawk, although I couldn't remember whether I'd seen Elizabeth.

"That's the question, isn't it?" She smiled. "Accident, suicide, murder. Everyone loves to speculate."

"Do you?"

"Not as much as my neighbors." She waved her hand vaguely toward the houses around her.

"But you must have an opinion."

"I think she killed herself."

"It seems the most logical," I said. "Although isn't it hard to drown yourself? A very painful way to die."

"Maybe she was one of those who needs pain."

It still seemed painful. There's the pain of a cut and the blood leaving your body, but in those instances, you lose consciousness gradually. The pain of not breathing seemed too awful to me. Maybe I'm a coward. If I were of the mindset to want to terminate my life, I would definitely take the easy way out. Something that didn't hurt. But I never would. I like being alive and can't imagine ever not liking it.

"She could have fallen in," I said.

"Yes. Drinking like that, it's a possibility."

"Did the police talk to you?" I said.

"Once. I've seen them at your place a few times." She studied my face, trying to tame her curiosity. She obviously wanted to know why they'd been back and what they were asking, interested despite her proclamation that she wasn't one to speculate.

We all speculate. We all want to know what happened and why…with everything. But especially death, or scandal, or tragedy. It's a compulsion. We have to know. It's why neighbors and co-workers and church members gossip. That insatiable need to know what's going on, to insert ourselves into the lives of acquaintances and strangers.

It's the reason pulp magazines and online gossip sites thrive. It's the reason people love reality shows, and those background stories they tell about Olympic athletes. We're like dogs and cats that check each other out with aggressive, invasive sniffing. We sniff with our words.

"They've talked to us twice, so far," I said.

"That must be irritating."

"It is. None of us knew her, so it's a complete waste of our time. And of course they don't tell us anything, they just keep asking questions."

"It's an unbalanced relationship," she said.

I nodded.

"In several ways. Do you think they'll be back with more questions?"

"Until they get whatever it is they're looking for," I said.

"What's that?"

"It sounds like they want to have a murder investigation."

"Or just be sure it's not that."

"True," I said.

"I suppose they want to understand Sean's relationship with her."

This was interesting. I didn't want to spill what I knew. If she knew nothing, if she was fishing, and the detectives talked to her again, it could go badly for Sean. But maybe she knew more than I did. It certainly sounded that way. I didn't want to admit my ignorance.

"I'm sure you aren't aware, since you didn't live here," she said. "There was something, although not much. I'm probably reading into it."

"You think he killed her?" My voice must have changed tone because she put her hand on my forearm and squeezed.

"Oh, no. Nothing like that. No, I didn't mean to imply that. He's a nice man. And I don't think anything happened between them, but…she was an attractive woman. I saw him looking at her, many times. Longer than necessary. When she wasn't aware of it."

"That's not so unusual."

"It wasn't just a man looking at an attractive woman. There was a deeper longing to it."

"You can tell that from a glance across the street?"

"He stood there for a very long time. It wasn't his expression. I couldn't see that, of course. But something in his posture."

"Do you think there's a chance she was murdered?"

"There isn't a lot of murder around here, until this." She gestured across the street. "No, I don't think so. The detectives just have to be thorough. In this area, where there's not a lot of crime, they probably make more of the situation than necessary. But most likely it's just being thorough. And I suppose that's what we want from them."

I smiled.

"Going for a walk?" she said.

"Yes. Do you want to join me?"

"I have some things that need taking care of. Maybe next time." She patted my arm, turned and walked to the house just beyond where we were standing. She started up the front path and unlatched the iron gate. She didn't turn to wave good-bye. I wasn't sure how there could be a next time. It was doubtful I'd ring her bell or that she'd ring mine.

21

The next morning I went for an early run. When I got back, I spent an hour in the weight room.

After that, I felt ready to work. I'd been getting paid all this time, of course, but since the day Karen's body floated into our lives, Sean hadn't said much about actually sitting down at our desks to get busy moving the app out the door and into the world. I don't kill myself to do my job, but I'm not a slacker who needs to be micromanaged. I knew my job, and I needed to get to it. Building a social media presence takes forever, and I was extremely late ramping it up.

I took a shower and made espresso. I cooked chicken sausages with buttered whole grain toast for breakfast. I ate at the bar, alone in the vast room with its fifteen-foot ceiling. As far as I could tell, Sean and Gavin hadn't come out of their rooms at all.

I went into the office and settled at the desk. I opened Twitter first, because it's easier to deal with. I scrolled through the thousands of tweets since my last visit. I re-tweeted a few witty comments and a photograph of a sea turtle. I followed five more people. I switched over to Facebook and opened the draft of a post I'd spent a few days composing before Karen turned up. The post said TruthTeller was a visionary company both with our app and our work-style which was our lifestyle. It had a line or two about Sean's utopian vision of working and playing together, making strong connections, feeling the creative aspect of work pervade your life. It ended with an invitation for others to comment on what they liked and didn't like about their own work environments and their relationships with their colleagues.

Once I had it worded exactly right, I posted it along with a photograph of the office I shared with Tess. The photograph showed a portion of the desk, the corner of the enormous computer screen, and the window shutters, angled so the giant birds of paradise and the trunk of one palm tree could be seen through the openings between the slats. I pressed the button to pay thirty-five dollars to boost the post.

I returned to Twitter.

It didn't take long for me to get off track, swept into the raging waters of Twitter. I read about a man who had fallen from the tenth floor of a hotel in a beach town south of Sydney. The death was suspicious because police weren't sure whether he'd fallen, jumped, or been pushed.

I was reading about a woman who had gone missing in Aruba years ago, and the new evidence in her disappearance when Sean knocked on the door frame.

"You're at it early," he said.

I smiled.

"Gav and I are going downtown. We're meeting with the device product manager."

"Sounds good."

"We'll eat downtown. Back by three or so."

"I have a lot to keep me busy."

He nodded, already turning away. "If the detectives come by, don't let them in."

"Can I do that? As an American?"

He gave one short laugh. "Tell them if they need to talk to you, it has to be out front."

"Sure."

He left and I returned to Twitter. The TruthTeller account had almost a thousand followers now, but not a lot of engagement. I was going to have to find something more provocative to tweet about if I was going to make this work.

In my experience, most businesses don't seem to worry much about engagement or enthusiasm. It's as if someone told them they must be on Twitter, so there they are. There's no real purpose. They tweet, they get a few favorites and retweets but they don't expect to sell a lot, don't expect new customers, just a slight connection with existing customers. They're simply sitting ducks for customer complaints. What we were trying to do — finding new customers and potential customers — was a long, uphill battle. A hill that might be impossible to scale. Being outrageous mattered on Twitter. I knew I'd think of something, eventually. Whether Sean approved of whatever I thought of would be another uphill battle.

After two hours, I was bored. And tired of sitting in one spot.

I went into the billiards room and played a game of pool with myself, trying to think of what I could be, what persona I could take on to capture attention on Twitter. Funny was best, but I wasn't sure I was all that funny.

I picked up my phone and checked Facebook to see whether the post had generated any comments. Ten likes. That wasn't too bad. I hoped it got more traction soon. I'd thought the photograph would help, but maybe it wasn't interesting enough. I needed to figure out something to produce in video.

I went upstairs and walked to Sean's bedroom door. After finding me in his room twice, he'd said he was going to start locking it. I was too cavalier about my boundaries, he said. *His* boundaries, was what he really meant. I pressed the handle and the door opened. His obsession over the detectives must have taken his mind off more petty intrusions into his privacy. I smiled and walked into his room.

Everything looked the same — immaculate and uncluttered. The bed was made so precisely it looked un-slept in. It was a very nice bed, a solid, comfortable mattress and lavish sheets and pillows and blankets and comforter. I wondered if he'd ever had sex in that bed. There hadn't been a woman around as long as I'd lived there. None of us went out much, so if he'd gone to see a girlfriend, or a hooker, it had only been a once or twice. A girlfriend was unlikely.

I went to the chair facing his statue of a naked woman. I sat down and pulled out my phone, tapping into Facebook again. There were three more likes. I put the phone on the floor by my feet and leaned back. The statue was so lush and smooth, it was hard to take my eyes off it. I loved it and wanted it for my own, which was not going to happen. But I liked spending time in his room looking at it.

The carving was a truly remarkable piece of art. The kind of piece you can't keep your hands off. The kind of piece you want to possess. I stood and walked toward it. I ran my palm from her elbow down to her armpit, and then along her side to her waist.

Artwork is such a personal thing. One person adores a painting or a sculpture and another thinks it's ho-hum or even hideous. Some art is more generally liked. This statue, I imagined, was one of those pieces that it would be hard not to like, although my father immediately came to mind as a candidate for the hater category. He didn't like nudity in art — it was unnecessary. I wasn't sure where my mother stood on the subject.

I ran my finger up the indentation around her spine.

When art speaks to you, it takes you over. It's as if the mind of the artist is embedded in the wood and metal and paint. That mind emerges and speaks directly to you, entering your body and becoming part of you.

Most people, religious extremists aside, would be spoken to by this statue, I was sure of it.

I adjusted the shutters. I crossed the room and picked up my phone. I opened the camera app. I framed the statue and snapped five photographs, shifting my position a few inches each time. It would be perfect for getting conversation going on the Facebook page. Of course, Sean would kill me if he saw it there.

22

San Francisco

The evening after her failed meeting with Detective Gorman, Tess took herself out to dinner alone. She wanted to revel in her own company and mull over her new revelation — that she was caring more for a dead man than she was for herself. As if she'd woken from a confusing, torturous dream, she suddenly was no longer bothered by the inexplicable circumstances of Steve's death. In the end, it was his fault. All of it, even his stained reputation. Why hadn't she seen that earlier? Maybe the shock? Whatever he did to get himself into that situation, whatever deviant individual he'd gotten mixed up with — it was on him. She had no obligation to polish his memory.

She wanted to laugh at the absurdity of her behavior. Now, she didn't give a flying fuck whether Alex had slept with the guy. She didn't care if he'd gotten into heroin all on his own or if some hooker had lured him into it. How stupid did he have to be for that to happen?

She chose a French restaurant. She wanted the tranquility of classical music and the refined, exquisite taste of French cuisine, not a thick steak or seafood — a hearty dinner that would remind her of Steve's preferences. She wanted light cream sauces and tiny portions of whipped potato, and delicate baby green beans. She wanted tender veal or perhaps a small piece of mouth-watering chicken breast, perfectly cooked.

She ordered a split of champagne. It seemed appropriate. She was celebrating her freedom from the burden of a former lover and former colleague, a man who was entitled and condescending. He'd taken over her life as surely as if he were still alive. He'd consumed her mind as surely as if they were still sleeping together and she was a weak and needy woman who couldn't breathe without a man to make her feel as if her existence had purpose.

Still, despite all of that, she did need a man. Maybe that was part of the problem. It had been months since she'd split with Steve. There'd been no one except those few casual encounters when she'd started her vacation in Australia. Being trapped in Sean's house wasn't good. She needed to talk to him about it. His vision for togetherness had the potential to become toxic. Human beings weren't just about work and games and food. Surely he and Gavin felt the same. She had no doubt Alex felt that way — it was clear in her restless behavior. This wasn't healthy. They needed balance.

The first glass of champagne went down smoothly and too fast. After that, she drank it slowly and enjoyed her meal, thinking of nothing in particular, except for the occasional flash of pure pleasure in the food and champagne. Ideally, the delicious meal should be completed with a lovely few hours in the arms of a naked man. She sighed and drank the last of the champagne.

When she entered her condo, Jen was watching TV and sipping from a glass of white wine.

"Mind if I join you?"

"It's your house." Jen smiled.

Tess didn't try to correct the distorted view. She went into the bedroom and stripped off her heels and nylons and suit. She took off her bra and put on a T-shirt and leggings. She washed her face, removed her makeup, and brushed her hair.

A glass of wine was waiting on the coffee table when she returned to the living room.

Jen picked up the remote and paused her show. "How was it?"

"I didn't accomplish anything."

"I'm sorry."

"It's fine. I had a revelation. I'm done thinking about it."

Jen smiled. She held out her glass. Tess touched her glass to Jen's. "To being done," Jen said.

"Tomorrow I'll take Damien to the vet. And get everything arranged for his trip."

"I'll miss him," Jen said. She looked into her glass. She swirled the wine slightly and took another sip. Without looking up, she said, "Does this mean we should find another place to stay? Now that you don't need us to take care of him?"

"Not at all. I still don't want to sell. It's better to have it occupied."

"Isaiah and I feel kind of guilty...not paying anything."

"I don't even think about it. I've been lucky in my career. And I'm not paying rent in Australia." She laughed. "So it all works out."

Jen smiled and finished her wine. "Do you want more?"

"Sure."

Jen went into the kitchen and returned with the bottle of Chardonnay. She topped off Tess's glass and refilled her own.

Watching Jen now, it was impossible to remember her as a hooker. She'd become an entirely different person, or maybe returned to the person she'd always been. Tess liked to think that the opportunity to live in a nice place, free from worrying about money, had played a small part in Jen's transformation. Her confidence, her ability to concentrate on doing well at work were a result of not having to think about rent and bills. And returning to a comfortable home, a nice bed after working as a bartender, had surely helped.

Tess pulled her legs up onto the couch and leaned against the back, relaxing into the cushion. "Are you and Isaiah…" She felt her face grow warm. Why? Maybe because she really didn't know Jen all that well. It was none of her business, and she didn't want to come across as if she believed that providing housing gave her a right to pry.

"No."

"How did you know what I was going to ask about…"

"It's obvious." Jen smiled. "The look on your face. And the way you stopped in the middle of the sentence." She took a sip of wine. "I don't want to wreck my friendship with him, for one thing."

"Tell me to MYOB if you don't want to say, but do you have anyone in your life?"

"There's a guy I met at work. We went to a concert, watched a few movies. We hang out."

"Boyfriend?"

"Not really."

"Do you want him to be?"

Jen laughed. She took a swallow of wine. "I don't know. Things are good. He's fun. I don't feel like I should bring him here. So…I mean we hang out at his place."

"I appreciate that," Tess said. She hadn't said that no one else should stay in her condo, but it made her feel more secure, knowing her wood floors and nice furniture wouldn't get banged up by potentially careless strangers, too many people. It was easy for one visiting friend to turn into three or four. The place was big enough. "Not coming here doesn't mean you can't be a couple."

"I know. I'm not sure why I said that." Jen laughed. "I guess I like it here, I like how my life is right now. As long as I have someone to hang out with, nice sex, I don't need more. Not right now. Not after how my life was. I like it that things are a little predictable."

Tess nodded. She leaned her head back and looked at the ceiling. She understood Jen's feelings — the desire for some sameness, not too much excitement. She wasn't lonely, far from it. At the same time, it wasn't just sex she desired. Along with it, she wanted a companion, someone who belonged to her.

23

Sydney

The minute Sean and Gav got into the car after their meeting, the frustration over his lack of control began to plague him. When they got home, he'd taken a late afternoon swim which cleared his head for a grand total of thirty-seven minutes while he was in the water. As soon as he'd dragged the towel across his shoulders, the irritation returned.

Once again, significant, meaningful work on getting the app to market had stalled. It wasn't as if he needed the money. He was well beyond that phase of life. He had enough that he could never work again. What he wanted, what he *needed* was to contribute something important to the human race. It sounded both trite and rather pompous, as well as somewhat needy, but it was a basic human drive, wasn't it? The desire to make an impact in the world was the same instinctive need that drove human beings to procreate. So far, he hadn't felt much of a nudge in that direction, but he wanted to contribute something to the world. He wanted his ideas to take root and live beyond him.

The app would improve lives. It would make people happier and more productive on a daily basis, more fulfilled in the big picture. In addition to the app, his vision for the ideal workplace had the potential to transform humanity. The vision was nothing new, it actually resembled feudalism in some ways, although he rejected that comparison. His model was the way agricultural societies lived and worked. But his ideas were even more focused on building community. Rather than parallel work with occasional spurts of shared effort, his vision was for something more transformative. Especially in this world, with technology taking over every relationship, there was a greater need for physical presence and live interactions with other human beings.

He picked up his mug and took a sip of hot chocolate. The uncovered living room windows looked out on the dark backyard. Nothing moved, proven by the fact that the lights around the pool and garden area hadn't come on for nearly an hour. He took another sip of chocolate.

Maybe all these roadblocks had a purpose. He'd read self-help books that suggested roadblocks had larger significance than their mere existence. They proved that what you were pursuing was important — the roadblocks were tests of character and will. But a dead woman in his pool? Detectives looking to spin a murder narrative? Just when he'd gotten the team back on track after the other deaths next door, this had to happen. Death was surrounding them, trying to take them out, kill their contribution to the world. At their ages, death should be the furthest thing from anyone's mind.

"Are you brooding?"

He turned. Alex stood in the opening between the living room and foyer. She wore a long white dress and her feet were bare. She looked as if she was going out, but not. At dinner, when they'd gorged on meat pies and beer, she'd been wearing jeans and a T-shirt.

"Going somewhere?" he said.

"Just here." She crossed the room and sat on one of the armchairs, facing the black glass, hardly looking at him. "What are you brooding about?"

"I'm not brooding," he said.

"I think you are."

"Think what you want." He put the mug to his lips and swallowed some chocolate.

"Are you lonely?"

"What's that supposed to mean?"

"It's not a trick question." She laughed. "It's fairly basic."

"How can I be lonely with a house full of people?"

"It's not that full."

He shifted his position, trying to face her, but it didn't make any difference. He still couldn't make eye contact because she was turned away from him. "I'm not lonely."

"Do you have a girlfriend?"

"No."

"Why not?"

"None of your business."

"Touchy," she said.

"I'm not. I'm just tired of people prying into my life."

"People?"

"The police. You."

"It's not the prying. You don't like it that you can't control what's happening. That Karen chose your pool for her death. She really got you there."

"She wasn't trying to *get me*."

"You know that for sure?"

"Yes." He took a long swallow of chocolate and put down his mug.

"Why no girlfriend?"

"This is truly none of your business."

"I think there's one flaw in our living situation. It was prompted by a comment on our Facebook page, by the way, in case you want to know."

"A comment about what?" He did feel like people were prying. No one wanted to know about the app or his revolutionary vision for work. Of course, that was Alex's job. Maybe if she did her job instead of gabbing around, trying to cause trouble...he supposed that wasn't fair. Had she really caused trouble, or did she simply get under his skin? He thought his attitude toward her had become more accepting after Lisa's death. He'd thought...

"I posted an overview of your work-live-play theory on Facebook. I thought people might be intrigued by how unique it is, relatively speaking. A back door into stirring up their interest in what we have to offer."

"Good idea, on the surface."

"Someone suggested that it sounded like it would cramp your sex life, unless there was something going on between the employees, and if there was, the experiment was doomed."

"Maybe posting that wasn't a good idea for kicking things off. Maybe you phrased it wrong. At this point, I think you should stick to talking about the app."

"You thought it was a good idea until I told you what the comment was."

"I said, on the surface."

"Well it's a good way to test the water. You think people won't find holes in the purpose or the function of the app? We need to be ready for criticism as well as interest."

He shrugged. He folded his arms across his ribs and

slumped further into the sofa cushions.

"It got me thinking. About sex," she said.

"I don't want to discuss sex with you."

"Not appropriate?"

"I just don't."

She smiled and turned toward him. "You seem awfully upset. Brooding."

"I'm frustrated, yes. Okay? I never know when the police are going to pop up with more questions. I have no timeline for when they're going to be finished with this charade. I have no idea, really, what they're looking for."

"A murderer."

"She wasn't murdered."

"That first night, you seemed pretty certain it could be a serial killer."

"A knee-jerk, unthinking response. It was shock talking."

"Maybe. But they seem to think there's something to it. Especially so soon after John."

"The odds of that are extreme. Two murders, right next door? I don't think so. She was grieving, she got drunk and drowned — accident or intentional, I'm not sure it matters. She wasn't murdered. End of story. The questions are inane."

"You're getting quite wound up about it."

"It's aggravating. I want it to stop."

"There's nothing you can do about it."

He sighed.

"Maybe if you had other things in your life, besides this app, you'd get a bit of stress relief."

She gave him a tiny smile that sent a chill through his chest. Was she coming on to him? He didn't think so, but there was something behind her words. Of course he wanted sex. He thought about it all the time, too much of the time. Swimming helped, basketball helped. Focusing on work put his mind on a different plane, a higher plane. But she was right about that, the digging into his life was making it harder to control his desire because it disrupted his routine.

He was not going to discuss it with her. And he refused to succumb to those desires right now or for the foreseeable future. Men had managed it throughout history. Monks. Priests, although a fair number of them apparently hadn't managed it at all. That kind of sickness had nothing to do with him. Lots of Buddhist monks led blissful celibate lives. They focused on other things, altruism for one. Simple tasks.

It was the same as going without food for a period of time — equally possible. Of course neither fast could be carried on indefinitely, but there was something healthy and cleansing about it. If more of the human race tried to control their impulses, the world might be better off. There was a spiritual achievement that came from denying the constant demands of your body and he was determined to find that realm of existence, even for a short time.

He stood. "Nice talking to you." Without picking up his mug, he left the room, crossed the foyer, and climbed the stairs. He'd sleep off his frustration and everything would be better in the morning.

24

Portland

It was just before Thanksgiving when Tony's poems took a sharp turn toward the physical. The first one came written on a folded sheet of thick white paper instead of printed inside of a greeting card. The words didn't rhyme and there was no meter, but the lines were cut off at odd places to give the appearance of a poem. It wasn't clear whether he'd chosen words he couldn't rhyme and still properly express his feelings, or if he thought he was inventing some new form of poetry, or trying to copy more sophisticated styles.

Whatever the case, there was nothing threatening or overly disturbing about the words, but they still made me uncomfortable. I couldn't say why. The poem talked about my smile and my eyes. That was nothing new, but the final line declared that he wanted to touch my hair. He wanted to put his hands in it and feel it like cream on his skin. He wanted to sleep with it on his pillow.

It was a nice enough image, although my dark hair and the color of cream didn't quite fit, but possibly that was artistic license, as they say. Our English teacher might have been impressed. What troubled me was that it sounded more like a definite plan than a simple rapturous admiration of my appearance. I couldn't put my finger on it, but something about his desire to feel my hair on his skin, the comment about his pillow, went beyond normal affection. It wasn't sinister, but it felt slightly perverse, almost as if he wanted to possess my hair, keep it with him all the time. It crossed my mind that he wanted to sit behind me in church and cut off locks with a pair of sharp, heavy shears.

Dark strands fall over my fingers
Smooth. Soft. Perfect. Dripping.
I'll make your hair part of me, cream across my skin
The scent wafts through my dreams
Beside me on the pillow.

I briefly thought about asking one of my brothers for an opinion about the poem's meaning, but how would they react? They did a good job ignoring the fact that Tony sat beside me at youth group, keeping that information from my parents. But how much protective instinct had my father instilled in them? He gave them lectures regularly regarding their duty to look out for the weaker sex. They viewed the sitting together as irrelevant, but they might view that arrangement differently if they knew about the poems. Revealing the poems might push them into betrayal.

Despite the unsettling nature of this new poem, I still liked being around Tony. I liked his attention. I didn't want to stop that, yet. But I didn't want to face a cleverly designed punishment from my father.

A friend would be better. A friend who wasn't in my youth group, someone from school who knew nothing about religious restrictions on girls' interaction with members of the opposite sex. I had three friends in my English class. We were the four oddities in the class who loved reading the assigned novels, while most of the other kids skimmed and bluffed their way through class discussions, or located information about the books' characters and themes online.

At first I considered showing the poem to all three, but then I decided it might be hard to keep the poems secret if an entire committee was offering opinions.

During lunch, I asked Cheryl to walk with me to the football field. When we got to the bleachers, we climbed up the benches to the fifth row. We sat down and I showed her the poem. She thought it was beautiful. She wanted to know more about Tony. I told her about the other poems but that this one bothered me.

She didn't see the problem — the poem was wildly romantic. It would make her feel beautiful if someone wrote words like that for her. She said I was lucky. Her eyelids lowered and she let out a sigh that was half desire and half envy.

"You don't think it sounds like…I don't know, like he wants to cut off my hair?"

She laughed. She tucked her own, short blonde hair behind her ear. "It's a poem. You're not supposed to take it literally. Besides, he didn't say cut it, he said…"

"I know what he said, but it gives me the creeps."

At our age, back then, a lot of girls weren't taught to listen to their instincts. I certainly wasn't. All direction came from the Bible via my father and church leaders. A fair number of girls still aren't taught that skill. Girls are taught to be nice, to be polite, to not say things that are mean or hurtful or rude. They're taught to smile when they're angry and say *thank you* when they're dissed.

"I don't understand why you're upset," Cheryl said. "It's sweet."

"I'm just not sure." Speaking those words made me realize that I *was* sure. The poem gave me the creeps, and her lack of recognition of what was wrong solidified that inside of me.

"Will you ask him to write a poem for me?" she said.

"He doesn't even know you."

"You could show him my picture."

"No."

"Is he your boyfriend? I guess I should have realized that. He likes you a lot, he's in love with you."

"You could say that."

She sighed and tucked her hair behind her ear again.

I put the folded sheet of paper in the pocket of my backpack and zipped it closed. "He acts like he's my boyfriend."

She nodded.

"But I don't think I want a boyfriend."

"Why not?"

I shrugged. "It seems like a lot of work."

She laughed. "You're a freak."

"Maybe I am, but I'm not sure I want any more poems."

"You could break up with him. And then give him my…"

"I'm not showing him your picture. And I can't really break up because we're not together. We're just…"

"It looks like he wants to be your boyfriend. He's so romantic."

I wanted to smack her. The more she talked, the more the poem gave me the creeps, the more I wanted nothing to do with him. That was easier said than done in a youth group that our parents required us to attend. And how would I even do it? I couldn't break up when there was nothing to break.

25

Karen woke. It was still dark, except for that bluish light. They were still flying, engines humming, TV screens flickering, passengers occasionally rising out of their seats and creeping toward the bathrooms. All of it backlit by that blue glow. The blue light was supposed to be soothing, but now, after all the champagne, and with the longing for sunrise and for the endless flight to be over, the color was making her nauseous. She closed her eyes but the blue tinge bled through the delicate skin of her eyelids.

The champagne had made her sleepy, which had been nice while it lasted. She looked at her watch. Four and a half hours to go. It was torture, even in first class. There was a sense of time standing still. She felt as if the drone of engines and that sickening light would be with her for the rest of her life.

No one should ever fly to Australia. It was too far. Just because human beings were capable of doing something didn't mean it should be done. They were defying the laws of the universe by soaring in a torpedo-shaped hunk of metal, packed full of human lives and their most urgent possessions.

A bottle of water and a plastic cup were sitting on her table. The flight attendant had anticipated her waking dehydrated. She twisted off the cap and took a sip. She tapped through channels on the screen in front of her. With hundreds of choices, there was nothing she wanted to watch. A thriller while she dangled in space would be too upsetting. An action movie would make her want to leave her seat, work her arms and legs, aching to feel her body doing something besides sinking into itself. A drama would make her weep. It might force her to think about her marriage and her dead husband. It was all over for good now.

She definitely could not watch comedy. She was not in the mood to laugh at the world. She felt the world, or God, or whatever being was in charge, owed her an apology.

Two years ago when John announced he was ready to retire, and that he wanted to live in Australia, she'd recognized right away he was serious about the retiring part. She had not realized he was equally serious about Australia. She'd laughed and said they knew nothing about Australia. All their friends and social activities were right there. Why on earth would they move to the opposite side of the globe?

It turned out not to be a suggestion. It was a done deal, he'd already made an offer on a house that she would *fall in love with*. She would *love* Australia, *love* the climate, he was sure of it. He seemed to believe she could love a lot of things, while he loved nothing.

Sometimes, most of the time, she'd wondered why she hadn't left him then. The simplest answer, maybe an excuse, but maybe not, was that she wasn't wired that way. She was his wife, she went where he went. She kept his house and cooked his food and loved him with all her heart, even though he'd cut part of it out of her body when he refused to allow children into their lives.

Being torn away from her friends hadn't been as painful as she'd expected. When she considered who she'd be leaving behind, she realized they weren't close after all. None of the women she spent time with had children, so there were no larger family connections. The bonds were superficial — lunches and tennis, shopping and bitching about men and their idiosyncrasies.

Karen felt even less connected because she'd held herself apart from some of those conversations. John's idiosyncrasies were beyond the norm, not something she wanted to mention in a group. Talking about a husband who pestered his wife over the years for a threesome in bed, laughing with your friends about his persistence, was not at all the same as a man who wouldn't use the same bathroom as you when you had your period, who really didn't even want sex, unless it was made antiseptically clean. A man who mostly complained about the unpleasant smell of your genitals, as if that odor seeped into the sheets and blankets and carpet and drapes of the bedroom and he couldn't be anywhere near it.

In Australia, she'd found new tennis partners to play and gossip and lunch with. They were interchangeable with the women in Chicago. Maybe when you didn't share much about your life, and nothing about your feelings, everyone was interchangeable.

They'd been living in Sydney for a little over a year when she discovered what John really desired. And it wasn't her.

He'd bought that telescope immediately after they moved into the house, while she was busy shopping for furniture and artwork to try to soften the bleak landscape of the house he'd purchased. The house was deadening — brand new and solid white — tile, carpet, ceilings, walls, appliances. It was like living in the eye of a blizzard.

Once they'd moved to Australia he stopped even pretending to share a bedroom with her. By then, his rejection was no longer a sharp pain, a quiet ache at times, but not the fierce, unrelenting pain she'd felt years ago. It was almost a relief not to have him beside her at night, that slender thread of hope that he'd be affectionate, that he'd find her desirable. That he would need her.

That's what it was really all about — being needed. No one had ever needed her. No children. Not John, and not her friends. Not her parents, who seemed to need only her brother and his three adorable children.

One night, something woke her. It might have been a sound or a voice in her dream because the house and the neighborhood were utterly silent. The silence of death, brought on by all that white, she'd thought at the time. It was disturbing and unnatural. She hadn't been able to fall back to sleep. After twenty minutes or so, she'd gotten up, pulled on a silk robe, and walked quietly down the stairs. Instead of pouring a glass of wine, she'd gone to the liquor cabinet and taken out John's eighteen-year-old scotch. She poured a tiny sliver into a glass. It would help her sleep better.

With the glass in her hand, she'd wandered around the first floor, thinking about the sterile environment — a metaphor for their marriage. Clean and blank.

On the second floor landing, she paused, wondering which room he was sleeping in. She turned to her left and looked out at the balcony adjoining the lounge. The telescope that was normally kept in the corner wasn't there. How strange. She took a sip of scotch.

She moved down the hallway. The second door on the left

was ajar. She stepped into the open space. The telescope stood at the far side of the unfurnished room. John wasn't sitting as he usually did, he stood behind the scope. Instead of pointing at the sky where it belonged, the telescope was angled down, the end of it staring directly into the window of the house next door. The garden and fence protected the interior of the house from neighbors and for that reason, the blinds were open.

From where she stood, she could see the light was on.

"What are you looking at?" She sipped her scotch, only mildly curious and already feeling the effects of the liquor, her eyes heavy, her muscles softening.

John jumped away from the scope as if she'd shouted his name.

His sudden movement made her hand shake. Scotch splashed up the side of the glass. Her hand grew weak and the glass slipped out of her fingers. It thudded on the carpet, gold liquid spreading across white.

"God damn it!" John rushed to the spot on the floor. He tore off his T-shirt and knelt down, trying to blot out the spill.

Karen walked to the window and looked into the telescope. The woman next door was lying on her bed, her arms stretched out and her legs crossed casually, one knee bent. She was naked.

"How could you be so stupid?" John said.

"How could you?" she whispered.

They didn't fight about it. She told him she was going home. Even now, disgust at what he'd been doing made her throat ache.

26

Sydney

After Sean left the living room so abruptly, I sat there for a while longer. I wasn't hungry. I didn't want a drink, even smelling the hot chocolate Sean had been drinking didn't stir my desire. The only thing I could think of was Gavin's body.

The few times we'd had sex we were in my bedroom. His was closer to Sean's and the risk of being seen was greater, although there was risk all around. And there were things in his room that weren't necessarily inviting. The tip of his older sister's finger being the main thing — torn off by a dog and held hostage by Gavin until it was too late for repairs. It was payback to his sister for rupturing his peace of mind throughout his childhood, coming into his room and into his fantasies and nightmares, her constant presence breathing down on him. She hovered over him while he slept, peering into his dreams.

I understood his feelings, but I was unnerved by the preserved finger.

Could I have sex in a bed where a dead finger rested beneath me in a jar of formalin? The jar was enclosed in an insulated box. It wasn't as if the flesh inside was decaying. I couldn't smell it. I never even had to look at it again. But it was one of those things that, once you've seen it, is almost impossible to get out of your head.

Still, once we were naked and stroking each other's bodies, would I be thinking about that finger? Not likely. In fact, after the first long, deep kiss it would fade to the back of my mind.

The other thing was that camera, recording all the comings and goings in his room, watching for intruders who might have a mindset similar to his sister's.

I stood and went upstairs. I knocked softly on his door. He opened it immediately. I stepped inside and he closed it.

"Wow," he said, eyeing my long, white dress. "Very mystical, or angelic, or something."

I pointed at the camera in the corner of the ceiling above his bookcase. "Is that thing recording us?"

He shook his head. "I turn it off when I'm in the room."

I pulled the dress over my head and dropped it on the floor.

"Wow, again." He smiled and came to me, putting his arms around my sides.

His hands were warm on my skin, his jeans rough and his belt buckle cool against my bare hips and belly, but a good kind of rough. We kissed for a long time and then moved toward his bed. I took off his clothes and we fell into each other, all of our thoughts overcome by the touch of skin and the spreading desire inside of us.

After, we slid under the covers and I rested my head on his chest, his arm around my shoulders, and fell asleep.

I woke first. I'd only slept for about twenty minutes. I tickled his armpit to wake him. No response. I pinched his nipple. He opened one eye, a very clever trick, I thought. I closed my eyes and tried to see whether I could do the same. I couldn't.

"Do you think this is ever going to get off the ground?" I said.

"TruthTeller?"

"Yes."

"Hard to say."

"Sean gets distracted too easily. He acts like it's his whole life, as if it's all he cares about, but then he doesn't push to move things forward," I said.

"He does get sidetracked. A lot." He sighed and pressed his chin against the top of my head.

"I like it here. I don't want to leave."

"There are other jobs. Your visa could be re-done."

"Yes. But this one is different. And so far, I like what I'm doing."

"Me too."

"Isn't your job always the same?"

"In some ways, yes. But there are different angles, the details of what's required for each application aren't the same."

I turned over, letting my neck rest on his upper arm, my head falling back slightly. "I was wondering, why aren't you a part owner?"

"Don't want it."

"But why?"

He didn't answer. I waited for a long time. Still no response.

"Don't you want to be rich?" I laughed softly, so it didn't sound as if I was too curious or too pushy or too greedy. It's a fine line — interest in other people, and nosiness.

"No."

"Most people do."

"Is that right?" He twisted his hand and rubbed my upper arm. "Is that what you want?"

"Yes."

"You're not going to get that here, so maybe it doesn't matter if this all collapses," he said.

"We're not talking about me," I said. "You do all the work, you're the one who'll make this a technical success…"

"Or failure…"

"Does it have problems?"

"No. Not yet," he said.

"That's kind of negative."

"Realistic."

"Do you think it doesn't have a chance, is that why you didn't want a stake?"

"I don't want to be married to Sean. Breaking up a company is like getting a divorce. I don't need that."

"I've never known someone who didn't want to be paid what they deserved for their work. I don't get it."

His shoulders moved beneath me, a careless shrug.

"Do you have a lot of money already? Is that it?"

"Not everything in life is about money. Don't you know that?"

"It sure makes everything in life better."

"No, it does not. It can ruin things."

"Such as?"

"Love. Friendship. Human kindness. Peace of mind."

"How does it ruin your peace of mind?" I laughed. "It's the opposite."

"I just don't want too much money, okay? I want to be secure, comfortable. I don't need a house like this, for example. I don't need a yacht or three homes or…"

"You're a long way from a yacht."

"Am I?"

I pulled back slightly. I'd come close to letting it slip out that my digging through Sean's drawers had revealed his and Tess's salaries. "I just thought it was interesting, when Tess told me you weren't an owner. It's your app."

"It was Sean's idea, I'm just implementing it."

"If you say so."

"Let's not talk," he said.

I agreed and we started kissing. This time, it didn't wipe all thoughts from my mind, so I suppose I'm more captivated by some things than others. A severed finger I can temporarily put out of my mind and carry on as usual. Knowing someone who didn't want to acquire all the money he possibly could wouldn't leave my head. It circled around, trying to come to grips with a person who thought so differently than I did.

In some ways, it made me feel very alone.

27

The next morning at nine-fifteen, Detective Martin and Detective Bender showed up at the front door. Sean answered. Their voices were audible in the offices but I couldn't make out the detectives' words, only Sean's.

Why do you want to know? Followed by — *What's this for?* After a pause of several minutes, he said, *Fine. Please be quick about it, we're trying to get some work done here.*

A moment later, Sean appeared in my office doorway. "They want to talk to you."

"Both of them?"

He nodded.

"Why?"

"They won't say, obviously." He moved into the room, closing the door quietly. "Be careful what you say."

"Why?"

"Because they're cops. Because they're overstepping. Because, just because."

He sounded like my father. I laughed. "Because you said so?"

"This is serious. If this does turn out to be murder, we don't want to get caught up in it."

"We're already caught up."

He glowered at me.

"No worries," I said. "I can handle it."

He didn't look convinced. He opened the door and I went out to the foyer.

"Where can we talk?" Martin said.

I led them to the living room.

"This isn't private."

I sighed. "We can go in the workout room, but you'll have to stand."

She nodded.

I led the way, entering the room before them and sitting on the bench. I was not going to stand. If this took half an hour, they could shift their weight from foot to foot, I'd be comfortable. And maybe they'd get tired and give up.

"We're having trouble with the timeline," Martin said.

Bender snickered.

Her jaw tightened and she turned her head slightly, forcing him out of her peripheral vision. "What time did you say you discovered Mrs. Norths' body?"

"I didn't say what time."

"Why not?"

"I told you, I didn't notice the time."

"I find that difficult to believe," she said.

"It's the truth."

"We have a text sent from her phone and if we can verify what time you found her, it will help us…"

"She didn't notice the time," Bender said. His voice was rough with a mocking undertone.

"I'll handle this," Martin said. "I find it difficult to believe you didn't check your phone or a clock," she said. "You wake in the dark and you get up and aren't curious about the time?"

I shrugged.

"This isn't a game," she said.

"I know, I just don't have anything to say. That's what happened."

"Most people would check the time."

"Would they?"

"I would."

"You're a detective."

"I think most people in the general population would check the time. They'd be startled or annoyed to be awake before dawn and they'd want to know."

I stared at her.

"Do you realize that no one in this house has an alibi?" she said.

"Do we need alibis?"

"If we determine she was murdered, yes, you do."

"Well we were sleeping. How can you have an alibi if you're asleep? Other than that, I don't know what to say. I didn't know her. The others didn't know her."

"Yet, her body was found in your swimming pool."

I was on a merry-go-round, the same questions as before, over and over, gliding in a circle, up and down, nothing changing. It occurred to me what a boring job detectives have. Most of the questions are trivial and they repeat them ad infinitum. It would drive a normal person mad.

"You have no explanation for that?"

"I don't."

"It's unusual behavior. Her clothing was in one of the bedrooms of her own house. You don't find it odd that a woman would strip naked on a chilly winter night, enter the yard of a virtual stranger, according to all of you, drink half a bottle or more of expensive scotch, and then go for a swim? Think about that for a moment. Think about the details of that. Imagine each step of that unbelievable chain of events."

I thought, although I wasn't sure what direction this thinking was supposed to take. Of course it was strange behavior. It didn't prove she was murdered or even that she had anything to do with Sean. It was just that — strange.

"This is a woman whose husband has just been murdered. Even if they're separated…"

"Divorced," I said.

"She was still mourning her loss. On some level, she was mourning, yet she drowns in *your* pool."

"It's not my pool."

"She drowns on this property."

I smiled. "I'm really confused about why you keep asking the same questions. We didn't know her."

"But the location of her death doesn't make sense."

"Lots of things don't. Isn't that true of crime in general? Does it always make sense?"

"This is not normal behavior."

"Is committing suicide normal behavior?"

She sighed. "Surely as a woman, you're troubled by…"

"Is that why you're talking to me and not the others, because I'm a woman?"

"Please answer the question. I'm truly curious. Aren't you troubled by her strange behavior?"

I thought about this for a moment. I'm confused by all emotionally-driven behavior. I don't understand people who get carried away by sorrow or love or anything at all, really. It's self-defeating. Most people confuse me and I don't understand half the things they do. I understand doing things that benefit yourself — seducing a man, looking for good restaurants, finding entertainment, meeting people that are fun to hang out with, playing verbal games at parties, working to improve your financial situation... I don't understand getting upset and letting your feelings dictate your choices.

When I decide to kill someone who's robbing a woman of dignity, who thinks women aren't equally deserving and capable members of the human race, I assess the situation and decide what to do. I don't get hysterical, I don't rant and rave about it, I don't fume and cry. I remove the problem.

"You see what I mean?" Detective Martin said. She obviously misinterpreted whatever look I'd allowed to creep over my face.

"I honestly don't know why she would go out wearing nothing but underwear when it's cold." I also knew she couldn't swim and refused to be around water, but that was my personal information, a tiny advantage in this game, and I wasn't about to give it to them.

They moved toward the door. Bender opened it and held it for Martin. She stood aside and gestured for him to go first. For a moment, there was a silent standoff, then he went out.

"Give some thought to how perplexing this situation is. Give us a call if you think of something that explains it. Until we can resolve this question, we'll continue pursuing a murder line of thinking. Especially following her husband's murder. Something isn't right here. Greater cooperation and concern from you and your housemates will be helpful. And think again about whether you checked the time when you got up. Most people would."

She smiled, turned, and walked out, leaving the weight room door open. A moment later I heard the front door close.

28

I closed the door to the workout room and reclined on the bench. Even though I was wearing a skirt, a long-sleeved T-shirt, and flip-flops, I strapped on the weight gloves and did four sets with the bench press. As I lowered the barbell after the last rep, the nibbling voice of the detective finally washed out of my muscles. I felt relaxed and in control.

I went to the kitchen and filled a glass with water. I grabbed a tangerine out of the bowl on the counter and returned to the office.

The tangerine looked like a tiny burning sun on the white desk. It teased me from the corner of my eye as I opened the TruthTeller Facebook page. I hadn't checked it for over twenty-four hours, which wasn't very effective marketing if it turned out we had a comment or two and I'd left them unacknowledged.

I sucked in air. There were over two thousand page likes, and three-hundred-twenty-eight comments on my post about our revolutionary but not very unique solution to work-life balance. I swallowed. I picked up the glass of water and took several long gulps. There were seven hundred thumbs up on the post, eighty-four hearts, twenty *wow* emoji faces, and doing their best to undermine all of that, three-hundred-twelve angry faces.

It looked like my schedule for the rest of the day had

been dictated by people who had a lot of strong feelings regarding work-life balance. I clicked onto the post and hit the link to expand the comment section, showing all. I would read everything before I responded with so much as a single white thumb enclosed in a blue disk. I needed to get a handle on what had happened. I needed to figure out whether I'd caused a huge problem for the TruthTeller brand, stirring up all that rage.

I started reading while I sipped water. The tangerine sat beside me, hopeful, but too much work to bother with until I digested all the noise over the work environment in a company no one had ever heard of.

When I was finished, the results fell into several basic groups — comments suggesting the commenters were singles under the age of thirty-five, marrieds of all ages, parents, the clueless, and the creeps.

How in the hell had all these people found our page in the short time since I'd posted the comment? Sure, I'd paid for a boost to more viewers, but still…I guess that's what they mean by viral, although I'd always thought viral added up to millions, not a few thousand. But the page was young. Who knew what might happen.

I was fairly certain this was not the kind of market entry Sean had envisioned. On one hand, he was naive to think it was so easy to interest people in a product that wasn't exactly cheap and whose value had to be described in more detail than most. I'd thought a mildly provocative comment would get us attention and I could transfer that attention to the app at some point. Now, I wasn't so sure.

Group one — singles under thirty-five — loved the TruthTeller work model. They thought we were ushering in a new age of Aquarius or some such thing, a post-corporate, post-authoritarian world. They praised and fawned over getting rid of business casual clothes and cubicles, lost weeks of their lives sitting in traffic, and office politics, replacing it with trust and humanity and holistic living. They thought we were brilliant, they wanted to know how they could send résumés for a chance to work at the company, they wanted our ideas, they wanted to know about zoning laws for businesses in the suburbs, they wanted to do fist bumps. They demanded pictures and video documentation for every minute of our workday.

Group number two, the marrieds, thought we were teetering on the edge of facilitating adultery. Such an arrangement as ours was *heads in the clouds*, delusional, subversive, unworkable for couples, married or not. It would tear apart relationships, it meant you couldn't have a job at a cutting edge company unless you became celibate or had incestuous relationships with your colleagues, and since you lived together like family, that's what those relationships were. A few mocked our good looks — at least those of Tess, Sean, and Gavin. My appearance was vague behind ball cap and dark glasses, but they guessed I fit the mold as well, and a few accused us of discrimination in favor of abnormally attractive people.

The clueless were just that, like clueless people in any internet forum.

The parents accused us of destroying the fabric of society. They said we were communists — how that applied, I couldn't work out. They said it would split families and was an unworkable model except for recent college grads.

The creeps wrote what you'd expect. Mostly comments

about sex and fuck-able office mates and orgies. I hid all of those from the stream. I wasn't sure if that also was a mistake, given our name was TruthTeller, but I didn't even have to think for half a second to know how Sean would feel about that kind of thing on our page. Toying with him had its entertaining side, but in the list of priorities, keeping this interesting and comfortable and very profitable job ranked higher. It would be fun to wind him up about the haters, but that could wait until the detectives were finished winding him up.

I went back through and began adding a thumbs up to all the remaining comments, even those that didn't have anything valuable to add to the conversation, the inevitable *cool, awesome, good luck* — throwaway comments to get themselves into the conversation, even though they weren't in a conversation at all.

I picked out a few comments and copied them into another document so I could compose responses with some thought behind them. Surely there was a way to change all of this into a discussion of our app. But if there was, I didn't see it right now. I'd been single-mindedly focused on getting attention. I certainly had that.

29

Flight #17 — San Francisco to Sydney

Tess had barely settled her belongings around her, slipped off her shoes, and crossed her legs before the woman seated beside her turned, flashing an eager smile.

"First visit to Australia?" Her accent said she was returning home.

"No. I spent two months there on a sabbatical of sorts, and now I'm living in Sydney on a work visa."

"Very nice."

"Do you live in Sydney?"

"I do. Only two kilometers from the harbor."

"It's a beautiful place," Tess said. It was best not to offer any information about her location. That might lead to more, and her living conditions were too unconventional. She didn't feel like explaining it to a stranger. Not yet.

"So what are we drinking? Oh, and I'm Angela."

Tess laughed. "I'm Tess. Do you always get right down to business like that?"

"Absolutely. Don't mess with my alcohol, my food, or my sex life."

"Sounds very straight-forward and simple."

"Yep."

Angela raised her hand and caught the flight attendant's

eye. "Are you serving cocktails yet?"

"You know we don't until after takeoff."

"Just checking. They change the rules for flying every day, I thought it was worth asking." She winked at Tess.

"That rule never changes." The attendant gave them a tight smile.

"Never say never," Angela said. "Well I guess we'll have to get acquainted and wait an hour or so until cocktail time." She leaned toward Tess. "I did have a flask with me, but they wouldn't let me keep it in my carry-on."

Tess couldn't believe it was even worth trying. "Since you get busted for a rogue tube of lip gloss, I don't imagine a flask would get through," she said.

Angela laughed. "I never give up. So why were you in San Francisco?"

Tess explained about Damien, the preparation with the vet and filing for a permit to bring him into Australia. Jen would work with the vet to crate and ship him once the details were finalized. He'd have to stay in the Melbourne quarantine facility before Tess could drive down and pick him up. She worried he'd be traumatized from the travel, from being away from friendly care. Angela confidently assured her the cockatoo would be fine. She laughed, like everyone did, about the idea of a native Australian bird being in quarantine before it was allowed into Australia.

They talked about work through takeoff and the ascent to cruising altitude. *The ascent until cocktail time*, according to Angela. She worked for a music production company and as a result traveled *everywhere*, the main reason she liked her job. Tess told her about traveling for CoastalCreative, great for the decade or so that she'd done it. She'd visited a lot of amazing places she never would have reached on her own — Delhi, Johannesburg, all the major cities of Europe, Singapore and Hong Kong and Seoul, and of course, an annual trip to Australia, and two trips to New Zealand. She'd only been to South America once — São Paulo.

By then, they had their drinks, and Angela touched her whisky sour to Tess's glass of Zinfandel, taking a sip without making a toast.

"I got tired of it," Tess said. "On one hand you have this amazing, exciting cosmopolitan life lived all over the world. You eat in fantastic restaurants, stay in luxury hotels. You never have to drive — you can work or talk while someone else fights traffic. But the dark side is that you don't have a real life. It's almost impossible to have a relationship, not to mention friends you see on any kind of regular basis."

Angela nodded. "I suppose. I never really think about it. I'm having too much fun. Are you married now?"

"No. You?"

"Divorced. A long time ago. Not sure I ever want to step into that dance again. I like being on my own. Of course, a regular man, even a partner, would be nice. It is hard to manage, you're right about that."

"Why are relationships so hard?" Tess sipped her wine.

"I don't have a clue. Ours is working quite well, don't you think?" She giggled.

"I meant with men."

"I know what you meant. Just sayin'."

After an array of appetizers, their dinners arrived — linguini Alfredo with mushrooms, green salad, and fresh sourdough rolls.

Angela ordered a glass of the Zinfandel. "And the fixings

for my next whiskey sour." She gave the attendant a coy smile and turned back to Tess. "Anyone on the horizon?"

"I don't know."

"How can you not know?" Angela's voice was a muted shriek, not loud enough to get heads turning in their direction. "Either there's a man on the horizon or there isn't. So that means, you must have your eye on someone."

Tess swallowed the last of her wine. She twirled up some pasta and put it in her mouth. After she chewed and swallowed, she took a sip of water.

"Quit stalling," Angela said.

"It's kind of difficult."

"Uh oh. Married? Boss? Therapist?"

"I guess you'd call him my boss, but we're more like partners." She ordered a whisky sour for herself and halfway into it, she decided she could be blunt with her thoughts. The odds of ever seeing Angela again were rather slim, despite their easy bond. How many people had she met on airplanes over the years, and never even exchanged contact information at the end of the flight? Hundreds. And those conversations had been equally entertaining and often satisfying.

She felt as if she had un-sprouted friendships dotting the globe, lost opportunities for girlfriends and possibly her soul mate. You never knew. It was completely possible. Her throat closed up for a moment, then she let the thought subside.

"So are you going for it?"

"I don't know. It's so inappropriate. Especially in our living situation." She explained their incubator environment.

Angela thought it sounded fun — for a month, followed quickly by utter claustrophobia. "Of course you're drawn to him, though. I mean, living like that, working so closely. It's the best aphrodisiac there is."

"Maybe."

"Life is too short to be indecisive. If you like him, grab him." She laughed.

They talked for another hour, through a dessert of chocolate cake and two more drinks. It was three in the morning San Francisco time when Angela announced she was going to sleep. She put a teal satin sleep mask over her eyes, stuffed pillows around her neck and head and was breathing deeply within three or four minutes.

Tess was wide awake. Images of Sean flowed through her mind. She was calm and tipsy from whisky and wine.

She'd been aware of his looks the moment she first saw him, but not in a way that made her consider being attracted, just a casual noticing, the sort of thing that happened with any good looking man.

It was so inappropriate, but also so true that life was incredibly short, literally racing past your eyes. And what were they all so damn worried about? Inappropriate according to what standard? Much of that was company policy, built around protecting the corporate coffers from harassment lawsuits. It was inevitable that people working together were attracted to each other. They found common ground, they had a shared vision and passion. It was quite natural.

Starting a relationship with a colleague was healthier than meeting someone in a bar. You had similar interests and goals, and a friendship on which to base your physical attraction. You couldn't control where someone was in the hierarchy. Working together was working together, peers and subordinates and superiors. The lines were only in org charts. Why were the so-called rules of life frequently upside down?

Would it destroy the success of the app? His vision? She'd never had the slightest hint from him that he was interested in her. Was he trying to be appropriate as well? Was he not attracted to her at all? It was impossible to know.

She'd have to give it more thought. She ordered a shot of whisky straight, hoping it would help her sleep, but it was a long time before she did.

30

As the flight closed in on its long-awaited end, Karen realized she didn't want to go to Australia at all. She looked out into the darkness. Soon, the light of the sun would spread over the southern hemisphere. It was one of the most beautiful things she'd ever witnessed. When she'd taken this flight with John, he'd shrugged his shoulders at the profoundly welcoming sight. For someone obsessed with viewing the solar system, his disinterest in the sun was jarring.

When she'd boarded the plane this time, she believed the trip was required. She had to deal with the house, dispose of the contents, put it up for sale, or for auction, which was the normal process in Australia. But now she wondered — did she really? She could have hired someone to handle all of that for her. Instead, she'd endured this endless flight and the flood of memories and she was no closer to figuring out where she was headed after this, or what had happened to her life.

It felt as if her life as an individual had never existed. She'd been a daughter, a wife, and a friend, but none of those labels really stuck. Now she was an estranged daughter and either a divorcee or a widow, depending on how you wanted to look at it, and someone everyone used to know but had lost touch with.

Her accomplishments were limited to approximately twelve hundred games of tennis, six thousand dinners prepared and cleaned up after, possibly more. The same number of breakfasts. About four hundred toilets cleaned, until they'd hired a housekeeper. Countless loads of laundry, trips to the grocery store...

She didn't want to think about it. What was the point? All the things she'd done, defined by numbers multiplying days and months and years, summed up to absolutely nothing.

The list of non-achievements should have made her cry, but it didn't. She felt nothing.

There was only one alluring feature of her trip to Australia — she could finish things off with that sexy, charming, aloof, inscrutable Aussie next door, with his long hair and shark tattoo, his nicely shaped arms and narrow hips.

It had been so long since she'd had sex. So long. Possibly, it had been forever. John was the only man she'd been with, which meant it was highly likely she didn't even know what real sex was. The thought was sickening. She'd had a few opportunities when they'd lived in Chicago and John was at work into all hours of the night, but she'd been a faithful and attentive wife back then. Most of those so-called opportunities had been minor flirtations, she wasn't completely sure they would have gone anywhere. They were fun, and there was a bit of guilt, although it wasn't the burning, searing kind, just a mild sense of knowing she was having thoughts she shouldn't.

The first time she'd seen Sean, she'd felt her legs wobble and her stomach settle into a puddle of warm syrup. He was gorgeous. And that voice, that accent. Of course, they all had that, but Sean had something else — an air of someone tormented, a man who had such ethics and dreams it made him ache as he tried to shape the world into what he thought it should be.

All of that was a fantasy of course, she knew very little about him, but it was what she imagined, observing his expression as he pushed his hair out of his face, watching him through her bedroom window as he swam in his pool. She was almost as bad as John, peering out at the neighbors when they didn't know they were being observed. At least she didn't breach the boundaries of their homes, invade their sex lives, drool over their naked flesh. Although she did drool over his naked chest and back, watching the muscles slither under the water as he made his way up and down the length of the pool.

She pressed her face against the window of the plane, shockingly cold as the frigid air at thirty-thousand feet pushed back from the other side. It was utter blackness out there. Where was the rest of the solar system? Why didn't she see any stars winking back at her? Was it the angle of the plane? Or had the entire universe been sucked into a black hole during the interminable time she'd been strapped to her seat?

The darkness was absolute. Her eyes strained to penetrate the solid wall of black. They ached and watered and still she tried forcing them to see something, anything out there. Flying at night was the most terrifying of all. In the daytime, she tried not to look out the window much, tried not to think about how far away the earth was, tried not to think that the fluffy clouds that looked as if they might catch the plane in a warm, pillowy embrace were nothing but vapor.

This entire flight had taken place at night — leaving LA at

ten-forty, flying into the darkness. The glow of sunlight didn't appear until nearly thirteen hours had passed. In the dark, it felt as if the few hundred people surrounding her were the only human beings left in the universe. It felt as if they'd been abandoned by God and all the comforting security of the earth. There were thirty or forty gallons of liquids left, maybe. Some snacks, the breakfast food. The plane had minor first aid equipment, but that was it. She was adrift with strangers.

They were so alone in the universe. *She* was so alone. Even people she'd known for decades indulged continuously in superficial chit chat. Beyond silly jokes and complaints, no one talked about what really mattered. Sex. Death. What comes after, whether anything at all comes after. And why did she equate sex and death? No one really talked about either one. For all the comedy and movies talking about sex, for all the complaints about men's needs, as if women had none, there was never any real conversation. Yet it was the force of life, ending with a foreshadowing of death.

Tears filled her eyes. She hadn't been able to cry for the paucity of her own life, but now, she was crying for the isolation of a plane full of strangers.

31

Portland

Clearly Cheryl was not going to provide any insight on how to divert Tony's newly disturbing fascination with me. I didn't need romantic envy that, in reality, was a rather clueless take on boys and relationships and the world. My gut told me the poem was off key and I needed to get away from him. I didn't need an echo chamber for my own instinct after all.

It turned out to be one of my first lessons in how aloofness inflames passion.

First, I stopped sitting beside Tony during Sunday morning services. Each week I found a cluster of girls and managed to insert myself into the middle of the group. If I couldn't maneuver that before he came wriggling down the row of chairs, I moved to a new row and snuggled up between my brothers, no doubt confusing them with my sudden affection.

Avoiding being near him resulted in an onslaught of poems — two a day on the days I was at church, each one shoved inside my backpack, and finally, a poem handed directly to me.

The poetry had moved on from my hair to embrace other features. He wanted to run his finger around the edge of my nostrils. He wanted to feel the softness and taste the sweetness of my earlobe on his tongue. Also candidates for his mouth were my toes and fingers — each one named.

On Sunday morning he was waiting outside the doors into the main auditorium where the worship services were held. He asked me to walk to a quieter place with him. I said *no*. He touched my arm, turned his liquid eyes on me with a blend of tearful regret and steel-cold demand. I moved out of reach, skirted around my brother Eric, and darted into the auditorium.

Tony followed. When I'd settled down between Jake and Tom, Tony shoved an envelope at me. It was one of those brown six-by-nine envelopes with a metal clasp. It was sealed and the arms of the clasp were spread through the hole — double security.

"What's that?" Tom said.

"I have no idea."

"Open it."

"Later." I crunched it in half, shoved it into my purse, and yanked the zipper closed.

"Come on, I want to see."

"Church is starting."

"Since when do you care about that? Whatever is in there looks more interesting than church."

"I seriously doubt it."

"Everything is more interesting than church. Come on, let me see." He grabbed at my purse strap.

I gave him a cold look. "I said no."

He turned and faced the front, slumping down in his chair, stretching his legs out and spreading them slightly so his knee encroached on my space.

That afternoon, I closed my bedroom door and pulled the

envelope out of my purse. I stood the clasps up straight and tore open the flap.

Inside was a single sheet of paper. There were eight or nine tissues stuffed on either side to make the envelope appear fuller than it was. I had no idea why he thought he needed to conceal the fact there was a single sheet of paper. Maybe it was his way of persuading his parents he needed a larger, seemingly more secure envelope.

I pulled out the creamy stationery and unfolded it.

There was a single line, running from the bottom left corner to the upper right, written in blue ink — *Your eyes are so juicy, I want to put them in my mouth and suck on them.*

I tore the sheet in half. I tore the pieces in half again. I kept on until the note was in tiny scraps. I couldn't even call it a poem. It was a cross between a line from a horror movie and a bizarre kind of threat. It made me feel ill. I wished I hadn't eaten the glossy hard-boiled eggs my mother served in a bowl alongside the ham and cheese sandwiches she'd made for lunch.

The next morning at school, I dropped the scraps of paper from the poem into the trashcan in the girls' bathroom. I ripped up the envelope and put that in a different trashcan. It didn't have my name on it, but I liked to be thorough, even then.

Wednesday night at our mid-week Bible class I told Tony I wanted to talk to him. We went out into the hallway. The long empty space with its thin carpet and high ceiling echoed around us.

"I don't like your poems," I said.

His eyes filled with tears.

"Don't send me any more."

"But I…"

"Don't. My father will be angry if he finds out. I'm not supposed to…" I didn't want to call him a boyfriend, that was headed in the opposite direction from where I needed to go.

"But I love you."

"You can't love me. You hardly know me. And I'm dead if my father sees your poems."

"There's nothing bad in them."

That was debatable, but I wasn't up for a debate. I wanted him to stay far away from me with his weird poems and the even weirder way he stared into my eyes, making that single-line poem run through my mind. It felt as if he'd permanently placed his words inside my head and I'd never be rid of them. I wanted to scrape at my brain the way you'd scrape over initials carved into the bark of a tree.

"You can't love me because I don't love you back," I said.

"I can't help it."

"Yes, you can."

"Love is put in our hearts by God," he said.

"I think that's general love for the human race."

"I can't live without you."

"You've lived just fine without me. We only see each other at church anyway."

"I want to see you more, I want to see you every day. I want to be together every minute of every day. Forever."

"That's not possible. Please stop."

"I can't stop." His voice shook. He spoke softly. "You're all I think about."

He reached out to touch my arm. I backed away from him. His arm remained extended, his fingers curving down slightly. With his long nails, his hand took on the appearance of a claw. It looked terribly uncomfortable, but he didn't move, staring at me, almost as if he didn't notice his arm was even in that position, didn't notice the threatening quality of his hand.

"You have to find a hobby. And leave me alone."

He started to cry.

"Don't be a crybaby."

Tears poured down his cheeks. He didn't sob or gasp for breath, just a steady, silent flow of liquid.

The door to our classroom swung open and Mr. Bartz, the head youth leader, stepped into the hallway. "What's going on here?" He moved toward us quickly.

"We're just talking," I said.

He looked at Tony. "Are you crying?"

"He has something in his eye," I said. "I told him he should have you look at it."

Mr. Bartz moved closer. "Let me see."

Tony ducked away. "It's okay."

"Come back here."

"It's okay. Really." His eyes were suddenly dry. They looked empty, the pupils shrunk to tiny specks.

"Then both of you get inside. You're aren't supposed to leave the room." He glared at me.

"I was just trying to help," I said.

"Get inside." He opened the door and held it while I walked through. Tony followed me, then Mr. Bartz, letting the door fall closed with a crash.

Tony didn't look at me as he hurried to the opposite side of the room and took a seat. I walked down the center aisle and chose a chair in the front row. I was relieved to be rid of Tony and his poems.

32

I had a breakfast of sausages, potatoes, fried tomatoes, and English muffins ready for Tess when she arrived from the airport. Since she'd flown first class, maybe the food was better than what I'd experienced when I spent over half a day of my life in the air, but I doubted it was that spectacular. It's still kept in foil wrapped trays on an airplane, how good can it be?

Sean came into the house with her, grabbed a bottle of orange juice from the fridge, and went to the office, insisting the bowl of oatmeal he'd eaten before he went to pick her up was more than enough.

She and I ate in the dining room.

"I really want to shower, but this is good," she said. "I didn't realize how hungry I was."

"Food always comes first."

"You're probably right." She stabbed her fork into a piece of sausage and put it in her mouth. She picked up the Tabasco and dribbled some on her potatoes.

"What happened in San Francisco?" I said.

"Not much. The condo looks great. Isaiah and Jen said to say *hi*. Damien should be okayed for travel in about three weeks."

I smiled. I could care less about her condo and the details of Damien's travel arrangements. I wanted to know what had happened when she and Ted made a team attack on the San Francisco Police bureaucracy.

She continued eating.

"And…?" I said.

She looked at me.

"What happened with Detective Gorman?"

She shrugged. "Nothing much."

"So are they going to look into it further?"

"I really don't want to talk about it." She smiled. "I actually missed this place, I didn't realize how much I'd fallen in love with it."

"Australia, or Sean's house?"

"Both." She ate some potatoes, chewing slowly, looking around the room as if she were taking tiny sips of it to moisten her mouth along with the food.

"You're not going to tell me anything about what happened? What the next steps are?"

"No."

"Why not?"

"I'd rather not get into it."

This could mean she was finished obsessing over it. It could also mean they'd talked about me and she wasn't supposed to discuss it. She wasn't supposed to let on that she'd been told to keep quiet. I wasn't sure what to think, but if I kept pestering her, it wasn't going to get any information to come out. "What's new with Jen?"

"She seems really happy. She likes her job. She's seeing a guy, but nothing too serious. I kind of thought she and Isaiah might…"

I laughed.

"You don't get to claim him," she said. "You broke up with him."

"I know. That's not why I laughed. I just think it's funny that you assumed since they were sharing living space, they would hook up."

"I didn't assume anything. I thought they might go well together."

"Why?"

She shrugged. "I just did. No reason."

"There must be a reason."

"You sound very possessive." She smiled.

I finished my sausage and started on the last of the potatoes. "Did it feel strange being in your condo?"

"A little."

"Did you see anyone else, besides Ted and Gorman?"

"I had a drink with Cynthia Latimer."

I nodded.

"I had a nice dinner with Jen and Isaiah."

"Did Ted try to lure you back to CC?"

"Actually, he assumed that's why I was there."

"So was he upset when you told him the real reason?"

She shrugged.

What was going on? She'd rarely been so withholding of information. She acted as if there was something she couldn't tell me. Was Gorman putting extra effort into finding the woman who had entered Steve's condo with him the night he died? Had she convinced Ted to have someone review Steve's mobile phone records? Were they going to be asking me questions?

"What have you been up to?" she said.

"Twitter. Facebook. Detectives."

"Sean said they're still asking questions."

"Constantly."

"How is he taking that?"

"He doesn't like it."

"How has he been?"

"Distracted. Touchy. Brooding."

She placed her utensils across the plate and pushed it away from her. "Great breakfast. Thanks."

"No worries."

"What kind of questions are they asking?"

"Just the same things. Wanting us to speculate about why she drowned in Sean's pool."

"Maybe because her house doesn't have a pool," Tess said.

"Good point. You should tell them that. They'll want to talk to you again."

"I'm sure."

"Does Sean talk to you much about how he's feeling?" she said.

"Not really. You sure have a lot of questions about him."

"Just trying to assess the landscape." She pushed her chair away from the table. "Now I absolutely need that shower. And then back to work." She yanked the elastic band out of her hair and shook it loose.

I picked up both plates and carried them to the kitchen. I put them in the dishwasher and cleaned up the pans I'd used for cooking. When they were dried and put away, I wiped down the counter and went out to the patio.

I still missed the chair where Karen had presumably lain before taking a dive into the pool. I liked the idea of her thoughts lingering inside the cushion, finding their way into my head. It had occurred to me that if I figured out a more convincing scenario for her death, the cops would leave us alone. Maybe.

33

The best course of action for getting Facebook traction was to continue focusing on the positive responses, ignoring the clueless, the complaining, and the near-murderous. Maybe leaving the mild end of the haters' comments would had worked in my favor — maybe, by now, the fans would have smacked them down for me.

I wanted to solidify those who were enthused about our work environment. I wanted to draw them in further. It was a delicate dance because it wouldn't be wise to post too many pictures that would enable anyone, hater or fanatic fan, to locate Sean's house. I also didn't want to bust open Sean's privacy, even though I was sure he would agree with my overall strategy of talking about our work environment. It had become clear that his utopian vision was almost as important to him as the app. The guy was a real crusader.

Eventually I planned to shoot videos — interview my co-workers, capture them playing water volleyball and shooting pool. I wanted to keep myself behind the camera ninety percent of the time and only include shots the others took where I remained shadowy.

I scrolled through the photos on my phone and stopped at the picture of Sean's wood statue. Without a doubt, he would not want that photograph on Facebook. But it was so alluring. It would spark conversation about art, feminism, sex.

Discussing sex on our company Facebook page was definitely a risky idea, but I didn't think there would be much I couldn't handle. And if it got out of control, I'd simply hide those comments. After all, it was our page, and I was in charge of social media.

Stepping outside the boundaries was required to get attention. Everyone knows it doesn't work to just put ads up or talk about yourself, make lame comments about your products or observations of life. That works when you're already a name brand. Being provocative was critical at our stage of invisibility, and this photograph was nothing if not provocative.

I adjusted the image lighting to make the figure more prominent. I cropped off the shutters on the left side, leaving the panels of light on the floor. I uploaded the photo and put a comment that our CEO had fine taste in art, which made our environment aesthetically nurturing. Even if he was pissed about the statue itself, he couldn't get too upset about being featured as someone with good taste, a man who thinks holistically about his employee's needs. His good taste would reflect well on the brand. It would draw positive attitudes to the app and his creative nature.

I smiled at my marketing finesse.

A lot of this I was making up as I went along, but I'd read enough about social media to have a few ideas. Mostly, it's social, and social interactions happen in your gut, no app to let you know what you're really thinking.

I posted the comments I'd composed, responding to a few of the most enthusiastic fans — the ones who wanted to send résumés and the ones who wanted to emulate what we were doing. There was one comment from a woman who wanted to blog about our venture. Her theme was cutting edge workplaces and ideas for the next decade of the twenty-first century.

I switched over to Twitter, fired off a few pithy thoughts, retweeted a ton of stuff, trying to add comments of my own with every fourth or fifth retweet so that TruthTeller was seen as a content provider, adding value, instead of an entity echoing everyone else.

After Twitter, I went into the weight room and did a mini lifting session — two sets for my shoulders, arms, and abs. I got a glass of water and cut up some lime, dropping a wedge into the glass. I returned to the office and opened Facebook. I smiled at the screen, thinking about what an easy job I had — easy and impossible. Trying to sell in a social situation opens you up to hate and shunning, but having a job where all you have to do is browse the internet and socialize with virtual friends was a dream.

The Facebook page itself had ten new likes, and the image of the statue had eighteen likes, several of them hearts, and a few *wows*. I drank my water and surfed the web and wondered why it was taking Tess so long to get into the office. She'd made it sound like after a quick shower she'd be at her desk. Instead, it had been at least an hour and a half since breakfast. Maybe she'd fallen asleep.

A moment later, I heard the slap of flip-flops on the staircase. I closed Facebook. It was too early to get into a conversation with her about the lower level details of my strategy. I opened Twitter and began scrolling through the followers of Australian trend-setters, looking for new people to follow. It made sense to start in our small corner of the world rather than trying to reach the entire planet in step one.

Tess walked into the office. She looked around. She went to the window and adjusted the shutters. "I feel like I never left."

I smiled.

"You look busy," she said.

"I am."

Since I was working at the desk, she sat at the conference table and opened her laptop. As I watched her scrolling through email, tapping out a reply here and there, as I wondered what was happening on the Facebook page while my attention was elsewhere, I felt we were looking over each other's shoulders. In such a large house, why hadn't Sean figured out a way for each of us to have our own office? This was far too much togetherness.

34

It was close to lunchtime. Finally, Sean felt his muscles relaxing as he read through the revised contracts the attorney had sent. He'd been alert and focused, the most clarity with his work in days, a week, whatever it had been since Karen literally floated into his backyard. It looked as though they were finally moving past the chaos. He felt he could breathe again, and it felt good to have his mind occupied with something that didn't reek of death.

Beside him on the desk, his phone vibrated with an incoming text. He finished reading the page before turning to look at it.

Sydney Police.

Aw shit. He stared at the phone. He could postpone opening the message, but of course his curiosity would eat at him and he'd lose all the concentration he'd worked so hard to muster this morning. He unlocked the phone.

Detective Martin here. I'd like to come by for a chat. Is 1:30pm today convenient?

A chat. He laughed out loud. Why did they pretend this interaction was one step from a block party? And asking if it was convenient…as if he were permitted to say today wouldn't work. He'd be lucky if she allowed a time shift of thirty minutes. The only power he had left was to let her stew for a few minutes before he replied to the text.

He returned to the contract. He read the same paragraph three times before giving up and putting the papers back in their folder. He replied to Martin with a simple *ok*.

When he opened the front door at one-twenty-five, Detective Martin stepped over the threshold and walked ahead of him to his office as if she believed she had free run of the house. He was annoyed before he even took a seat, the chair she rejected, at his own conference table. She asked him to close the door. He stood and closed it and remained by the door, determined that he'd win this territorial battle.

"I have some questions about your housemate, Ms. Mallory."

He gave her a single nod.

"Please have a seat."

"I've been sitting all morning."

"I'd like you to take a seat."

It required all his self control not to utter a crisp *fuck you*. He sat on the edge of the chair, leaning forward, elbows on his kneecaps.

"Are you in a relationship with Ms. Mallory?"

"What does that have to do with anything?"

"So I should take that as affirmative?"

"I didn't say that. I want to know why it matters to you."

"I have questions about the information she's provided and your relationship with her might color your answers."

"My answers are my answers, uncolored by anything."

"This will take longer if you lead the conversation in circles."

"I'm not in a relationship, and I can't imagine why you'd think that."

"Thank you. Ms. Mallory tells us she woke well before

dawn but she didn't look at the clock so she can't tell us what time it was. You told us you were roused by Mr. Dirkson at six-twenty."

"That's right."

"And you're still certain that was the time?"

"Yes."

"There would be some pre-dawn light at that time."

He shrugged.

"Was there?"

"I don't recall."

"There is, sunrise was at six-forty-four that day."

"If you say so."

"Ms. Mallory might have woken any time between approximately three a.m. and six, or later. From what we retrieved off Ms. North's mobile phone, she may have been in the pool as early as one a.m., and Ms. Mallory may have discovered her immediately. Possibly, she could have been alive. I need to know how much time elapsed between her discovery of the body and waking you. I need to know what she was doing during those minutes, or…hours."

"Why don't you ask her?"

"I'm asking you."

"I have no idea what time she woke up."

"Were you aware of any activity in the backyard before Mr. Dirkson woke you?"

"No."

"Think hard."

"I said, no."

"I'm certain there's a timeline issue here and I need it resolved before we can determine how to proceed with this case."

He stared at her. Bender was right, she was making more of this than necessary. Still, it was entirely possible Karen had been murdered. Her husband had been. Maybe they were mixed up in something that got them both killed. Drugs, most likely. John was a bit of a nutter, it made sense that he was on something. Of course, dealers didn't use the shit they sold, did they?

"Do you have any thoughts on the matter?"

He sat up straighter. "I don't."

"You don't seem to want to help us find out what happened to Ms. North."

"I'm answering your questions, that's all I can do. For what it's worth, I believe she killed herself." He wasn't at all sure, but it seemed safer.

"Ms. Mallory is not being truthful with us."

"How do you know that?"

"Everyone checks the time when they're woken from a deep sleep."

"*Everyone?*" He hated people who talked like that, made assertions based on their own habits and viewpoints, projecting their behavior onto other people. Terri had been like that and it constantly annoyed him. She made accusations and assumptions about his motives and desires based on her own thoughts. The trait hadn't done anything to enhance their relationship.

"Wouldn't you? In fact, you did do that. You were very precise with the time that Mr. Dirkson knocked on your door."

"That doesn't mean every single person on earth has the same habit."

"I think they do."

"If Alex said she didn't check, I think you should take her at her word. You shouldn't be assuming a lie just to fit your theory."

She waited for several minutes before speaking again. "We're not going away, Sean. We treat every unexplained death with dignity and care. There's a reason a dead woman ended up in your swimming pool and I would think you'd show a little more concern for ensuring she receives justice."

"I think being allowed to end your life in peace would be fitting justice."

She stared at him, waiting for him to say more, to trip himself up, most likely.

"Why don't you want to know the truth?" she said.

He glared at her and said nothing.

Finally she stood. "Please think about that timeline. Try to recall whether you heard any talking or splashing, anything at all, coming from the backyard. Try to think about Ms. Mallory's general habits and whether you believe she's that casual with the time.

35

Returning to Sydney

Entering the house where she'd lived for such a short time — John's house, not hers, the house where she realized her life had been an illusion — hit Karen with more force than she'd anticipated.

First, she'd forgotten the awful whiteness of it. John couldn't tolerate dirt or decay or imperfection of any kind. It was one of the things that had occupied her days and deadened her mind in their early marriage before they could afford a housekeeper. She'd spent hours every day cleaning the house. And he'd loved her for it, or so she'd thought.

This house was cleaner than anything she'd be able to achieve on her own. It required a crew to keep the purity of those white tile floors from being marred by the smallest piece of grit. You could lick those floors and come up with your tongue germ free.

The white made her eyes ache. She wanted to close them, unable to find a pleasing focal point. In contrast to the relentless white, the homey, comfortable furniture and artwork she'd chosen in an effort to tone down the bleakness took on the appearance of a horror movie set — so obviously out of place, you knew immediately that something wasn't right.

She left her suitcase standing in the entryway and began walking through the house. It wasn't as pristine as it had looked at first glance, there were a few signs of the police and their lab technicians — crushed carpet fibers, a smudge near a light switch, and an empty takeout coffee cup on the counter beside the gleaming white fridge.

She made two trips through the rooms on the first floor, pausing a long time to look out at the rainbow arrangement of blooming shrubs and flowers in the backyard. It had been her idea to plant them in an arc of red to purple. John hated it. He said it was foolish and contrived, but he'd left them alone, even after she was gone.

Going up to the second floor where his body had been found would require courage that had slipped to the pit of her stomach. She returned to the kitchen and opened the fridge. It was empty except for a few bottles of beer and sparkling water. She took one out and unscrewed the cap. The sound of her throat taking in the liquid echoed through the room. She was suddenly aware of how empty the house was. No life but her own. She replaced the cap and left the bottle on the counter.

Staying here until the place was ready for sale was too much. She didn't care what happened to it, how much it sold for. She wanted it sliced out of her life. How was she going to sleep in this place for even a single night? She hadn't considered that. She couldn't imagine even lying down in one of the so-called guest bedrooms. She couldn't fathom getting her eyes to close and remain shut.

She returned to the entryway and opened the front door. She stepped outside. The patio furniture looked unused. She'd never once sat out here. Had John? It was doubtful.

She crossed the patio and looked up and down the street. Maybe Sean would come outside. She didn't feel comfortable ringing his bell, but if they ran into each other…She closed her eyes for a moment. She needed to go to the store, stock up on food and a few bottles of wine. Maybe she would spend all her time on the front patio. Eventually he'd come out. She could even sleep here if she had a nice soft blanket and a pillow or two. There was a long bench with a back and thick cushions that would do just fine. It would offer better rest than the airplane.

A magpie landed on the lawn and began moving toward Sean's yard with large hops. To the birds, nothing had changed. They didn't know the occupant was dead, didn't know the house was a mausoleum even when he was alive. All they cared about was the availability of food. She walked toward the sidewalk, longing for another person. She'd only met a handful of neighbors, all of them superficially, like every human connection in her life. She wondered if they'd even realized she was gone until the police showed up and began spewing details about the home's occupants throughout the neighborhood.

She crossed the street, hoping that by sheer force of will, Elizabeth or one of the others might choose this moment to come outside for a handful of fresh cut flowers or a late morning walk or a dash to their car for a trip to the store.

The sun was directly overhead and she felt the prick of sweat on the back of her neck, but she was going to stand here until another human being appeared, if it meant standing here all day. She couldn't go back into that whiteness, couldn't climb those stairs until she stabilized herself with some normality, even an empty exchange of niceties about the weather.

After forty minutes, she was rewarded. Elizabeth Strand's front door opened and she stepped onto the porch. As if she'd been watching Karen all along, she immediately lifted her arm and waved. She walked toward the front of her yard and they met in the shade beside a magnolia tree.

Elizabeth touched her elbow. "It must be so difficult."

Karen nodded. "We were divorced, but still…"

"I know." Elizabeth moved closer and gave her a light hug. "You won't be selling the house, will you?"

"I am."

"Australia really is a lovely place," Elizabeth said, "Even if you never had the opportunity to experience that."

"I imagine it is. I can feel it. But…"

"People make too much of the so-called energy inside a house. A death, even this kind of death, doesn't damage the house. That's archaic superstition. There's no reason you can't stay. You'd be welcomed."

Karen wondered if that were true. She hadn't felt particularly welcomed when she'd lived here with John. Although maybe that was on her. How often had she done this, walked outside and lingered, waiting for others to make an appearance? Maybe never. She was always rushing out to the car and rushing back inside with an armload of groceries or other purchases, going to the mall, out to dinner…

"They have no leads. I'm not sure how much they told you," Elizabeth said.

"I know. It's baffling."

"Do you have any idea who might hate him so desperately?"

"We only socialized casually with a few people. Mostly,

John kept to himself. We both did."

Elizabeth smiled. "Yes. He tried to be neighborly, but he was awkward. Helping where it wasn't necessary."

Karen laughed. She shook her head, wondering how much Elizabeth knew about John's awkward neighborliness. That was the understatement of the year, maybe the decade. She laughed again. Awkward. Had he ever aimed his telescope to see inside of Elizabeth's home? Of course, she was too old to capture his prurient interest. It sounded as if she was unaware of what he'd been up to. They were all in the dark. Probably the police didn't even know. How would they?

"Does Sean still live there?" She pointed at the house beside hers.

"Yes. Why do you ask?"

"Just curious." She sounded too curious.

What was wrong with her? She was forty-six years old. Sean was thirty-two at best, possibly younger. It wasn't unheard of, but still, she was acting like a silly middle-aged cougar who thought she still had it. Sure you heard about relationships with an age gap that large, but it was rare. And it was nothing but a horny, curious guy who wouldn't say no to any woman who showed interest and took the lead. She sighed.

"Are you okay?"

She shrugged. "I don't have the energy for this."

"It's only jet lag. You really should stay. You could make a fresh start."

Karen thought about stripping all that white out of the house. She could get a red cooktop and oven. She'd seen that once. A charcoal gray refrigerator to complement it. One wall in the kitchen painted a pale gray, the living room painted sage green. She'd tear out that white carpet and replace it with…

The intensity of the sun seemed magnified. She squinted, feeling she could hardly make out the features of Elizabeth's face. There was no reason to go back to the states. Redoing the house with an explosion of color would provide a certain victory over John. She could bring life to something that he'd sucked the marrow out of. It wasn't a bad idea.

"You're thinking about it. That's good." Elizabeth smiled.

"But the room where they found his body, I'm not sure I could…"

Elizabeth grasped her forearm, pulling her closer. "I told you, that's nothing. The house is made of wood and plaster and concrete. He's no longer there. Trust me. You should stay."

Karen moved her arm gently out of Elizabeth's grip. "I can't make any decisions right now. It was nice seeing you."

"Come over for a cup of tea. We can talk more," Elizabeth said. "Thursday?"

Karen nodded hoping the movement of her head looked vague — friendly and a little grateful but promising nothing.

The minute the front door closed behind her, she started toward the stairs, determined to do it without thinking too much. Elizabeth was so confident there were no ghosts in the house. This was the twenty-first century. It was imagination, fueled by childhood stories and cultural superstitions. The mind could believe anything, if you thought about it too much. The house was silent enough — like a tomb.

As she made her way along the upstairs hall, she paused and opened the door to each of the bedrooms. She left them standing ajar. Nothing had changed, two of the rooms were empty, three were minimally furnished as guest rooms. The master bedroom was another story. She'd heard of this, but the police hadn't warned her of course, and she'd forgotten, never thinking it would apply to her.

The room was shocking. The sheets had been stripped off and taken to the lab to inspect for fibers and hairs and the potential presence of DNA that didn't belong to John. The room smelled of something she couldn't name, and she didn't care to figure it out. It wasn't pleasant. There were dark smudges on the walls and doors from fingerprint powder. The carpet had been torn up in two of the four corners and it was still folded back, like the skin of a man's chest undergoing an autopsy. At least there wasn't any blood. She'd heard of murder scenes soaked with blood, left for the family to clean up.

She backed out of the room and closed the door.

She walked down the hall to the lounge area. The door to the front balcony was partially opened. She slid it along the track and stepped outside, eager for clean air. She leaned on the half wall and looked out at the street. Something felt wrong about the balcony. She turned slowly. The table was near the doors. A few feet away was the chair where John sat when he was actually using the scope for its intended purpose. But the telescope wasn't there.

Surely she hadn't missed it in one of the other rooms? She knew she hadn't, but all the same, she went back inside and walked down the hall again. When she'd confirmed what she already knew, she searched the closets on both floors. She opened all the cabinets in the garage and then went back upstairs and looked under the beds.

The telescope was gone.

36

Sydney

It's not that detectives are easy to mislead. I imagine it's the opposite. Never start off assuming someone isn't smarter than you and never assume they don't know how to do their job. And especially with cops, they can pretend to be innocent and naive as they lead you exactly where they want you to go.

I wanted to come up with a scenario that explained Karen's death. It might allow the detectives to step away without embarrassment. Maybe they were as tired of the repetitive questions as we were. For all we knew, they, like every working person, had a boss pushing them to deliver something impossible. Much like being friendly on Facebook and expecting that to turn into millions of sales for your phone app.

Not that I didn't believe that was theoretically possible, but it was somewhat far-fetched.

I went for a short run because I got a later start than usual.

After a three-mile loop, my hood was off, the zipper down, and I was nearing Sean's street. I crossed over so my route would take me past Elizabeth's house. I'd noticed she came out early every Friday and dragged the hose to the curb where she watered a triangle of earth filled with new plants. It surprised me she didn't have a drip system. Maybe she did and just liked giving the hands-on care while they were young.

Each time after watering, she got in the car and drove down the street, staying away until late in the afternoon. Not that I was spying on her.

I slowed my pace. She wasn't out in her yard yet. I hoped I hadn't miscalculated. I began walking, taking my time. A moment later, she emerged from the shadow of her front porch and went to the faucet. She walked across the lawn, the black hose uncoiling as she went.

When she reached the triangle of plants, I was there.

"You're out early," she said.

"This is late for me. I usually run before the sun comes up."

"Oh, my. That is early. I'm a night owl."

I smiled.

"Has the Karen matter been put to rest?" she said.

"No. They keep circling, looking for signs of murder."

"Like I said the other day, thoroughness. It's very important, although sometimes overdone."

"It's getting old," I said. The longer they hovered, the greater the chance they were looking at John's murder and Karen's death as a single entity, the closer they might get to asking me more difficult questions. I was confident there was no trace of me at John's. The telescope was safely hidden in my enormous closet, the size of a small room itself. Unless they got a warrant to search the house, but nothing like that had been mentioned. Still, I wanted them out of there. I needed them out of there. I didn't fret and fuss and complain like Sean, but I understood him completely. They were a nuisance, and they were too curious about things that didn't matter. It's always the things that seem not to matter that trip you up.

"I talked to Karen the day she died," Elizabeth said.

"Does Detective Martin know that?"

"No, I don't know why I said anything. It's not important."

I didn't think the detectives would agree.

"It feels uncomfortable. Sad. To know those were her last hours on earth."

"What did you talk about?"

"I suggested she stay in Australia, that she shouldn't let superstitions about ghosts keep her out of that beautiful house. And it's such a lovely neighborhood. I did wonder about the man who killed John, wondered if he might return...but I didn't say anything to her about that. I wonder if I should have."

"That seems unlikely, don't you think? How would he know she was staying there?"

She nodded. "It does seem unlikely. But your mind races to all kinds of possibilities, searching for the answer. And we'll probably never have it."

"What else did you talk about?"

"She asked about Sean." Elizabeth smiled. "I think she was drawn to him as much as he to her. But with a boy who looks like that, anyone would be." She smiled.

Apparently getting the hots for a good-looking guy didn't fade when you were in your seventies.

A moment later she gave me a tiny wink, but it could have been an involuntary tremor of her eyelid. It was very tiny.

"I think the liquor bottle wouldn't be there if she was

murdered. I think she drank a lot and either fell into the pool, or walked in," she said.

"Did she seem depressed?"

"I don't think suicide is always depression. It's an acceptance of finality, of the ultimate end, and maybe you're tired of waiting for that. Some people want to take their fate into their own hands."

It was a rather gloomy view of life, and yet her face looked content and mildly happy every time I glanced at her. She was an unusual woman.

"Did you give the detectives your opinion?"

She laughed. "They could care less about my opinion. They only wanted to know what I saw or heard. Maybe that's why they don't always solve their cases. Too much emphasis on what they find with their five senses and not enough of their other senses."

"I thought cops relied a lot on instinct?"

"So they say. But it seems to me they also miss quite a bit."

I moved toward her fence and leaned against it. She aimed the hose at the last plant. "I think it's pretty clear what happened. She wanted to seduce Sean…"

Her accent on the word seduce was so charming, I almost giggled.

"…he said no, and she decided she'd had enough of the world. The simple answer is usually the right one."

It sounded plausible when Elizabeth said it in her calm, even voice, but immediately the questions arose in my mind. Why sit in the dark hoping he'd happen to look out and see her? And drowning herself made no sense. Karen hated the water.

Still, did I believe it enough to suggest it to Detective Martin or Bender in the same assured tone the next time they started asking me again what time I'd found her?

I hadn't given the time because there was a gap while Gavin and I considered what to do. The gap would make them wonder what I'd been up to during those minutes that stretched to half an hour. It would make them consider my potential as a killer. Hiding it might have been a mistake. They knew I was keeping something back. I think they had more instinct than Elizabeth gave them credit for.

37

After breakfast, I told Tess I was going to work from my bedroom so I could concentrate without distractions. She took it easily instead of demanding to know why I considered her a distraction. Perhaps she felt the same way. Sharing a workspace is okay on an occasional basis, but there's a definite distraction caused by another physical presence, even if your officemate doesn't talk. It's the awareness that you're being watched and listened to. Maybe it's the brainwaves of the other person becoming a tangible presence in the space around you. Perhaps it's just the reduced level of oxygen when two sets of lungs are able to consume only fifty percent of what's available.

I needed privacy because I couldn't let her glimpse the photograph of that statue on the Facebook page. She still hadn't seen the statue in real life. She hadn't seen it because she refused to invade Sean's space, which was very upstanding of her, but she didn't know what she was missing.

Oddly, she hadn't asked any specifics about how TruthTeller's social media presence was moving forward. She'd seen me using Twitter but hadn't wondered about the number of followers or shown any interest in whether we were getting engagement. Maybe she was still jet-lagged. More likely, her head was in California, working through whatever had happened there. Her silence around her meeting with Gorman concerned me even more than the chance of her discovering the statue on the Facebook page.

I sat on my bed, raised the cover of my laptop, and opened Facebook.

There were over seven hundred likes and loves for the photograph. Even better, there wasn't a single blood-boiling angry face. Over two hundred people had left comments. Again, the value-add was low. Lots of single word statements such as *beautiful* and *gorgeous* and *breathtaking*. Quite a few had simply written — *I want*.

One woman who used a Siamese cat as her profile picture asked me the name of the artist. Two men asked the same question. Another woman with super short black hair and an elfin-looking face agreed that our CEO had fine taste and commented he must be an interesting guy.

I replied that he had a lot of vision.

Carmen Dunn, the elfin woman, must have been hovering over her page, because the thumbs up on my comment was almost instantaneous. Then another comment appeared.

Carmen Dunn: *How long has he had the statue?*

I couldn't comprehend why that mattered. I wrote back that I wasn't sure, but would try to find out. She asked whether I knew the price. It was still odd, seeing my name mashed up with the TruthTeller name to help keep myself as private as possible on Facebook. I wondered how long it would take until it felt natural.

Alex Teller: *Are you interested in making an offer?* I put a winking emoji.

Carmen Dunn: *Maybe. It's stunning.*

Alex Teller: *I agree. It's hard to take your eyes off it. The picture doesn't do it justice.*

Carmen Dunn: *It looks like one-of-a-kind. Is it?*
Alex Teller: *I don't know that either, but it does, I agree.*
Carmen Dunn: *You should find out.*

I added a few emojis with different types of smiles. I love emojis, I can paste a little digital sticker on someone's page or in a text message and avoid speaking words that might trap me. It's so much easier to tell people what they want to hear in person or over the phone, but writing it down risks having it come back to bite you, word for word. Emojis erase all of that in colorful little shapes, sharing assumed communication. I can put a tiny glass of wine and everyone assumes I'm suggesting sharing a glass of wine. But am I? Maybe I'm suggesting you drink too much, or I need a drink after talking to you, or what you just posted sounds like you're drunk. It could mean ten different things. The yellow smiling faces are even more versatile. The potential for miscommunication is staggering.

Carmen Dunn: *Will you?*

In this case, I guess the emojis weren't as effective as I'd thought. She was going to push for a direct answer. There was no way Sean would sell the statue. I hoped she was just joking around about making an offer, but her other questions suggested she seriously thought she could have it.

Alex Teller: *To be clear, it's not for sale.*

Carmen Dunn: *I'm still curious.* She added a smiley face of her own.

By then, others had added a few more comments. I went through and ticked the thumbs up on all of them. I created a new post showing a photo of the biofeedback device. Above it I added a comment about how curious people are about their own psyches, how mysterious our own minds can be, even though we exist right inside of them. I hoped the innocuous shape and texture of the device would prompt people asking what it was, opening the door for a low-key, friendly, no pressure, barely discernible sales pitch.

Checking out Instagram had been on my to-do list for a while, so I spent a few minutes looking it over. I quickly decided it wasn't the right fit for TruthTeller. I sent email to the rest of the team telling them my decision. Better to focus on two channels and do well than too many and accomplish nothing. They all responded within two or three minutes, agreeing with my reasons.

It was strange, sitting alone in my room, emailing people who were one floor below me, people who ate meals with me and slept down the hall from me. Not much more ridiculous than doing the same with people ten cubicles away or a floor below in an office building, I suppose, but still…there was something about the living together that made it more senseless. If we were living together, we didn't need to exchange email at all, and yet, we did.

38

Sean opened the door in response to the third chime of the bell. He'd hoped it was someone he wanted to see, even a package would be welcome, but he'd known in his gut that it was a police officer.

Detective Bender.

No polite phone call asking if it was convenient. Just a guy suddenly standing on his front patio, wanting more of him, inflated with his power to constantly disrupt their lives.

"What's up?" Sean said.

"Got a minute?"

Some consideration after all. Was the guy implying Sean had a choice? Bender wasn't going to shove his way in no matter what Sean thought about it? He was so taken by surprise, he stood there for an extended minute, staring at the detective. A kookaburra burst out laughing, forcing Sean to smirk.

"Do you?" Bender said.

"Yeah. Sure." He stepped away from the door, holding it back so Bender could enter the foyer.

"Why don't we sit on your front patio. It might be better."

Sean stepped outside and closed the door. "Something to drink?" he said.

Bender shook his head and they took seats facing each other.

Bender leaned forward slightly, as if he planned to share a confidence. "Just wanted to tell you not to let Martin get under your skin."

"She doesn't."

Bender gave him a don't-bullshit-me look. "She doesn't have anything."

"Are you supposed to be telling me this?"

Bender laughed. "What do you care?"

"I'm just surprised."

"I told you, she's trying to make a name for herself. Wants to prove she's tough and hard-driving. She had a kid about eight months ago. Her fourth. The woman can't keep her legs together." He snickered.

"The boss told her the same and all she did was whine about being harassed. What's harassing about that? It's a fact. Hard to be a cop and take care of babies. So she has one case since she came back from leave and she wants to make it something big."

Sean stared at the other man, who returned the look without flinching, seemingly unaware of how offensive his comments were. The look on his face was almost eager, waiting for Sean to agree, to take it further. Did he talk like that to Detective Martin's face? Did she realize what was being said about her?

He hated the questions, the undercurrent of suspicion, but he didn't doubt her ability to do her job. And he certainly didn't think she wasn't deserving of her position, from what he'd seen, she was a decent cop. Finally, he spoke. "I guess men manage to have children and careers."

"She's the mother. Can't be a mum and a good detective. And she's not being a good detective, letting her imagination go wild on this. It's clear as day that gal got drunk and drowned."

"Good to know."

"And just so you know, Martin's comparing notes with Detective Joyner, another gal cop. They're taking over, I'm telling you. And these girls get all emotional, stirring each other up so they think they have a murder when they have a drunk and a swimming pool. Joyner is the one on John North's murder. Now that one's clear. Murder for sure. You know right away what it is. Murder screams at you."

"Someone else asked us questions right after it happened," Sean said. "But there hasn't been anything since. It wasn't Detective Joyner."

Bender gave a short laugh, a harsh sound like he was simultaneously coughing and spitting out chewing tobacco. "Reassigned to a girl. Happens all the time. Females are getting close to half the force. Taking over. Wrong job for the weaker sex, if you ask me. Can't fight, can't run, easily intimidated by the criminal element, prone to crying. It's risky and a bad idea all around. It's distracting when you're trying to work, and all these women are wiggling their bums in your face." He laughed to himself. "And you have to watch every fucking word you say. Everything offends them. You have no idea."

Sean's thoughts circled back to his previous fear — was this a trap to get him to bond with Bender? Was the guy inserting himself so that Sean felt free to confide? If nothing else, he might be hoping Sean agreed so he could be reported for denigrating a police officer, if that was an offense. Surely the guy didn't really think this way about his colleagues, about women in general. He was about forty. Too young to have ideas that were decades out of date.

"I want you to know, I have your back. I'm working on her, trying to get her to wrap it up. I know she's interfering with your business, and she's way too curious about you and the girls living here. Very curious. She must be jealous. Wishes she was a swinging single again." He laughed. He slapped Sean's knee. "To tell the truth, so am I."

For some bizarre reason, some twist of his brain, Sean couldn't respond to the suggestion that they were all having group sex, which if it wasn't directly in the words was definitely on Bender's face. All he could focus on was the phrase — *tell the truth*. It made him think of their app, sent his mind wandering to other things — worry about the launch schedule, wondering whether it would be as successful as he'd dreamed. The slow-down in momentum filled him with irrational fear they'd somehow passed their window of opportunity.

"If there's anything you can tell us about this Karen North…"

He'd been right. Suddenly the conversation was back to questioning him. The other had been an elaborate detour, a definite trap. "I didn't know her."

"So you said, so you said." Bender nodded as he spoke. "The faster we can get some definitive info, the sooner I can get Martin to back off."

"I've said everything I know." The lie had been repeated so often, it no longer felt like a lie. Again, TruthTeller wafted through his mind. He couldn't change his story now. And he was still confident it didn't matter. There was nothing he knew that pointed to murder.

Bender grinned. "Nothing like confronting the facts to

puncture the fantasy Miz Martin is weaving in her mind." He shook his head. "I know this scrutiny is tough, mate. I can see you squirm. If there's something dicey that happened, you banging both the girls in your house, this Karen getting involved…information is power. The truth will set you free."

"I've told you the truth." That lie was more difficult, it stuck in his throat. Perhaps because it was new, and perhaps because it was more blatant in some ways. If this guy had so much power over Detective Martin, why couldn't he just persuade her on his own?

Bender stood. "If you think of anything…" He slapped Sean's shoulder and handed him a business card. "*Anything,* call me. If you want to get something off your chest, call me. I can expedite this, but I need the details."

Sean stood and shook his hand. "There's nothing else." He still took the card. It would seem uncooperative not to.

39

I was sitting on the living room couch, my eyes closed, listening to the birds. The door was open just a crack to let in their voices but keep out most of the cold air. Usually they quieted in the afternoon, but today they were still at it. Maybe they sensed the mood in our house, the mood in the entire neighborhood — chattering and fretting.

The front door opened and Sean stepped inside. He closed it and stood staring at the door handle as if he didn't want to let go of it. After more than a few seconds, he moved away. He shoved his hands in his pockets. He wore jeans and a pale green and white striped button-down shirt. His feet were bare.

"Sean!"

He looked over at me, shoulders hunched as a result of his pocketed hands.

"We have over two thousand page likes."

He scowled. He pulled his hands out of his pockets and took a few steps toward the living room entrance. "What?"

"The TruthTeller Facebook page — over two thousand people have liked it."

He walked closer. "We need a hell of a lot more than two thousand customers."

"We just started." I smiled. "And that's a lot. The Facebook page is to get the word out, not a measure of how many people buy the app. Not everyone is going to interact on social media.

"Okay. That's good, then. How did you find them? Are they interested in the app or just the name of the company?"

I didn't answer, waiting to see whether he'd actually enter the room so I didn't have to keep raising my voice to be heard across the rather large space. After a long pause, he did. He sat on the floor, looking up at me like a pre-school child drinking in his teacher's face, waiting for story time.

"I post a lot of stuff. Not all of it's about the app. If it's always about the app, it turns into an advertisement and people tune you out. It's *social*." I smiled.

"I get that, Alex. How did you find them?"

"Quite a lot of them because I wrote about your vision for work-life balance."

He smiled, but he looked tired, as if he no longer cared all that much.

"Anyway, it's a huge step forward. You should be excited."

"Will do. If you say I should be excited, I'll get excited." He put his head in his hands.

What a drama queen. I waited for him to explain the reason for his despairing pose.

"Detective Bender popped by," he said.

"What did he want now?"

"I can't be sure. Either they're definitely trying to trap me, or he's an ass."

"What did he do?"

"He said some pretty shit things about Detective Martin. Said she couldn't keep her legs closed, if that's not too crude to repeat. She has four kids."

I waited.

He lowered his hands and looked up. "I didn't mean to offend you."

"I can handle it," I said.

"He hates having women on the police force, I guess. Thinks those jobs belong to the guys. He still thinks the murder angle is just Martin's push to make a big deal out of it."

"Do you think that?"

"I honestly don't know. She wants something from me. She has a reason they aren't drawing the obvious conclusion."

"Female intuition?" I smiled.

He laughed. "Could be. But that's not a real thing."

"Intuition is absolutely a real thing. I just don't think it's confined to my half of the human race."

He looked at me hard, as if he was assessing me, bringing all his intuition to bear. I could see him replaying our complicated relationship in his head.

"Not to change the subject," I said, "But I was curious, is that statue in your room the only one of its kind?"

He nodded. "Yes. What brought that up?"

"Did you commission it?"

"No. Why do you want to know?"

"Curious. I'm a very curious person."

He folded his lips together. He leaned back, pressing his hands against the floor behind his hips to prop himself up.

"Can I ask what you paid for it?"

"I don't think you need to know that."

"No worries."

"No worries? What the fu…" He shook his head slightly. "Never mind. I want these endless police queries about every minor detail of my life to stop. It's getting on my nerves."

"So you said."

"Aren't you tired of answering questions?"

"I don't really care," I said. "It's boring, repeating the same answers, but I don't care."

"He implied there's a new detective looking at John's death who might want to talk to us too."

That I cared about very much. I waited for him to say more. The chatter of the birds seemed to grow louder, filling the room.

He shivered. "Why is the door open?"

"So I can hear the birds."

"They're plenty loud enough with the door closed. And it's too cold."

I looked at his bare feet.

He held my gaze as if he expected me to respond immediately to his discomfort.

I crossed my legs. "You don't know how it is for an American. I love listening to them. I wonder how Tess's bird will take to it. He's used to being sealed up inside a high-rise condo."

"It's a bird," he said. "They adapt better than we do."

"You need to use the pronoun. Tess doesn't like anyone calling him an it."

He smiled.

He really was quite gorgeous. That smile made me melt. It washed away all the snipe-like things that came out of his mouth, diminished the aura of arrogance.

"So Bender doesn't want any women to be detectives?" I said.

"It sounds that way. For a fairly young guy, he's a bit of a dinosaur."

I nodded. He was more than a dinosaur. I thought about Martin trying to work under those conditions. The guy actually came to our house to slam her behind her back. Unless she was in on it... But I doubted it. I could think of other ways for them to play that game without trashing women. "What else did he say?"

"That women aren't equipped to be detectives — too emotional, not enough physical strength. That sort of thing."

"Did you call him on it?"

"No. I want this to be over, not prolonged by an argument over something that I can't do anything about. If that's how he sees things, that's how it is. There are lots of guys like that."

He was right, of course, but that didn't mean they didn't get called on it. Sean had been so uncomfortable with Barry's behavior after all that happened with Lisa, as if he wanted to make sure to polish the reputation of mankind, but now, he didn't care. I suppose he cared more about his own comfort. His frustration consumed all his thoughts.

"You know part of this is your fault," he said.

"How so?"

"They don't believe you. They don't believe that you don't know what time you found her. Not having a time makes it seem that we could have known for hours, that we tried to cover up a murder."

I leaned back and put my heels on the coffee table, crossing my ankles. My feet were also bare.

Sean stood up. "Want a beer?"

"Sure."

He went to the kitchen and returned with two bottles of Tooheys. He sat beside me on the couch, handed a beer to me, and clicked the neck of his bottle against mine. He took a swallow. "At any rate, did you?"

"What?"

"Did you lie?"

I took several moments to consider how to answer this. The lie rose easily to my tongue, but I didn't want to shut the door on wherever he was headed. "I don't think that matters."

"You're right. We agree on that. Do you think there's a way to get rid of them and their pointless questions?"

"Not that I can see, and I've tried."

We drank our beers in silence. Even the birds had quieted now. The cool air continued to flow into the room, but Sean had apparently forgotten about that.

I sucked on the top of the bottle, sticking my tongue inside to feel the cool glass gripping my flesh. I removed my tongue, tipped the bottle up, and swallowed some. "Did you lie?"

"We're on the same page," he said. "It doesn't matter."

So, Gavin and I were right. He lied. He and I both lied. And it hadn't helped anything. Did the detectives sense it from both of us? My chest burned with curiosity to know what he'd lied about. Clearly he had some sort of relationship with Karen. I didn't think he'd killed her. He didn't have it in him, and he was too intelligent to do something like that in his own pool. Had he talked to her the night she drowned? Had they had a thing between them before she left Australia? There were several possibilities.

If I revealed my lie, he would return the favor. And mine was quite innocuous. It truly didn't matter at all. "I do know what time I woke up. It was three-twenty-six. I had a cigarette — on the balcony. I didn't see her right away. And then Gavin and I talked about it before we woke you. But that doesn't mean what they think it does."

He nodded. He gulped down the rest of his beer. "I saw Karen by the pool. She was drinking right from the bottle. She didn't see me, and I didn't go out there." He stood and walked out of the room. He returned with two more beers, setting one on the table. He stood facing me and drank half the contents of his bottle.

40

Portland

My relief at being rid of Tony and his cannibalistic poems lasted exactly three days. After church on Sunday, as I was walking to our classroom, safely surrounded by three other girls, I reached into my purse. My fingers brushed across the hard corner of a box.

The purse strap had been looped over the arm of my chair and the purse itself sat beside my feet during the church service. I hadn't seen Tony anywhere around me. I watched the back of his head during the entire first half of the service. Once the sermon started, I suppose I'd lost track. He must have moved to a seat behind me. It still didn't explain how he'd gotten something inside my purse, but there it was. The explanation didn't really matter.

I told the girls I needed to pee. They entered the restroom with me. They stood near the mirror, talking about the virtues of short hair, while I went into the farthest stall.

The small box was wrapped in red paper with a white bow stuck on the top. I tore off the paper and stuffed the bow and paper into the sanitary disposal box. I lifted off the lid off the box. Inside was a folded scrap of paper. Beneath that was a collection of ten fingernail clippings. I closed my eyes as a wave of disgust passed through me. After a moment, I opened my eyes and turned the box upside down over the toilet. I flushed.

The note contained one word — *You.*

As I tore it into strips, I thought about its possible meaning. In its own way, it might have been the most compelling poem he'd written, the most powerful use of words ever scrawled with ink onto a piece of paper. It was flattering with a rather ominous tone. He was consumed with me. There's something powerful in that, and something frightening. No one wants to be the center of another person's universe, their god, the dictator of their soul. It's too much responsibility, the thought of the expectation alone is enough to crush you. And what did the fingernails mean? Would he cut off other parts of himself, eventually giving every fragment of his body to me? Considering his comments about my eyeballs, was he suggesting he might take parts of my body for himself? Or was he just intending on trimming away parts of himself that he intuited I might not like until there was nothing left?

With a second flush, I sent the note down the toilet. Two strips of paper remained. I flushed again. I went out and met the other girls. I turned on the faucet and squirted soap into the palm of my hand.

"Are you okay?"

"Yes." I scrubbed my hands and rinsed them.

"I heard the toilet flush three times."

I grabbed a paper towel and dried my hands. "Everything is fine."

All through Sunday School class, I thought about those fingernails. I remembered what they'd looked like on his fingers. His hands were beautiful, except for those hideous, feminine to the point of freakish fingernails. A bit of moist black dirt was always lodged under the thumbnails. I imagined that without the excess nail, his hands looked more aristocratic, less fiendish. I expected he looked more like a normal boy.

I pictured him taking the nail clippers out of the bathroom drawer, inserting his nail between the blades, and squeezing the lever. I saw the nails falling into the little box, the kind of box normally used for jewelry. The only thing missing had been the square of cotton fiber to keep the nails from rattling around.

What had it felt like when he scratched his skin with those long nails? Did they bend from the effort, or raise welts along the underside of his arm? Was it hard for him to work on a keyboard or hold a pen, nails clacking against the keys or pressing into the flesh on the inside of his hand? Most of all, what had possessed him to think I would enjoy that *gift*? I couldn't imagine why he thought that might draw me closer, awaken feelings of love inside of me.

When I closed my eyes briefly as we bowed for prayers, which were scattered liberally throughout our ninety-minute class, I saw those nails, raking across his cheek.

I tried to think about what I was going to do. I thought I'd been pretty clear that I didn't like his poems and didn't want to spend time around him anymore. On one level he got the message because there hadn't been another poem. Just that word — so innocuous and so threatening, so full of things that couldn't be described.

He was a poet. He'd made that clear. His face had the look, if there is such a thing. He was the type of person who comes into the world with an exposed heart. Every drop of rain feels like a torrent of hailstones, and every bleating horn carries the same raucous, head-splitting intensity as an approaching army in thick, iron-toed boots, carrying deadly weapons.

Someone so sensitive surely must have realized I didn't have the same feelings as he did. There was no love, no undying devotion that made me take risks or turn my nights over to dreams of him and my days into fantasies that carried me, floating up through the ceiling and outside of the classroom.

As we sang the final hymn — Onward Christian Soldiers, every single verse with that plodding cadence, every single week — it occurred to me that he was sensitive to the things that touched his body, wafted into his nostrils, traveled through his mind. He was completely clueless about my thoughts or feelings. All he knew was what *he* wanted, he couldn't read even the most obvious signals from me, much less listen to and absorb what I had to say. He was too busy hearing and seeing the fantasy me he'd constructed inside of his head, too busy feeling his own feelings.

Still, I had to say something to him. I had to try to make him hear.

Most girls might ask their parents to intervene, but doing that would create more restrictions on me. It was too high of a price for ejecting Tony from my life. Some girls would ask the leaders of the youth group to put a stop to his excessive push for attention, bordering on stalking. I wasn't about to make myself indebted to one of them, to provide an open door suggesting they had a right to muck around in my life. Once they thought I needed them, needed their guidance and supposed wisdom, they would think they owned me.

There had to be some way of speaking that would open Tony's ears to absorb the words, fit them into his view of the world, and get him to leave me alone. I did not want to receive a gift-wrapped box full of toenail clippings.

As the words to the final verse billowed around me, I knew — Tony needed someone else to love!

I set about putting my friend Delia in his path. I suggested to Delia that she should stop wearing a hairband, to let her hair fall loose around her face and shoulders. I stuck myself to her side so that every time Tony looked at me, he saw Delia. I talked him up to Delia, pointed out how beautiful he was. I mentioned he was quiet and what a nice change that was from the norm. She agreed. I told her he was sensitive and he seemed like he needed a friend — she should become that friend. I went on about his thoughtful poems.

On Tony's side, I pointed out Delia's thick, straight hair. I told him Delia adored poetry. I told him Delia thought no boy could ever be interested in her. I spoke softly — *she's lonely.*

Once they began sitting beside each other during our gatherings, I gradually moved myself out of the picture. One day, I stopped him as he was turning into the boys' bathroom — a great bit of timing that would keep our conversation short.

I cooed at him that it was great to see the love between them.

Tony looked at me, his eyes round, flecks of amber in the dark brown, looking as if they could shatter into a million fragments. "I don't love Delia. She's a friend. She needs me."

"But she…"

He put up his hand as if to place it over my mouth.

"There's only one girl for each boy. God planned it that way, so we'd all find completion. A boy has to hunt until he finds her. I'm blessed that I already have. There will never be anyone but you. You."

"That's not going to happen. I don't love you."

Tears dribbled out of his eyes. He stared at me. I gave him a tiny smile and turned away. I walked quickly across the classroom and out the side door to where my father's car waited every week for me and my siblings.

41

Sydney

After so many years traveling all over the world, Tess was disgusted with herself for mishandling her jet lag on both ends of this trip. The morning she'd arrived back in Sydney, she'd napped after breakfast. As a result, she was now staring at the thin white numbers on her phone — one-sixteen a.m. — ready to start the day.

The time difference between San Francisco and Sydney was brutal. When the US was still on daylight savings and Australia was heading into winter, the gap was eighteen hours. To fly home, you boarded the plane at ten p.m., flew all night and then into a second night as you crossed the international date line, leaping ahead in time, three a.m. becoming evening of the following day. She wondered if that's why people were willing to believe in the idea of time travel. Returning from Australia or Asia to the United States, you lived the same day twice, like traveling back in time.

She sat with her pillows propped up behind her, feeling as energized as if she'd just completed her morning workout. If she were in California, she would have finished an hour ago. She'd be at her desk, looking out over the bay, if she were also back in time working at CoastalCreative. How dramatically her life had changed — she lived in another world now, literally.

She threw off the covers and got out of bed. She went into the bathroom and brushed her hair, a somewhat random act since she'd done it before she went to bed. She supposed it was in lieu of brushing her teeth or splashing water on her face, both of which would have finished off sleep for the rest of the night, extending the jet lag another day.

She went downstairs to the liquor cabinet in the dining room. She took out Sean's bottle of Macallan's single malt scotch. She poured herself a shot and a half and eased the cork back into the top of the bottle. She went out to the back patio and put the glass on the table. She dragged one of the lounge chairs close to the edge of the shallow end of the pool — about where the chair had been located when they found Karen North's body.

Holding the glass of scotch in her left hand, she settled herself onto the lounge chair. She closed her eyes and took a tiny sip. The liquid burned her throat and sent warming alcohol through her bloodstream. Already she was calmer, able to face the possibility that sleep might not return for an hour. She took another sip of scotch.

Why were her thoughts drifting toward mourning the death of a woman she'd never met? She supposed she didn't like the idea of someone dying alone, of having her body dragged out of the pool, bloated and heavy. Like Steve. Dying alone. Most people did. Even if you were in a hospice, the odds of someone being there the moment you took your last breath had to be fifty-fifty at best.

And here she was thinking about Steve again. She refused to fall into that. She'd resolved it was no longer important. He was gone and she was moving forward. In a few years, he'd be an infinitesimal sliver in the landscape of her life. He died alone because he chased women away with his unrelenting male superiority. He died alone because he did something stupid, whatever that something was.

Not thinking about him. She was not going to think about him.

She got up and walked to the edge of the pool. She sat down and put her feet on the top step. The water was warm. It soothed the tendons and skin of her ankles. It seemed to have an immediate effect in reducing the swelling in her feet from sitting on an airplane for nearly fifteen hours. She took another sip of her drink. It was going down fast, but it didn't matter. The faster she drank it, within reason, the faster she'd be back in bed, dreamless. Free from thoughts of death.

The water lapped softly against the tile and undulated around her ankles. She drank the scotch and let her mind drift into nothing but noticing the warm glow of alcohol, the water on her skin, the hardness of the concrete pressing against her tailbone.

It wasn't clear how much time had passed when she took the last swallow of amber liquid from the glass. She had a nice buzz and was confident her pillow would now feel comforting. She stood and stepped out of the pool. Leaving the lounge chair where it was, she walked deliberately across the patio with that hyper-sensitive awareness of her feet and hands and the shape of her face that comes with alcohol.

She left the glass on the kitchen counter and started toward the foyer. She paused and turned back. She got the scotch and poured another shot in the glass. At the top of the stairs, she took a sip. She pressed her hip against the railing and leaned forward, looking down into the dark foyer.

The sound of a door unlatching made her turn too fast. Her fingers squeezed around the glass with so much force she worried she might crush the thin sides, more fragile than a water glass.

Why would someone be leaving their room at this hour? Everyone had a bathroom with their bedroom. It must be close to two-thirty, possibly later. Whoever it was might be hungry, looking for a slice of cold pizza or even an extremely late nightcap, like her own. She took a sip of scotch and waited.

From where she stood, she could see the entire length of the hall — her own door to her left, the spare room, Alex's room, and Gavin's at the opposite end. The hallway made a right turn to the master suite so that Sean's door wasn't visible.

Slowly, Gavin's door opened and Alex stepped out. Even in the darkness, her shape and the gleam of her white T-shirt and pale pink sleep shorts obviously belonged to a woman.

Tess took five or six steps forward, hoping that even with the usual soundless response of the floorboards, Alex would sense her presence. It seemed very important that Alex know she'd been caught having sex with Gavin. And there was no doubt that was why she was creeping out of his room in the middle of the night.

Tess moved to her left and flicked on the light.

Alex turned. Her face registered no obvious surprise. She nodded her head. She slipped her hand in the waistband of her shorts, pulled out a key, and inserted it in the keyhole of her door handle. She opened the door and slipped inside.

Why, after all her obsessing over Gavin's locked room, was she now locking her own? Had Gavin told her why his was locked and she believed she needed to protect her space for some reason? Tess shivered. She turned off the light and hurried into her room, closing the door and locking it behind her.

42

Last night on earth

After she left Elizabeth, Karen spent the rest of the afternoon and evening wandering around the house, inspecting it as if she were intending to purchase it herself. For dinner she ordered takeout Singapore noodles and potstickers. She drenched the potstickers in chili oil and white vinegar while she drenched herself with Pinot Gris.

For half a minute, Elizabeth's suggestion that she remain in Australia had sounded tempting. Add that to the boy next door and her life seemed as if it could take a new, more satisfying direction. For half a minute. Maybe less.

Then she thought about living in this house. She could paint every wall a different color and it still wouldn't whitewash twenty years of rejection and loneliness and shame. Yes, it was shame. Every time her friends laughed and teased about their sex lives, her heart and lungs, liver and spleen and stomach and whatever else was inside her body burned at a temperature worthy of the Australian outback. There was no way she could live in this house. Not ever. She didn't even want to spend a single night sleeping here.

And the boy next door…yes, he was very good looking. Charming. But he was a *boy*. They'd have sex, possibly great sex, a few times and that would be it. She was close to fifty years old. There truly wasn't anything left for her.

She wished it had been different with Sean, but even her encounters with him added to her shame. That lie about checking with a mythical girlfriend before arranging a date for drinks. Did he think she was that stupid she wouldn't see the lie? He wasn't interested. He wanted to be rid of her, thinking his excuse wouldn't embarrass either one of them. It was there in the position of his arms and the way his head remained rigid when she'd touched his hair.

She stood quickly. The chair skittered across the floor. She carried the food containers to the trash and dumped them inside without bothering to fold the flaps back in place. She left her plate in the sink and ran some water over it to keep the residue from hardening. She poured the last of the wine into her glass and went upstairs.

She went into one of the furnished guest rooms and sat on the bed. If she had to sleep here, this would be the room. Not the room she'd once shared with John, the room he'd used as his own after she left, the room where he'd been murdered.

For all her sentiment during the flight, she felt nothing, thinking now about his death, about someone wanting to kill him. She felt nothing at all — no regret, no love, no loss. It was as if he'd never existed.

The frightening part was — it also seemed as if she'd never existed.

She stood and went to the window. She opened the blinds and looked out across the backyard. A small portion of the pool next door was visible. She'd seen it in the daylight, the water was black from the painted bottom. Now, it was even more black, if that were possible. Like a murky pond, the kind they warned kids not to dive into because it was impossible to know what was beneath the surface.

She hated water. She'd never learned to swim. She didn't even own a bathing suit, she was that determined never to be near the water. The violent aversion filled every cell of her body whenever water activities were mentioned, when she was invited to a swim club or a pool party or a trip to the beach. She had no idea where it had come from. Maybe one of those things that happened prior to conscious memory. Some horrible trauma had marked her for life. Maybe her mother wasn't attentive, allowing her baby girl to slip below the surface in the bathtub for a terrifying moment.

Unremembered trauma might very well have been John's problem as well. His perverted view of women, his desire to look at them but never touch them, never be anywhere near them.

It was late now, after ten. All the lights in Sean's house were off. It was unusual. When she'd lived here, his house was lit up all the time, well past midnight. She shrugged and started to turn away. Something flickered at the corner of her eye. She turned back.

A disk of light shone out from one of the several decks on the second floor of Sean's house. She'd know that shape anywhere. She'd seen it often enough, coming up the walkway after a nocturnal walk, John on that concrete deck outside the lounge, surveying uncovered bedroom windows. Sometimes she felt he even turned it on her as she walked slowly toward home, loving her through his viewfinder, from far away, but never up close.

Was the missing telescope next door? Did Sean have it, and he was now watching her? The freakish thought seemed impossible, yet the shape of the reflection and its presence on a balcony were unmistakable. That telescope had dominated her life. She hated it. An inanimate object of glass and metal and plastic. The telescope symbolized everything wrong with John — it had stood in the house like an enormous phallic symbol. Of course she'd noticed its absence and of course she recognized the reflection it gave off when it was directed out at the sky, or elsewhere.

Had Sean murdered her husband? It didn't seem possible. He was such a gentle human being. You could see it in his eyes. You could feel it in the way he carried himself and the way he looked at you, even when he was lying that he had a girlfriend who needed checking with.

She should find out. She should walk over and ring the doorbell, no matter how late, and ask how he'd come to possess it. She seriously doubted John gave it to him. Even if he'd been looking at a more high-powered replacement, he wouldn't have let this one go until he had the new one.

Then, suddenly, she didn't care.

She wasn't sure what made her go into Sean's backyard. Curiosity, mostly. Did he have the telescope? Was he watching her? Was he exactly like John? Were all men disturbed in one way or another? Of course they weren't, but when your experience was narrow...If he wasn't like John, maybe he would come into the backyard.

After draining her wineglass and leaving it in the kitchen sink, she'd taken off her clothes, all but her red lace underpants. She wasn't sure why she'd undressed, maybe because she wanted to make her intention clear. Or maybe, in case Sean was like John. Was it that common? Of course it was common for men to want to look at women, but through a telescope? And surely Sean didn't share John's added anomaly of wanting nothing more.

It didn't matter. Here she was, lying on the lounge chair, sipping John's expensive scotch, feeling the cool air across her belly and breasts. She wasn't cold. It might be the liquor, it might be the desire thrumming through her body, hoping even though she knew it was foolish and humiliating and close to impossible, that Sean would turn the telescope on her, see her waiting for him, and come out to the pool.

She shifted on the chair, turning so she was in a more seductive pose rather than simply sprawled on her back, legs forced slightly apart from the slope of the leg rest and the fat cushions. She sat up a bit so her breasts weren't flat against her body and didn't look too saggy.

The bottle was nearly empty when she knew he wasn't coming out. She couldn't even be sure he'd seen her. She chose to believe he hadn't, that he wasn't delivering the final rejection of her life. That she could just enjoy the feel of her body in its near-natural state, the warm glow of the liquor, and the dissolution of her mind.

She might have drifted to sleep, might have simply turned off her brain, but she became aware again of her presence on the lounge chair. She stood and walked unsteadily around the pool to the deep end.

Why *did* she hate water so feverishly?

She inched toward the edge and dipped in her toes. It was so warm! She'd had no idea. It would feel lovely on her bare skin. She would slip into it and let it hold her. If it caressed her and made her feel loved, she would be happy. If Sean came down and lifted her out of the pool, she would be happy. And if the water took her down to the bottom and left her there, she couldn't see that she'd be unhappy. She stepped over the edge.

43

Sydney

The first thought that passed through my head when I woke was the memory of Tess staring down the hallway, holding a glass of scotch, her eyes wide with shock as I came out of Gavin's bedroom. She hadn't said a word, but I fully expected her to bring it up in her own sweet time.

It wasn't a problem that she'd seen me. I would have preferred to keep it a secret, but it didn't matter if she knew, nothing would change. She would consider it inappropriate, she would pull the mother thing on me, but I'd stopped allowing parental voices to drown out my own voice long before that instinct even wakes up in most people.

The lack of sex in this house was absurd. We were all adults — adults who needed and wanted sex as much as we needed and wanted our jobs, possibly more. What did she think was going to happen? Half of her problem was the lack of sex in her own life. Lately, she fretted and waffled over every little thing, and she seemed distracted and unsure of herself. She was not the woman I'd initially been impressed with — self-aware and self-possessed and driven to get what she wanted, *sure* of what she wanted. She'd always analyzed her desires, but this was different. I was certain the change in her was because she was antsy with desire. She would think a lot more clearly, and be more driven in her work, if her body wasn't aching for a man.

Even if she told Sean about Gavin and me, what could go wrong? Sean would complain about it, he might fret that it was disruptive to our work, but it was equally possible he wouldn't care. Especially now that he and I were on the same team, so to speak. After we'd shared our lies, we understood each other. There were bigger issues to deal with than who was sleeping in what bed.

I went for a run, followed by forty minutes in the weight room, then took a shower. When I walked into the kitchen to make breakfast, all three of them were there. No one was talking, absorbed by their phones. Four jars of jam stood on the breakfast bar beside a plate holding a stick of butter. The toaster had been moved to the bar. Crumbs were scattered about on the granite. The remains of English muffins sat on each of their plates and the aroma of espresso was strong.

"Anyone want another shot?" I emptied the grounds and began loading up a fresh supply. No one spoke up for a cup, so I prepared two shots for myself. I split an English muffin and dropped the halves into the toaster.

When my coffee was done and the muffin buttered, no jam, I sat beside Gavin. I turned my chair so I could see the patio and part of the yard beyond it. I hadn't brought my phone downstairs with me. I was curious to see what had happened with the Facebook page, but I wanted to view that alone, on the computer, not with a bunch of eyes staring over my shoulder.

One by one we finished eating and drifted out of the kitchen to the offices. Tess informed me she would be working in her bedroom for the morning. Glad to be alone in the office, I closed the door and brought up the Twitter page on the desktop computer. I wanted to prolong the anticipation of seeing what kind of engagement I had with the Facebook page. Browsing through Twitter had less riding on it. There were some favorites and retweets of my tweets, but nothing worth noting as far as a connection of some kind.

I opened Facebook. One-hundred-forty-three likes for the device post. It was thrilling to see, but there were only ten comments. None of them said anything significant enough that I could play off the comment to reveal more about the app. I'd have to think of a better way to spark curiosity. The tiniest step into a promotional tone had frozen everyone's voice.

Clearly the statue was the only thing generating interest — but there was no segue to the app.

The statue image had over two hundred more likes and thirty new comments. It took some time to respond to quite a few of the comments. They were starting conversations about talent and art, talking about wood carving and the years of practice and developing skill that allowed something so perfect to emerge.

There was a new comment from Carmen, asking if I'd found out the price of the statue and whether it was truly one of a kind.

I wrote that the price wasn't available. I thought that was rather discreet of me, instead of telling her what Sean had said, just in case. I told her it was definitely one of a kind.

The minute I clicked the post button, a thumb appeared on my comment. Carmen.

I couldn't figure out if the woman — assuming it was a

woman and not a man hiding his identity on the internet —
spent her whole day on Facebook, or if she and I just
happened to be in sync. I had no idea where she was located.

I clicked on her name. Her page was private, nothing but
her name and profile pic and broad details — *Married. Lives in
Queensland.* Lots of people keep their info private, so I didn't
think I should necessarily view this as an oddity, someone
who I should watch out for, or a simple set of questions from
a girl who just liked to keep to herself.

Another comment popped up below mine.

Carmen Dunn: *I'm asking because I think I've seen it before.*

Alex Teller: *I don't see how.*

Carmen Dunn: *Would you forget a statue like this?*

Alex Teller: *No.*

Carmen Dunn: *Trust me, I've seen it. The pose is distinctive and
so is the wood itself.*

Alex Teller: *Have you ever lived in Sydney?*

There was no response. I waited for several minutes. I
went back to Twitter, returning to Facebook fifteen minutes
later, but there was still no response. We weren't so in sync
after all.

I started writing up a short piece about what I loved
about the app, simultaneously trying to think about what the
visual might be. I worked on that for about twenty minutes,
then returned to the page again. Still nothing from Carmen.

I polished what I'd written. I put together a one-page
report for Tess about our social media presence and
engagement and the next steps. I was vague about the specific
posts, categorizing them as social posts, app-specific, and
work-life balance. When the report was polished and sent, I
did some tweeting and following.

I returned to Facebook and liked a bunch more comments. All inane. What was wrong with people? Did they think they got some sort of social cred for the number of times their profile pic and a few words showed up on someone else's page? Was it like talking to people in person, where some feel compelled to release their thoughts, even if they're irrelevant and repetitious? Who would want a digital record of a lifetime spent writing *cool* or *great* or *awesome* accompanied by a handful of emojis?

There was still nothing from Carmen.

44

Tess returned to our office at twelve-fifteen. She'd changed her clothes since breakfast. She wore a white turtleneck sweater and a dark brown pencil skirt and high heels. Her eyes were made up with thick, black liner and mascara and sweeps of shadow up to her brows. She wore small pearl earrings and her hair was tucked behind her ears, enhancing the pearls' iridescent sheen when the overhead light struck them.

She closed the door and sat at the conference table.

"Are you going out?" I said.

"No. Will you come over to the table, please? We should have a chat."

"A boss kind of chat?"

"A colleague chat."

I went to the conference table, pulled out the chair across from her, and sat down.

"You know I saw you last night, coming out of Gavin's room?"

"Yes."

"Why didn't you say anything?"

I crossed my legs. "What was there to say?"

"How long has this been going on?"

"What difference does it make?"

"Why would you jeopardize this fantastic opportunity by

doing something so stupid?"

I smiled. "How is it jeopardizing anything? And sex isn't stupid, it's natural. Although you'd never know that in this weird set-up."

"Sex has a way of complicating things."

"Not for me."

"Well then you're the first human being on the planet to believe that."

"Am I?"

She sighed. "Sean won't like it."

"That's too bad. I'm a virtual prisoner here. There are two guys available, I picked one."

She looked sympathetic. I could see her fighting to hide the expression of understanding, trying to remove it from her face before I saw it for what it was. Finally, she succeeded. "Why are you so careless with your body?"

"I'm not careless."

"You sleep with any man that gives you a second glance."

I smiled. "Not true."

"Steve. John. Now G…"

"Wrong on two out of three."

"Do you think I'm naive?"

"In this case, you are. I told you I never did it with either of them."

"I don't know about John, but Steve? I saw that coming a mile away. The way he fell all over you, the way you flirted… you played into his feeling of power."

"I don't recall flirting."

"Not overtly, but it was there. I felt it."

I laughed.

"At least give me the courtesy of telling the truth, of

treating me like I have a shred of intelligence."

I leaned my forearms on the table and stared into her eyes, not blinking, not smiling, my gaze boring into her pupils, holding them as if I possessed her eyes as fully as Tony had wanted to take mine. "I never slept with Steve. It may have been headed that way, but he OD'd before anything happened."

She didn't shrink from my stare.

I leaned back. "What happened in San Francisco, anyway? Did they find out anything about the woman who was there the night he died? Are they reopening the case? What's going on? Why aren't you talking about it?"

"Don't change the subject. My point is, you're jeopardizing your future here by sleeping with Gavin. Why can't you show a little discretion?"

"I don't have a car. I'm stuck in this house. I needed a guy. Gavin's nice, he's interesting, and kind of mysterious, don't you think?"

She didn't speak for several minutes. She managed to hold my eyes for about half of one of those minutes, then she turned toward the window. Her hair slid forward, covering one of her beautiful earrings. She tucked it back into place, as if she wanted me to see the earring and admire its warm glow. Without turning back toward me, she spoke in a low voice. "Why are you suddenly so interested in Steve's death, after nagging at me to let it go? Maybe I did let it go."

I could only hope. I felt like the dead bodies were piling up and I couldn't keep dodging so many curious minds. They didn't go so far as to consider whether I played a part, but they were just too interested, and although I enjoyed the challenge to some extent, it was starting to feel like more work than I wanted. "Did Detective Gorman tell you the trip was a waste of time? Is that it?"

She shrugged.

"...and you don't want to admit it."

"I want to talk about you and Gavin, not the past."

Not the past. That was a good sign. Maybe Gorman had listened to me after all, maybe he'd gently let her down, maybe he'd made her finally see this was one arena where she couldn't have her way. In the business world she had leverage, power, people did what she asked. The law enforcement world had its own rules. Using heroin had been the perfect choice for killing Steve. The drug was too prevalent to raise many questions. I felt mildly relaxed. It looked like it was finally done and I could stop thinking about it.

"Don't you see that two members of this company having sex will put a strain on everything? It's obvious what could go wrong. I understand that you let your hormones take over, but now you need to step back."

"Is Sean having this same conversation with Gavin right now? Are we horny teenagers being yanked apart and confined to our rooms? Or am I being singled out because I'm the girl?"

"Sean doesn't know anything about this, as far as I know. And I hope he doesn't find out. He would be so disappointed. His vision..."

"I know what his vision is. And he's an idiot if he thinks we can live like monks."

"He said we should feel free to get away from time to time," Tess said.

"He says it, but everything works against it. This group feels like a cult."

"Don't be stupid. The only difference between this and a thousand other start-ups is that we're working in a house instead of sharing the floor of an office building. The hours are the same, the eating and blowing off steam together is the same."

"But we sleep here."

"I knew people at CC that slept in their offices a few times, when a big product rollout was coming and they were too tired to drive home."

"That's creepy. And they didn't sleep there every night. They didn't live there."

"It's called having a vision. It's called dedication. Passion."

"So passion for technology is fine, but passion for another human being is inappropriate and threatens the project?"

"Don't twist my words."

I hadn't twisted anything, but I kept that thought to myself.

"What if you have a fight? What if you decide it's not working? What if he goes out and finds another woman and you're heartbroken?"

"It's just sex. What's there to fight about? And I won't be heartbroken over anything." I wasn't sure I could say that for Gavin, maybe his heart could be broken, although I had the sense we were both after the same thing.

"I don't understand why you're so lacking in discretion. I really don't."

"What did discretion ever get anyone? It's just another word for doing what other people want you to do, letting someone else dictate your life."

She shook her head — that maternal look of

disappointment again.

"Don't you want a guy?" I said. "When was the last time you had sex?"

"Yes, a relationship would be nice. But I don't just walk around looking for some guy to fuck like I'm a stray cat."

I laughed.

"It's not funny."

"I think it is."

"Obviously I can't tell you what to do, but if Sean finds out...Do you care about this job?"

"I'm liking it."

"And you're paid very well, not to mention you hardly have any living expenses."

"I do like that."

"Well, Sean..."

"That's why it feels like a cult. Sean is the owner of the company. That's all. He can talk to me about my job performance or my work hours, he can put pressure on me for team-building bullshit. But he can't make me do those things and he sure as hell cannot dictate who I have sex with."

"He's not trying to dictate."

"Good."

"He doesn't even know, but if he finds out..."

"It doesn't matter. It's none of his business." I pushed the chair away from the table. "Did you read the social media report I sent?"

"Not yet."

"I wanted you to look at it before I send it to Sean. See how discreet I am — not going over my boss's head?" I smiled.

She laughed, but I could tell she was pissed. And frustrated — with me, and probably with her own sex life.

45

We all ate lunch at the same time, drowning in the same heavy silence that had pervaded breakfast. This time, my phone was with me. I fooled around on Twitter, still wanting to avoid the Facebook thing while others were watching. The Facebook effort required more thought and more strategy in answering questions. I had to plan ahead how I would lead commenters in the right direction. It's more intense and more personal than Twitter.

I rinsed my plate and put it in the dishwasher. As my contribution to our communal living, I wiped off the knife that had been used to spread mayo on our turkey sandwiches. I grabbed a bottle of lime flavored sparkling water and went up to my bedroom. No one asked where I was going.

I sat on the balcony and smoked a cigarette. The cloudy sky made the tropical plants more vivid. Unbleached by sunlight, the green seemed to pulse with life. My phone buzzed — Detective Martin. I'd hardly caught my breath from the assurance that questions about Steve's death were finally put to rest, and now more questions were coming my way.

The detective would not let go. She must have good instincts, pursuing my questionable story with such diligence. It was such a trivial thing — not looking at a clock. But she was dead certain in her belief that no one woke in the middle of the night without checking the time. She was probably right.

"It's Detective Martin," she said.

"Yes."

"I'd like to have a quick chat with you this afternoon. What's a good time?"

"Two is good."

"Excellent. I'll see you then."

"Should I tell the others?"

"No. Just you."

She sounded cheery and pleasant, as if we'd arranged to meet for a glass of wine or a walk beside the harbor. Possibly, it wasn't anything important. I was pretty sure I was wrong about that.

She rang the bell precisely at two. I was sitting on the bottom step of the staircase. I stood and opened the door. We went into the billiards room and she closed the door behind her. We sat in two armchairs angled toward each other, the huge oak and green felt table filling the center of the room. The cue ball sat near one corner, but the rest was swept clean of colored balls.

"I wanted to check whether you've been able to recall looking at your clock before you discovered Ms. North's body."

"I didn't check the time. Why do you keep asking?"

"You know…" She leaned forward, one elbow on her knee. "It's a man's world. It might be the twenty-first century, but even now, terrible injustices go on. Men still run the show, and it's unbelievable the punishment inflicted on women who speak up, or try to threaten their privilege, or go against their wishes. Even women who don't speak up, women simply trying to do their jobs and live their lives."

I had no idea why she was saying this or where she was headed. What did the state of worldwide gender imbalance have to do with checking the time? I waited for her to get to the point.

"I wonder if Mr. Farmer, is pressing you to hide something from us."

"No."

"It's difficult to go against what your employer asks."

I nodded.

"You agree?"

"To some extent. Not always."

"So you feel strong enough to stand up to your employer, to tell the truth even when it makes him look bad?"

"Absolutely."

She glanced down at her mobile device resting in the palm of her hand. "So will you tell me the truth?"

"I did."

"Mr. Farmer is an obvious control freak. Even a strong woman like you can get tied down, bullied."

I gave her a meek smile.

"I have strong instincts. And my instinct is telling me something isn't right in this house. Are you living here freely?"

I laughed.

"You think that's funny?"

I wasn't about to tell her there was nothing free about it. She would take it the wrong way, since she seemed to be stepping around the idea that this was some kind of forced labor, at best, or sex slavery, at worst.

"We do what we have to do," she said.

I nodded in pleasant agreement.

"Even I've experienced harassment from my employers."

"Okay."

"It might seem hard to believe, but you'd be shocked. My boss says all kinds of inappropriate things to me and there's nothing I can do."

"Aren't there places for reporting that?"

"Those ruling authorities can have their own male bias. It's systemic."

"I guess so."

"I'm subjected to sexual jokes and touching that I don't want, and all kinds of...things. My point is, an employer can exert heavy pressure to keep you from speaking up."

This was getting interesting. She'd decided to play the girl card, trying to get me on her side. She hoped I'd spill my guts to her simply because she was female. She thought her story would encourage me to tell mine. I didn't have a story, of course, but she assumed that I did. She assumed I was living with two men who controlled the shape of my life. It had its problems, definitely. But that was a big leap to assume I was here against my will. Far from it. I had a good deal and I knew it. My bank account was growing quietly and quickly.

"I thought Australia was highly evolved, cutting edge in their approach to everything. Health care. The environment..." I said.

She laughed. "We are."

"But?"

"Some men feel their jobs are being taken away. That's how a lot of them view it. Women are moving on male territory and there's less for them."

"No man ever wanted the kind of jobs I've had, so I

guess I haven't experienced that."

She nodded. She put her digital device on the table between the two chairs, pushing it toward the center as if it no longer mattered. "It's tough. Bender tells me all the time that I must give good blow jobs, since I have the lead role."

"Ew. Why do you work with him?"

"It's not as if you get to choose your colleagues, right?"

"Then report him."

"Like I said, my superior is worse."

I tried to imagine worse, but I didn't ask and she didn't try to prove it.

"You're sure there isn't a government office where you can file a complaint?" I said.

"And end my career?"

She straightened and pulled the device back toward her. It seemed as if she'd wanted it out of earshot, and now she was done with her confession. Maybe she hoped she'd revealed enough to get me talking. She was definitely playing the girl card — *We're a team. We're all in this together. You need to rat out the guys you live with because surely you've experienced these things. We all have.*

We all have, that's true. And I'm all for female bonding. But in this case, the cop card trumped the girl card. She was still a detective, she was still investigating a death, and she was still asking questions of me and my roommates, pushing to uncover lies. Who knew where her questions might lead. But I wasn't going to confess and I wasn't going to rat out Sean. I did wish I could do something to get Bender out of her life, but a cop? That would take some doing.

46

Tess didn't like admitting that Alex was right, but before Alex even mentioned it, Tess had known what the problem was.

Going without sex was like going without exercise. Or food. But mostly exercise. Your body began to lose fluidity. You became weak and anxious, limbs trembling. Your body knew, even if your mind wasn't aware. Your interior landscape became a wasteland. Of course your body wouldn't atrophy without sex like it would without exercise. Ceasing movement caused your body to collapse into itself, to lose mass. Deprivation of sex turned it into a tangle of unfocused anxiety.

She'd ended her relationship with Steve in a rather unthinking way, suddenly tired of his arrogance, suddenly aware that although she enjoyed being in bed with him, she did not enjoy his personality at all. She'd walked out not even knowing at the start of the evening that was her plan. Since then, there'd been those few guys at the start of her vacation in Sydney — partying in pubs and a quick trip back to her hotel room, a farewell before the sun came up. It seemed like years ago.

She stripped off her clothes and studied her body. Spending time thinking about its neglect was too sad. She yanked on her swimsuit and grabbed a large towel out of the linen closet. She went down to the pool and dropped the towel on one of the lounge chairs.

With the same force she'd used when she walked out of Steve's bedroom that night, ages ago, in another life, she walked to the deep end of the pool and dove in.

She swam five lengths without stopping.

She paused in the shallow end and tried sitting on the second step. It was too high, forcing her shoulders above the water where they were slapped by cold air. The bottom step was too low for sitting without breathing in water.

Just as she was about to propel herself forward in a butterfly stroke to burn even more energy than she had with the crawl, Sean emerged through the great room door.

"Mind if I join you?"

She shook her head.

"That's not very welcoming," he said.

"Don't be a child." She plunged down a few feet and swam under the water until she ran out of breath. She surfaced and looked over to where he was standing. He walked to the side of the pool and stepped down onto the first step. She was glad she'd put distance between her and the steps.

She continued treading water, watching him.

He was absolutely gorgeous. She realized now that she hadn't felt an attraction when she first met him because she'd been so consumed with her experience of the Great Barrier Reef. After that, he'd already made his proposal that she join his company, so she hadn't allowed admiration of his appearance, a deeper attention to noticing his body, to enter her mind. The most she'd done since was notice how attractive he was, but she kept that thought in a tidy little box — an appreciation of a work of art, almost.

Now, she wanted to swim toward him and touch his shoulders and arms and the firm muscles of his chest. She wanted to stroke his hair before he entered the water.

She cycled her legs faster, concentrating on the effort required, watching her hands skull back and forth, trying not to stare at him.

"Glad you're enjoying the pool." He took two steps down and stood for a few seconds before easing himself fully into the water.

She couldn't speak. All she could do was watch the water flow over his skin, study the vulnerable look that engulfed him after he dove under and re-surfaced, his hair slicked back, drops of water clinging to his eyelashes. Now that she'd let go of her discretion, if she wanted to call it that, she couldn't see anything but how desirable he was. And it absolutely was a letting go of discretion. Despite a life with quite a few indiscretions, she'd been pretty good at drawing a line between business and her personal life. Steve was the sole exception. Her mind had always ruled her body. Now that she'd cracked open that window, she was overcome.

Especially in Australia, out of her element, she'd focused on her career and what was best for the start-up.

Now, all of the restraints had come untied and she was flooded with alternate memories of their time together — his smile, the golden skin of his arms and the movement of his muscles when he did the simplest tasks, the way he walked, his slim hips moving inside slightly loose blue jeans, the way his T-shirt pulled up when he reached for something out of a cabinet, exposing the top edge of his boxers and his smooth, taut belly.

She thought of all the times he and Gavin had been in the

pool and she'd turned her head, thinking she was focused on other things, when really, she couldn't bear to watch without feeling a thread of desire wind its way through her core.

Her body was so weak with desire she could barely keep treading water.

Sean began swimming laps.

She rotated onto her back and kicked her feet, propelling herself toward the side of the pool. She should get out. Staying in the water and allowing herself to melt with desire wasn't going to have a positive outcome.

All of this was on Alex. She talked about sex like it was a relevant part of their jobs. She was so casual about the subject, she implied Tess was stupid for not thinking about it, for not putting her needs front and center.

What was Sean thinking? Did he notice her? Or Alex?

He seemed almost asexual in some ways. Not when she looked at him or observed his easy grace, the sure strength of his movements. But he never gave off a vibe that sex was anywhere in his thoughts. He looked at her and spoke to her with respect, treating both her an Alex like valued colleagues. There was no discernible difference in how he spoke to Gavin and the women. He could be controlling, dictatorial in some ways. He was optimistic and idealistic to a fault. But he wasn't flirtatious and he never once gave off the slightest tell of anything inappropriate. She appreciated that about him. But now...

He obviously did a much better job than she did keeping his life compartmentalized. And she was still certain he would be horrified if he knew what was going on between Alex and Gavin.

Did the two men ever discuss sex? Had they ever made

comments about her or Alex? All men did, possibly even more often than women realized. Maybe he did know about Alex and Gavin. Maybe she'd read that all wrong.

There was a sharp pain in her ear, as if water had gotten inside. It was a pain caused by turning something over in her mind so endlessly and so fruitlessly that her very nerves had begun to object to the effort.

She swam to the shallow end and walked up the steps. She grabbed her towel off the lounge chair and wrapped it around her shoulders and hips.

Sean paused at the deep end, grabbing the edge with his fingertips. "Didn't mean to chase you away."

She shook her head. "You didn't." It was close to the truth. Her own thoughts had chased her away. She couldn't be in his half-naked presence for another minute.

47

Sunday morning.

Easter.

Contradicting all the ads for clothing and hats, baskets with plastic grass, and the imagined scenes painted by artists who conceived of brilliant rays of sun cutting across arid landscape and shining onto the opening of a previously occupied tomb, Portland had torrential rain.

The choir and the soft rock band, the preacher and the men reading from the Bible all tried to counter the damp mood, but it was too late. A decent number of people had stayed home from church, possibly to allow their children to hunt for eggs indoors. Hunting eggs was frowned on by our church, but people did it anyway. For all the enthusiasm and devotion demonstrated by the members, they could occasionally be a rather disobedient group in secretive ways.

Gloom settled over everything. The hallways were dark along the sides, the fluorescent lights garish rather than warmly dispelling the shadows coming in through windows looking out on a black sky.

After the lackluster service, everyone trudged across the industrial high-traffic carpet to their age-appropriate Sunday School classes. All the high school kids met in a smaller auditorium, then broke up into groups by grade level and gender. Together, we were a crowd of several hundred.

We began with a few songs accompanied by an electric piano providing canned percussion, followed by a Bible reading that we'd already heard during the church service, but no one seemed bothered by that fact.

Next up was the opening prayer.

The high school leader, Mr. Bartz, walked to the stage and climbed the steps. He stood behind the podium, gripping the sides as if he needed to keep it from falling over the edge of the stage.

He asked us to bow our heads and we all obediently did so, even me. I did not close my eyes. I'd learned at an early age that not bowing caused too much grief. It led to being pulled out of the group, spoken to about my attitude and lack of humility and devotion. It meant glaring looks and wasted time and lots of conversations I wasn't interested in having. Bowing my head was easier. They couldn't see my eyes.

Mr. Bartz opened his prayer with a lengthy recap of the Easter story. He went on to pray for our purity, our self-sacrifice for others, our knowledge of the Bible, and a few of the other usual themes. Then, he paused.

"Today, we ask for grace upon the Marks family. We plead for comfort for Mr. and Mrs. Marks in their grief."

This was strange. He prayed with their surnames, as if god might not know who he was referring to. It was unusual to pray in the large assembly after the death of a grandparent. And he hadn't mentioned Tony yet...

"Have mercy on the soul of Tony. We know when he accepted salvation and fell at your feet in repentance, when he was buried in the waters of baptism, his sins were washed away then, now, and for all eternity. Even this sin. This most awful sin. Comfort his family. Restore their souls. Take Tony into your arms. We remain strong, knowing your blood cleansed his sin and forgave even the taking of his own life."

Everyone lifted their heads, eyes open. I imagine, if he'd opened his own eyes, Mr. Bartz would have seen a sea of faces with gaping mouths and protruding eyeballs. Surely he heard the unanimous intake of breath that passed through the room like the wind of the Holy Spirit that came to the apostles a few weeks after the first Easter.

Mrs. Bartz stood at the foot of the stairs, glaring at all those bulging eyes and rounded mouths. She deliberately closed hers and lowered her head, an example we were supposed to follow. No one did.

A few sobs could be heard. There were coughs and sniffles until it sounded like we were in a hospital rather than a Sunday School auditorium.

The prayer went on but no one was listening.

Tony was dead? He'd killed himself? We didn't care about the condition of his soul or the grief of his parents. From the growing orchestra of sniffles and quiet weeping, most cared only about their own shock and grief. And we cared about what had happened. How had he managed to kill himself? The means available to a high school student at our church where most of us had limited freedom, were restricted to water or rope, possibly a kitchen knife. Unless his parents needed pills to sleep. Unless an unsaved relative owned a gun.

I don't know about the others, but I spent the rest of the prayer time, the next two songs, and another Bible reading, picturing Tony in multiple horrible positions, all of them dead.

The whole thing consumed my thoughts. And talking to other kids later, I wasn't alone in that gruesome interest, even though they all had tears to shed, and grief-stricken expressions. I studied their faces closely, trying to form my lips into the same loose, trembling shape, concentrating until my eyes grew glassy, so I had at least some form of visible grief.

It wasn't that I felt nothing. Mostly, I thought Tony was stupid. You only get one life, why would he get rid of it so quickly, so casually? He hadn't even given it a chance. There was lots of talk by our teachers about depression and low self esteem and feeling excluded from the group.

No one suggested there was any guilt for contributing to his feeling shut out, yet they were overcome by sadness regarding his death.

In the midst of the tears and their sad faces, and for the boys, the stoic faces they thought gave them the appearance of men, with a few rapidly blinking eyes, they shared my fascination. They wanted to know how he'd done it. They wondered if he'd written a dramatic final note to the world. They wanted to know what it felt like and if he worried about people seeing him dead, turning away in horror.

The youth leaders reminded us repeatedly not to gossip. But they knew we were, which I suppose is what caused the constant reminders. They saw us standing around in small clusters, our voices low, the conversations devoid of the usual laughs that erupted out of nothing.

That night, my father filled our dinnertime prayer with an explanation of why suicide was a sin, explaining it to god in the same way the youth leaders had.

After homework at the kitchen table, I went upstairs to

get ready for bed. I spit out toothpaste and rinsed my mouth. I opened the bathroom door and my mother was standing there.

"I'd like to talk to you for a few minutes," she said.

"Sure."

We went into my room and she sat beside me on the bed. She placed her hand on my leg just above my knee. "I think we should talk more about what happened to Tony."

"Nothing happened to Tony except Tony," I said.

"What a terrible thing to say!" She began crying softly.

I wasn't sure what to do. I put my arm around her, creating an odd reversal — the child trying to comfort the mother.

"Why do you say things like that?" she said. "I came in here to help you. You must have feelings about this. Facing death at any time is so very difficult, but at your age…"

I thought about Gabriel, the missionary boy that died in Malaysia, supposedly for not obeying god. They hadn't been quite as sympathetic about his death.

"You said something *happened* to him, and nothing really did. That's all I'm saying."

"Okay, you're right, but it's a terrible tragedy. We have to address it."

"You said it *happened* like someone else was to blame."

"I don't think I said that."

"You made it sound like it came from somewhere else. Isn't that what *happened* means?"

She sighed. She sat up and moved out of the circle of my arm. "Do you want to talk about it?" she said.

"Not really."

"Do you understand why it's wrong to take your life?"

That was one point where we agreed. I did think it was wrong. We had different reasons for thinking that way, but we did have the same opinion.

When I didn't answer, she went on. "God gives us life. It's up to Him to decide when it's over."

"Okay."

"Do you understand? Tony was forgiven, of course, absolutely forgiven, but he still disappointed the Lord."

I waited for her to say more.

She put her arms around me and held me, speaking into my ear. "I know you would never do something like that."

I pulled away. "No."

She patted my leg. Without saying any more she left me alone.

I was confused. I couldn't understand why he would take away his own life. I couldn't understand why anyone would do that, ever. Wasn't living always more interesting than dying? Maybe it came of making too much of this amazing heaven we were all headed to, a place where everyone was happy all the time. Maybe a person's mind could become so caught up in all the wonderful things that were going to happen there, it didn't seem worth continuing with the mix of pleasant and unpleasant and sometimes awful things on earth. I really don't know.

No one told us what was written in Tony's note. I wondered if it was a poem.

It was too bad that he ended his life before he took more time to work on his poetry. He might have written something amazing.

48

Sydney

This time, Elizabeth was waiting for me when I finished my run. She called to me from across the street. I cut over diagonally to where she stood by her front gate.

"Good to see you again, Alexandra."

"You too."

I put my hands on my hips and stretched gently to the side.

"Do you go running every day?" she said.

"I try to, but it doesn't always work out."

"When I was young, running wasn't popular. At least not for girls. I swam. I think all Australian girls did. They still do."

I nodded. "Do you have a pool?"

"Of course. That's why what happened in your pool was so upsetting. To all of us. Most of us around here have pools. It's horrible to imagine it happening to you, to have a place that gives so much life and pleasure stained like that..." She shuddered gently, as if she'd dived into the water and her arm had brushed up against something dead.

"Is that why you're in such good shape?"

"Yes." She didn't smile or act coy. "What's the story with the detectives?"

"What do you mean?"

"I still see them at your house. Quite frequently."

"Their curiosity isn't satisfied. So they keep picking away."

"I would really like this to be over."

"We all agree on that."

"Why can't you be rid of them?"

"It's not so easy."

She took a step back. She put her hands on her hips, either to mimic my posture or taking a pose for lecturing me. "You all look like smart people. Can't you figure it out?"

"Apparently not." I laughed.

"I don't like having police around all the time."

"No one does."

She lifted her eyebrows slightly, suggesting I didn't fully understand her point. "What are they asking?"

"I guess they still think it's a potential murder."

"You're not sure?"

"I don't know what they think, to be honest. Their questions are all over the place and they pop by randomly, sometimes talking to just one of us, sometimes to everyone."

"That's concerning."

"Why?"

"I just don't like it."

She seemed to think I had some sort of power to be rid of them. Being smart, no matter how smart we all looked, had nothing to do with satisfying the detectives. In fact, maybe we were too smart. Maybe someone who didn't distort or hide the truth because they were so insistent on their right to privacy would have been rid of them much faster.

Elizabeth's curiosity was as intense as the detectives'. It wasn't really her business, and I certainly wasn't going to tell her about my shading the truth, or about Sean's flat-out lie.

"We're kind of stuck with it for the time being. Since they suspect there's some sort of tie-in with John's murder. And it sounds like we can expect another one joining the interrogation."

"It's an extreme coincidence, if it's murder. A man and his former wife, just days apart?"

"Exactly," I said.

"I believe it's more reasonable that she killed herself. Don't you?"

I shrugged. "Probably. Yes, I think so. Maybe you should talk to them again, impress on them that she seemed like she didn't want to go on, that she seemed checked out of life, something like that."

"Lie?"

"No, but the sense you had of her."

"I don't want to talk to them," she said.

"Too bad she didn't leave a note. She made it worse for us."

Elizabeth nodded as if she too believed Karen could have been more thoughtful. It was an unusual response. Most people would have considered my comment heartless. But she seemed as frustrated as we were, as if the detectives were ringing her doorbell every other day, wasting her time asking the same questions.

"It might help if you did talk to them," I said.

She shook her head. "No, I don't think so."

"Then they probably aren't going away any time soon."

"It's so obvious. It's like they're looking too hard for a connection. Her husband was murdered, and she couldn't cope with her feelings. Guilt, maybe."

"But in Sean's pool. And mostly naked. That's the thing."

"She didn't have a pool, she had to use someone else's."

I thought again about Karen's hatred of the water, at least according to John. Considering myself in that situation, drowning would be the last way I'd choose for ending my life. Of course, I'd never think of ending my life, so it was kind of an absurd train of thought. "Well, at some point they'll give up."

"Will they? How do you know?"

"They must have guidelines — how long they keep pushing for the answers they want to hear before a superior officer insists they move on," I said.

"Let's hope so. I don't know how they operate."

"Neither do I. Especially in Australia. I'm just guessing."

"Common sense," she said.

"Yes."

She turned and looked at Sean's house, furrowing her brow, but there was no need to squint, the sun was just then rising into a cloudy sky. She turned back toward me. "You can't think of any way to be rid of them sooner?"

"Like I already said, you're in a better position to do that. I never met her. And your age — I think comments from people who are mature are given more weight."

She laughed. "That's not the case at all." She paused for a moment. "My son doesn't like it that they're hanging around. It's almost like they're looking for things, trying to stick their noses into everyone's business. Police think everyone is up to no good and they're always looking at who they can sweep into their net. As if they're paid according to how many new crimes they can uncover."

I laughed. "You really think that?"

She nodded.

"Does your son live with you?"

"No. Of course not."

"You said…"

"He visits quite often."

"That's nice for you."

She narrowed her eyes. She looked at me for several seconds. I could see that she wanted to say more but wasn't sure whether she should.

"What is it?" I said.

"We're business partners. He's here nearly every day."

"Well if you're that concerned, why don't you tell them Karen was suicidal? Did she say anything that made you think she was, something you didn't mention when they first talked to you? Maybe something you forgot?"

"Not that I recall. But it doesn't matter, I'm not volunteering to talk to them."

I laughed. "What are you up to that you want them gone so badly?"

She didn't respond. Her face was blank. It was as if she'd given away far too much by getting into the conversation with me, and now she was going to draw a curtain over it all. She was like me — an instinctive aversion to police, to the ongoing stream of innocuous questions that might turn into something more. There was a reason for that, but I couldn't imagine what it might be.

49

Tess was not impressed with my report on our social media presence. She quickly and correctly noticed that it was all social and no marketing. She didn't think discussing Sean's revolutionary — but not — approach to living and working together was all that valuable. According to Tess, his approach was not going to change the world, and talking about it was attracting the wrong kind of attention to our page. It was a diversion from what we needed to do for a successful business — sell products, acquire loyal customers. She didn't care about changing the world right now. That was something that *might* come later.

She sketched out a Venn diagram and pointed out that I was wasting energy on less than five percent of potential customers. Of course she was right that someone intrigued with our work style wasn't necessarily interested in the app at all, unless they wanted to pose questions about what kind of company they wanted to work for.

Suddenly, her marketing expertise had kicked into high gear.

Shooting pool and eating meat pies and drinking beer as a team was going to demolish that team because there wouldn't be enough sales to sustain us, she said. Discussing philosophy on Facebook would do the same.

She sent me back to my computer to figure out a better strategy.

I still liked the idea of talking about our living situation. She didn't understand that you can make a name for yourself doing something else entirely that gets you noticed and talked about. The point was to rise above the noise without appearing to be overtly selling. But she'd been educated in a different world, one that was only starting to notice the sea change of the internet. When she was in business school, the curriculum still focused on pre-internet marketing techniques. Our customers, as she loved calling them, thinking of them as wallets rather than connected fans who would support products they loved with their dying breath…our customers cared about those things — Social responsibility. Alternative lifestyles. Work-life balance. Our customers lived online and they were looking for connections.

Still, I needed to do something to satisfy her, something that would impress her enough to get her talking me up to Sean.

Although he and I were in a truce with our mutual lies, it wouldn't last forever. If I was lucky, it would last until the detectives gave up. *If* I was lucky. Other than that, he still viewed me with suspicion and seemed ready at any moment to insist the company would be better off without me.

It wouldn't be the end of the world, I had plenty of money saved up, but I adored the house and I was enjoying Gavin. I loved the opportunity to continue stockpiling cash, spending hardly anything and making a normal, aka inflated, high tech salary. It was a very sweet situation that I needed to protect. Putting effort into that was worth my time.

I decided to demo the app. I'd do a *Facebook Live* event,

pose a question, and let our fans see how the app worked.

I would blast the date and time of the event all over Twitter, setting up automatic tweets to get it going. I was pretty sure I could get about ten percent of our page fans to attend. Ten percent seemed like a cautious, but optimistic goal. I'd lure them with some promise of a provocative personal question. Of course, I had no idea what that question might be, but I was confident it would come to me.

There was a sound behind me, the awareness of a change in the air, of someone standing in the open doorway of the office. I launched the screen saver and turned.

Gavin was leaning against the door frame. He gave me a lazy smile. "Fancy going to a pub?"

I'd been avoiding him somewhat and I wasn't entirely sure why. Maybe it was the realization that despite the dead finger of his sister in a bottle of formalin beneath his bed, the camera set to record anyone entering his room when he wasn't there, he was a guy burdened by more ethics than most, certainly more than any of his housemates.

"I would love to go to a pub." I smiled, enthusiastic about getting out of my luxurious prison, even if I was perplexed by the thing between us, by his mild desire to tell the detectives more than they needed to know.

I can't comprehend those kinds of views. Why on earth would you give the police information they didn't need? They had a job to do — figure out whether or not Karen was murdered. Since we all knew that none of us had murdered her, there was no reason to go telling them all sorts of peripheral stories.

Although, maybe she had been murdered by one of us after all. It could be Gavin was considering this possibility.

Maybe it was one of those murders that crosses the fine line of negligence. It's some form of murder, manslaughter, maybe or simply negligent homicide, I don't really know. If you see a woman fall into a pool, drunk, and you do nothing, that's murder. If Sean had lied about knowing her, lied about seeing her that night, how did I know that his confession of a lie wasn't a lie itself?

He was certainly overwrought by what had happened. More disturbed than was normal. I thought about his reaction in that light, tried thinking about how the rest of us responded compared with his response. It was his house, so that explained some of it. He was idealistic, so that was another fragment.

The image of him standing beside the pool, hands pressed to the sides of his head as if he needed to prevent it from exploding like a melon hit with a hammer came back to me. Was that normal? Even for a high-strung control freak like Sean?

I stood and walked to the door. Gavin and I didn't touch or kiss, I suppose in silent agreement that our relationship was to be kept secret. Except now the secret was shared by three. Once that happens, once a secret leaks out beyond one person, there's a risk of exposure. Leaking outside of two, that's usually the end of it.

50

The pub was dark. Even the well-placed lights didn't have much effect. Partially this was due to copper lamp shades which prevented even a single watt of light from escaping anywhere but through the circular openings at the bottom.

We chose one of the booths that lined two sides of the room. The third side was occupied by the bar and the fourth offered an open space to accommodate an air hockey game and three dart boards.

Gavin went to the bar and returned with two enormous beers in glasses that looked as if they would topple over if they weren't steadied by the pressure of fingers on the base.

"You'll like this one." He raised his glass toward me then to his mouth for a sip of foam with a touch of golden liquid.

He was right, it was tasty, although I found myself longing for a martini.

We talked about work and he told me a bit about his history of writing software code. He'd fallen in love with it when his parents shuttled him off to a Saturday workshop at the age of twelve. The intricacies of coding swallowed him whole, pushing all other thoughts out of his mind. He could spend hours on a problem, then suddenly come to his senses, realizing he hadn't eaten lunch and it was nearing dinnertime. He could work until two in the morning, never yawning, hardly glancing at the clock.

Our beers were nearly gone. He returned to the bar for two more and an order of *chips*. I watched him leaning on the bar and thought about Tess. Studying his back, the curve of his shoulders, I tried to guess how he'd respond if I told him Tess had seen me leaving his room. A large part of me thought he would dismiss it as unimportant. Most guys would. Most guys would laugh it off, proud of the attention. I was sure a significant part of him wasn't interested at all in what Tess thought of his sex life. At the same time, he took time to lock his bedroom every time he went downstairs, even for a cup of espresso. And there was that motion-detecting camera pointing at the space behind his locked door.

It wasn't as if we could control being seen. All the bedrooms opened onto the same L-shaped hall. It wasn't as if neither one of us had considered the rather strong possibility we'd be noticed at some point. Especially when we slipped into bed mid-day.

We'd never discussed telling the others or keeping it a secret, we'd never discussed anyone seeing us.

I had a sense he preferred that Sean not know. Not because he cared about Sean's opinion or had any concerns about jeopardizing his future with the company — Gavin was crucial to the app, unlike me. In fact, it wouldn't exist without him. But he seemed to like keeping Sean at a distance, despite their playful attitude toward each other in the water or around the pool table.

He returned and put the basket of fries in the center of the table. There was aioli sauce in a small ceramic cup, balanced on top of the fries.

I took a fry, swiped it through the sauce and popped it in my mouth. It was steaming hot. I tried to chew without touching too much of it to my tongue or the sides of my mouth, a delicate feat. To cool my mouth, I took a large swallow of beer. Finally my tongue was able to move again. "When do you think the detectives will be satisfied that Karen wasn't murdered?"

He shrugged. "Maybe never."

"Never?"

"Not until they figure out who killed her husband. Or maybe not until they're satisfied we've told them everything we know."

"We have."

"Not true. Sean lied."

"It's a small thing. It doesn't provide any insight into what happened to her."

"That doesn't matter."

"Why are you suddenly so perfectly ethical? You lied when you kept that piece of your sister's finger after the dog bite." I smiled.

He didn't return the smile. His tone was serious. "I'm not perfect, and I'm not judging him. I just said I won't lie for him. That's different."

"It is?"

"Absolutely. I want them to stop coming around, and until their instincts tell them they have all they can get from us, that won't happen."

"Instinct might be over-rated. They're suspicious of everyone. It's their baseline. They don't have any answers and don't have anyone to suspect, and we're handy. I've started to think there's nothing instinctive about it."

"Maybe."

"Even Elizabeth, the woman across from John's, is tired

of them."

"Of course she is."

"Why?"

"She sells dope."

I laughed. "What makes you think that?"

"I don't think it, I know it. Sean told me. Her son grows it and she makes edibles."

"How does Sean know this?"

"He met her son. Sean was looking to buy and asked him if he knew anyone."

"Isn't that a little risky? Asking a stranger a question like that?"

Gavin sipped his beer. "He didn't seem worried about it. And it worked out."

"She makes edibles?"

"Yup. Mostly baked goods, but some oils and tea, I think."

"Wow. She doesn't seem…" I paused. Maybe she did seem the type. I laughed again, remembering the expression on her face as she worried about the detectives. "So why won't you back up Sean's story?"

"No one wants them hanging around, but I'm more pragmatic than Sean. They can sense we aren't telling them everything."

"His lie isn't important."

"Doesn't matter." He shoved three fries in his mouth and chewed quickly. "It's their job to put together a story of what happened. It's like writing software — the smallest missing fragment can change the whole picture."

I didn't have more than the sketchiest knowledge of what was involved in writing software, but I did know that a misplaced bracket or missing semi-colon could cause an entire application to barf all over the screen. Maybe they were just doing their jobs, without instinct, just pushing forward to explain before moving on to the next puzzle. "Then why don't you push him to tell them he knew her after all?"

"It's his call."

I ate several fries, chips, rather, one after the other, chewing slowly, savoring the salt and comfort of deep fried potato and the sweetness and tang of the aioli on my still tender tongue. So Gavin wasn't all twisted up in ethics. I should have known. It was funny — he seemed more of a stand-up guy, and yet he kept a dead finger fragment under his bed, silently and secretly repaying his sister for years of torment. He wouldn't lie, but neither was he going to go out of his way to push Sean into telling the truth. Of course, telling the truth wouldn't solve the problem. The detectives didn't believe my answer either, but out of sheer stubbornness, I refused to adjust what I'd told them.

Sean was filled with altruistic vision and love for the ocean and the natural beauty of Australia, things you associate with ethics. But he'd lied to the police, then lied about the extent of his lie, and for all either of us knew, was still lying.

51

Thirty people had indicated they planned to attend my Facebook Live demo of the TruthTeller app.

That wasn't a great response. I could probably count on at least half of them not showing up. The good news was there were twenty-seven new page likes and enough favorites and retweets of the announcement blitz that I guessed some of the attendees had come from Twitter.

Even less enthralling than the anticipated demo audience was a new comment from Carmen below the image of the statue. I'd expected the discussion of the statue's value and the image itself to disappear in the feed, swallowed as all things social media are, in the second-by-second deluge of new thoughts and opinions and information.

The flood of human consciousness unleashed in digital forums is threatening to turn into a beast with a will of its own. Everyone is worried about robots taking over the world, becoming our masters and turning on us, as if machines can be good or evil, as if they even grasp those concepts. Really, people should be concerned about the monster of our collective consciousness, not a humanoid collection of chips and wires.

Human consciousness never sleeps, it never stops, it devours everything in its path.

Carmen was the primary contributor to the longevity of

the statue post. Of course, my replies to her comments weren't helping. Each little thumb and heart and laughing emoji pushed the statue back toward the surface, as if they were a team of lifeguards, making sure the photograph and its associated comments didn't drown.

Carmen: *I know I've seen that statue somewhere else.*

Two people had liked her comment. Two utter strangers who knew nothing about the statue, and as far as I knew, had never met Carmen, gleefully clicking *like*. To them, it meant nothing. But their liking had made the thread more visible once again.

I'd posted the photograph to get interest in the page, to increase traffic, to let people know that beautiful and cool things would be posted there in the future. I didn't want it constantly clawing its way back to the top where there was an increased chance that Sean or Tess would stumble across it.

Instead of liking Carmen's comment as I had in the past, giving her thoughts extra social clout, I simply replied.

Alex Teller: *I'm sure there are other similar works, but this is one of a kind. The owner assured me.*

As before, she was sitting with her fingers poised over her Facebook app. The response was immediate.

Carmen Dunn: *Nope. I've seen this one. It's very distinctive.*

I needed to keep her happy but shut her down. It was a delicate line, making her feel that I valued her comments, not making her sound stupid, or accusing her too harshly of being wrong, while gently, nicely encouraging her to shut up and get a life.

Alex Teller: *I'm so glad you love it. But the owner was definite about it. Thanks for being so intrigued, you have great taste!!*

Carmen Dunn: *You said your CEO is the owner…where did he get it?*

I stared at the screen. What was wrong with her? I considered sending her a private message, but she'd have to accept me into her account and I wasn't sure I wanted that either. I just wanted her to stop. Why was she so curious?

I clicked on her profile, studying her photograph as if there was some secret hidden in the image. Of course there wasn't. Could she be a slightly atypical internet troll? Was she trying to bait me into an argument that wasn't yet revealed to me, blow up our whole page by abruptly turning ugly?

My hands hovered over the keyboard. It's rare that I'm at a loss for words, but I honestly could not figure out what to type. I considered not replying. Ever. And just as that seemed the best solution, two thumbs up appeared under her comment about it being distinctive. Great. Between my responses, her persistence, and random people curious about our discussion, the statue would again appear in the page fans' stream of updates.

Maybe the solution was to post a whole bunch of additional content. Bury it myself as surely as if I were digging a grave. I could ignore Carmen. The likers of her comment would forget. They didn't care enough to add their own comments.

I posted a reminder of the live event coming in a few days. At the risk of over-promising, I wrote that the results of the demo would be shocking. I hunted through some other business pages and shared a post about an upcoming appearance of Jerry Seinfeld at the Sydney Opera house. I shared another post about meerkats. Everyone loves meerkats, and sure enough, there were five hearts and twelve thumbs within two minutes.

While I combed for other posts to bury the statue, my mind was fractured between deciding how to handle Carmen and what to pose as the question for my demo. It couldn't be a softball question about new clothes or dinner out. It had to be serious so the audience would see the value of the app for the most important decisions of their lives. It had to feel like something real, not a phony concern no one could relate to, not something that would be too generic about changing jobs. It had to have specifics to be real.

Two new comments popped up.

Jane Horner: *I can't wait to find out where Carmen saw the statue!*

Lara Merritt: *Our own real-life mystery.*

Immediately both comments received a thumbs up. I stared at the screen. I had the urge to post twenty or thirty kangaroo videos. Surely there was a way to make this topic die. At the same time, there was a prick of interest deep in my brain. Had Carmen truly seen the statue before? Was it possible she knew Sean? If she knew him, she'd been inside his bedroom. Or odds were leaning in that direction.

There was one way I could put a stop to this. And kangaroos and meerkats were not it.

I found an image of a woman looking perplexed, with a suggestion of fear. I wrote my comment and clicked the blue button:

Find out what TruthTeller is all about! Join the first ever live demo of this fascinating new app, due to be launched next month. I'll be posing a question of my own, allowing the app to dig inside my subconscious. The question? — Should I tell my friend I lied?

The question wasn't entirely truthful. The question I had

in mind was whether I should tell Detective Martin I'd lied. Definitely not a friend, but the slight adjustment of details would do for the public demo, and it wouldn't suggest to Tess that I'd lied to the police, although she might assume it referred to her.

Just as I was about to close the screen, another message from Carmen floated by.

Carmen Dunn: *Curiosity is killing me. Where did he get it?*

She followed this with a winking face. I closed the screen without liking or responding to her latest comment.

52

Despite my concern over the lack of attendees at our first demo, the event was a success. Seventy-five people ended up watching, a number that was decent considering the overt sales pitch. There was lots of engagement, with thumbs and surprised emojis rising like bubbles from the ocean floor as I walked them through the questions.

I told the viewers I'd entered the basic background info before starting the live feed. There was no way they'd want to sit through fifteen or twenty minutes of my personal history. Not to mention the fact I had no intention of putting those details out to the entire world. Not even Tess knew most of it.

In the end, the app informed me that deep in my gut, I knew my lie was harmless, that correcting the mistake served no purpose. The audience loved it. Hearts and laughing faces exploded across the screen. Twenty-four people signed up to be notified the minute the app was available for purchase.

I was impressed with myself — for figuring out a question that piqued curiosity and for entertaining people with an unexpected answer. The surprise made the app more appealing. No one called me on my over-hyped promise that the results would be shocking. Considering how new we were in the online world, I viewed it as a huge win.

Sean and Tess weren't all that impressed by the results.

I'd asked them to view the demo session from another room, leaving me alone in the office. I didn't want to be distracted hearing conversation in the background, no matter how low their voices, or seeing their faces and gestures that might throw my mind off track. When they easily agreed, I thought they understood I needed all my focus on the event.

Apparently not. Throughout the thirty-minute broadcast they'd sent text messages, telling me each time a viewer dropped out, as if they assumed my presentation had become boring, rather than understanding and expecting that of course some are going to get distracted or called away, or decide the app wasn't for them. In Sean's mind, the app was for every person on the planet.

Sometimes, he was idealistic to the point of madness.

As I was disconnecting the live feed, Tess walked through the office door. It made me think she'd watched the demo sitting on the bottom step of the staircase.

"Good job," she said.

"Thank you."

"Just a few concerns. We hope this event wasn't premature. The audience size was definitely not what we'd hoped for."

"I thought it was great, considering we don't have a huge following yet."

"How many sign-ups for notifications?"

She shook her head when I told her. "That's disappointing."

"Tess. It's social media. This isn't television advertising. The audiences will be small, especially in the beginning."

"I understand that in theory. But Sean's used to hearing about YouTube channels with millions of viewers."

"Well tell him to hire Katy Perry and maybe we'll have a few bil."

"We have to do better."

We?

I flashed a smirk at her. "You have to set his expectations better. He's delusional if he thinks that kind of attention can be acquired in less than two months. And he's delusional if he thinks we'll ever have a million viewers. We might sell millions of copies of the app, but not everyone is going to engage at the same level. I already explained that."

She nodded. "I know. I know. He's high strung."

My phone buzzed. A message from Sean. I tapped the screen.

Sean: *Please see me in my office. Now.*

I held up the phone. "He wants to talk to me."

"I'll go with you."

I shrugged. We walked out and took the seven or eight steps to the other office. I knocked and went in. Sean was sitting on the sofa his attention directed at the door. "I need to talk to Alex," he said.

Tess moved up beside me. "But I…"

"Alex. Alone. Close the door."

I knew then what he wanted. It had nothing to do with attendance at the live event or the audience reaction.

Tess left and I closed the door. I pulled out a chair and sat at the conference table.

"I've asked you this before so I have no idea why I'm asking again. I know I won't get an answer that explains, but I have to ask anyway — what the *fuck* is wrong with you?" He folded his arms and crossed his legs as if he were wrapping himself up into a torpedo that would fire itself at me, fracturing me into a million pieces.

It wasn't a good idea to pretend I wasn't sure what he was talking about. It would inflame him further. And it might backfire — make me look not very bright. There was only one thing that would have him this pissed off. "I'm trying to be provocative. That's what you do online, to get a following."

"I'm not your prop for whatever crazy idea you come up with."

"They aren't crazy ideas, Sean. I'm in charge of getting some online attention for this group and I should have some freedom to do it in a way that works. It's not as if I filmed you having sex and posted it."

He stared at me as if he'd suddenly decided there was even more wrong with me than he'd realized.

I stared back at him. We held each other's gaze, neither one of us changing expression or shifting our bodies. The air in the room was equally still. I wondered if his mind was racing madly, or if he was simply consumed by a slow-burning rage. She who speaks first loses, they say. I continued waiting.

"Take it down," he said.

I continued staring at him.

"Now."

"We'll lose visibility."

"I don't care."

"The post has a lot of comments. There's even been some…"

"I'll watch while you do it." He gestured toward the computer on the desk.

"Don't you want to know how it fits into the strategy?"

"No. I'm waiting." His arm remained extended toward the

chair in front of the desk. "And just so you know, Tess and I were working on a bonus structure. You can forget about a cash bonus when the product launches."

"That's rather bold of you," I said.

"I own this company. There's nothing bold about it."

"Is that legal?"

"You're a guest in this country. Are you planning to file a complaint?"

I smiled and crossed my legs. "Have you forgotten your little gut-spilling moment the other day?"

He laughed. "Is that some sort of blackmail?" He stood and took a few steps toward the desk.

I smiled. "I wouldn't use that word. You need to calm down and listen to my strategy. I know you think I invaded your space, but no one online knows that. The statue is cool and it shows something about our life here. And it's generating interest. It's also given…"

"Stop talking. Sit down at the desk and remove that picture."

"…it's given you some street cred, if you want to call it that. People are intrigued by your taste, and the fact that you care about art, not just technology. How do you know some of the attendees today didn't sign up because of that gorgeous statue? It's not hurting you. It's good for the company. If we want to get attention, we have to be willing to expose multiple facets of ourselves." I felt slightly ill saying that last part. I wasn't about to expose a single thing about myself, but I wondered if I wasn't inadvertently headed in that direction. Still, I'd deal with that when the time came, there was no point in thinking about it now.

"You had no right to take that picture, much less post it

online. I don't understand why you think you can do whatever you want."

I stood and walked toward him. He looked kind of hot, all angry like this. Maybe a little teasing would calm him down. He didn't seem all that concerned about me revealing his lie, which was a little surprising. He must be really upset about that damn statue's privacy. I stood close to him.

He moved away. "What are you doing?"

"If you're that upset, I wanted to apologize." I gave him a sweet smile. I put my hand on his upper arm and squeezed gently, hardly any pressure at all, just a slight note of comfort.

"You can apologize by getting rid of it." He moved away and pulled out the desk chair.

I sat down and wiggled the mouse to wake the screen. "I think this is a mistake."

"Stop arguing."

"After we discussed the stories we told the detectives, I thought you and I saw the world the same way."

He didn't respond. I wondered whether he was considering the question I'd posed to the app, wondering whether I'd lied to Tess or, more importantly, to him. Or if there was something else he was unaware of.

I clicked on the Facebook page. There were more comments posted on the demo event as well as more reactions. "The demo went well," I said.

"The statue."

I took my hands off the keys. I stretched my fingers and turned slightly in the chair. He was directly behind me so I couldn't see him. I eased the chair to the side, moving away from the keyboard.

"What are you doing?" He moved to my left. "Never

mind. Get up and I'll delete it."

"Do you really want to lose all those comments? Some people might think we're censoring the interaction and can't be trusted. That's not good for an app called TruthTeller. We might lose page likes over this."

"Don't be ridiculous. And if we do, we can live without them."

"That's not a very customer-centric view." I put my hand on his chest. The thud of his heart pushed against my fingers, accelerating slightly.

He moved away.

"Why don't you discuss it with Tess and Gavin? Shouldn't this be a team decision?" I said.

"You're taking my private life and turning it into a circus on the internet." His voice trembled, I wasn't sure whether from anger or imminent tears.

"Your whole life is this company and this app. Is the statue so important in that context?" I reached out and ran my finger down his forearm.

He yanked his arm close to his side. "It's one of my most treasured possessions. It means…" His voice trailed away. He looked out the window.

"Talk to the others. Give it some more thought. I'm serious, posting that picture gave your first set of customers a peek into who you are. Part of getting attention online is being vulnerable and open — your true self. People are drawn to transparency."

He stared at me. I couldn't be sure whether it was a look of hatred or if my bullshit had cut through to some deeper part of him, the part that needed this app to succeed, the part that wanted to leave his mark on the world.

53

Sean felt as if he'd had to physically shove Alex out of the office to stop her from touching him. His resolve was strong, and Alex was the last person on earth he should mess around with, but he wasn't a robot.

He didn't recall her being such a tactile person, so what was this with her hands on his arm, his chest, the way she stood too close? Her betrayal was extreme — hanging around his bedroom as if it belonged to her, photographing something that was his, something he treasured in such a personal way, and then posting it on the internet. He wasn't sure whether the problem was an utter lack of boundaries, or if she was trying deliberately to upset him, or she was just clueless about the feelings of other human beings.

He felt so exposed, and she rambled on about how that was a good thing! He understood the concept of transparency, but something had been stripped away against his will. He couldn't figure out if she was now threatening to expose what he'd said about Karen, or if she was trying to seduce him. She was a perplexing woman. He was constantly confused and off-balance around her.

He turned the desk chair and sat down. He scrolled to the photograph of the statue. It was a lovely shot, very artistic, especially when you considered it had been taken with a phone. Her management of the lighting coming through the shutters was superb. He leaned back and studied it, trying to think what to do.

There were a lot of comments, she'd told the truth about that. As he sat admiring the photograph, more likes and loves appeared below the image. He smiled. It was addictive. All these strangers, all over the world, liking and loving his artwork, admiring his taste. Were they seeing what a good person he was, attributing that good will to TruthTeller? It made his heart ache with pleasure, even though he tried not to think too much about how the statue had entered his life. That was the part he wanted kept private.

Even if no one he knew saw what she'd posted, his feelings around it were private and he didn't want them shared with strangers. Against his will! Alex had no way of knowing that, but she should possess the normal human instinct to mind her own business, to stay out of other people's things. Why didn't she post a photograph of something that *she* treasured? In all fairness, she hadn't brought much with her to Australia. He didn't know much about her life in the States, nothing significant. He wasn't exactly sure where she'd left her belongings, if she owned a home or…anything, really.

It didn't matter. And she was right about something else. He was the owner of the company. If anyone was to be out there, the public face, it should be him. She might be in charge of getting attention on social media, but the attention ultimately needed to be directed toward him. The spotlight needed to form a halo around *his* head, not hers.

He touched the mouse and clicked to expand the list of comments.

They loved it. All of them. Over a thousand people. It

was unbelievable. The comments were repetitious, but they were all good — *Beautiful. Gorgeous. An exciting work of art. I love it.* They went on and on. There were sixty-seven comments, all from people who were now theoretically interested in his app, his work philosophy…and *him*. It was intoxicating. He laughed softly, then turned abruptly to see if anyone was standing in the doorway, tiptoeing into the room while he was lost inside his head, muttering like a madman.

He took his hand off the mouse, picked up his phone, and sent a text message to Tess — *Can you recommend any websites or books about social media?*

Tess: *That's Alex's job. No need to worry about it. She has it under control.*

Sean: *I just want to understand it better.*

Tess: *Then ask her.*

He placed his phone on the desk. That was not going to happen. He had to sort his thoughts about her first. He didn't want to speak to her or be alone with her again until he had. He wished he didn't have to see her at all until his feelings and thoughts were arranged in a more orderly fashion.

He moved the mouse and clicked to reveal the next collection of comments that had been posted over several days. He felt a quick, involuntary intake of breath.

Carmen Dunn.

It absolutely could not be the same Carmen Dunn. There was no way in hell. What were the odds? The chance that she might stumble across a Facebook page for his app. How had that happened? It must be a different Carmen Dunn. It had to be. The name was unique, yes, but there wasn't only one woman named Carmen in the entire world. And Dunn was surely a somewhat common surname. She might not even be from Australia. There were lots of people with the same name. Even unusual names. He'd seen it all the time. Once, he'd Googled himself and come up with pages of Sean Farmers. On Facebook alone there had to be thirty or more, even with the same spelling.

He moused over the woman's profile picture. He squinted at the screen. That same pointed chin, those eyes — slightly too large for her face. Her hair was short, cropped up above her ears. And it looked darker, almost black. He remembered it as medium brown with streaks of lighter color, shoulder-length and wavy. This woman's hair was straight. But still. Those eyes and that chin.

What was he thinking? He knew it was her. He was trying to talk himself out of believing it, but he knew. He didn't even have to look at the minimal information that was available beside her photograph — Lives in Queensland. Married.

So, she was married now. Still in Queensland.

He clicked through her comments and it only took a few to make it clear she was looking to make trouble. The only thing that allowed him to let out a long slow breath was that Alex had been rather cagey about answering Carmen's questions. In fact, reading between the lines, it looked as if Alex was trying to shut her down.

At the same time, Carmen wasn't giving up.

54

Except for the initial, innocuous questioning right after John's body was found, I'd never had a police officer pay a bit of attention to me in relation to one of my murders. When I met those two cops in San Francisco, I'd thought at first they were overly interested in my background. For a while, I'd wondered if another set of detectives was watching me from the building next door to Tess's condo, but in the end, none of them made the connection. I'd never been asked a serious question.

To Gavin and Tess, detectives popping by and asking questions, repeating questions, silently staring as they waited for an important, case-changing revelation, was a simple annoyance. To Sean, it spelled a creeping sense of trouble he couldn't escape and a growing uphill climb to keep forward momentum for TruthTeller. But for all of them, one additional detective didn't much matter. Of course they wanted them to stop harassing us. *It truly is harassment*, Sean announced, repeatedly, with a very authoritative tone, his CEO tone. *They have no reason to be here. They just don't know what to do, so they're picking on us.*

Then, Detective Joiner showed up, unannounced. More of the same for my housemates, not so much for me.

It's not that lying is difficult, but there would be a whole new level to it when I was required to make sure the lies fit together seamlessly. Lying about what time I woke up to find Karen's body in the pool wasn't that important. In that case, I hadn't done anything. And lies I tell to skate from other problematic situations aren't as critical to survival.

This was different. If the new detective truly became interested in me regarding John's death, she would peel back every layer of every word I spoke.

Detective Joiner was clearly more interested than the detective who had started the investigation.

I was the last one she spoke to that morning, but I didn't have the last person advantage of knowing what the others had been asked, and more importantly, what they'd said.

She explained she was new on the case, but dispensed with asking biographical information. I suppose she already had that from the previous guy, or from Martin and Bender. Thinking of their names together echoed inside my head like the name of a cocktail or a high-end home decorating store.

"I understand you and the others went to Mr. North's house to do some stargazing," she said.

I appreciated her obvious clue that the others had already mentioned the stargazing, rather than asking more generic questions with larger potential traps. "Yes."

"How did that come about?"

"He invited us."

"He invited you, and you invited the others, correct?"

I nodded.

She studied my face for a moment. "Yes?"

"Yes," I said.

"Why did he invite you?"

"He liked looking at stars. I guess he liked sharing his interest with other people. He didn't say why."

"How did the invite come about?"

"I was finishing my run, he stopped me and we chatted. He invited me to look at the stars."

"That sounds like a bit of a rush. Did you think anything was off about it?"

"Off?"

"Did you think he was hitting on you? Is that why you invited the others?"

I held her gaze. "It never crossed my mind that he would be hitting on me."

She looked as if she didn't believe me, but said nothing.

"I invited the others because looking at the stars through a telescope sounded cool. And Sean is big on team building."

She was obviously unimpressed with team building. "What kind of telescope does Mr. North own?"

"I don't know." I felt something inside, a faint tremor in my stomach. I smiled. "It's white." I waited for her to inform me the telescope was missing. I waited for her to speculate about the killer taking it. I waited for her to say maybe robbery was the motive, although a rather odd set of circumstances — robbery for a complicated piece of equipment that wasn't on everyone's wish list.

"How many times did you speak with Mr. North alone?"

"I think twice."

"You think?"

"It was casual. I don't keep track of when I talk to the neighbors."

"But more than once."

"Yes."

"What did you talk about the other times?"

"The neighborhood. Being from America."

"I noticed your accent," she said. She gave me a half smile.

It was strange, thinking of myself having an accent. Theirs sounded so melodic, so charming. I wondered if they felt the same about ours.

"Did you ever see any unusual behavior around his home?"

"What do you mean?"

"Did you notice cars that were there regularly, witness any arguments outside, hear anything when the windows were open?"

"No. He kept to himself."

"That's what your roommates said."

I was glad we agreed. It was the truth, so it would have been surprising if they'd said something else.

"Did he ever act as if he was afraid?"

"Afraid of what?"

She looked at me as if I were dumber than dirt. "Afraid of being murdered."

"No." I liked that she was moving away from questions about me and onto territory that suggested John had acquaintances who might get violent, that he had secrets hidden inside that stark, secluded house.

"He never said anything beyond small talk? Never suggested that perhaps his wife might want him dead?"

"No."

"The telescope has gone missing."

I parted my lips in a suggestion of surprise. I kept my thoughts inside, refusing the temptation to offer possible explanations. It would suggest I cared, it might suggest I was trying too hard. It might suggest all kinds of things. I needed to find a way to better conceal that telescope lying on my closet floor.

As if she'd read my thoughts, she leaned back in the chair and studied my face, watching for the next micro expression. "Because of Mrs. North's death in this house, I think we'll be looking at acquiring a search warrant."

I nodded and said what was obvious, what was expected, even though it sent my mind scrambling for the things I needed to do. "That makes sense."

She studied me for several more minutes. "Did anything unusual happen when you were looking at the stars with Mr. North?"

"Not that I can think of."

"Was he disappointed that you invited your roommates?"

"No."

"How do you know?"

I smiled and gazed into the middle distance. "He was excited to talk about the stars. He was really into them."

"Possibly someone took his telescope for that reason. It has the appearance of a personalized theft."

I shrugged. "I don't know."

"There were other valuable items in the house. It's strange that the telescope is the only thing missing."

"I guess."

"Do you know if Mr. Farmer had other interactions with Mr. North? Before you moved in?"

"They'd met, but that was about it."

"And how do you know that?"

"That's what Sean said."

Her face remained calm but I sensed a cynical reaction beneath her placid exterior. I wasn't sure if I'd conjured up the cynicism in my own mind, but I didn't have much time to think about it. She immediately circled around to questions I'd expected at the start — asking about Sean's background, my background, a bit about Gavin and Tess. Most of her focus was on Sean. I suppose because he owned the house. Because it was his pool where Karen drowned. Because he'd known John the longest. Because, maybe she could tell he was lying. I'm much more practiced at it.

55

Portland

Everyone in our youth group went to Tony's funeral. It was a full-on funeral, not a memorial service like so many older people in our church specified in their final wishes. Tony's family wanted his poor, lifeless body front and center. That huge mahogany box that my father whispered, *probably cost twenty grand*, dominated even the large space at the front of the auditorium.

It sat at the foot of the stairs leading to the platform where the musicians and preacher stood. People who chose seats near the front had to walk around it. The minister would have to circle around it to climb up to his lectern. Beside the coffin was an easel with an enormous photograph of Tony, taken a few years earlier. He looked like a child still. On the opposite side were three more easels with wreathes of white orchids.

Coffins are such shocking things. I don't think you'd ever get used to seeing them. I suppose if you work in a funeral home, you must, but I can't imagine it. They are so obviously designed for only one thing — holding a human body, hiding the decay from view, giving funeral attendees the impression that what's inside is as beautifully preserved as the polished exterior.

My father said we should be glad they didn't go so far as to utilize the feature that allowed the top half to open, like Dutch doors, displaying the waxy face and stiff shoulders, giving you a shock that would stay with you the rest of your life. Seeing that box was nothing compared to the closed eyes and lips drained of color, sometimes painted a light rose to look vibrant, my father said. That very lifeless skin that you could not ever mistake for a person deep in sleep.

By the time my father was done describing it, we might as well have seen Tony in an open casket.

My father had plenty of time to offer his thoughts because most people milled about in the lobby, not wanting to enter too soon and sit staring at that box. It didn't prevent them from peeking through the open doors every few minutes, checking the display of flowers and mahogany container.

The kids in the youth group were instructed to sit together in the front section to the left of the stage. I managed to get in at just the right time. Lingering too long in the lobby might force me into the front row, those seats left for latecomers because no one but the super eager ever want to sit in the very first row. And going in too soon, claiming a second or third row seat, farther from the coffin, might invite an over-efficient youth leader to demand I move to the front row. Thankfully, a few of my classmates were the super eager types and there was a good showing in the front row by the time I entered the auditorium.

Most of the kids wore regular clothes, celebrating life, as they say, with blue dresses and pale green shirts. I wore black — my father's choice for the entire Mallory family. My brothers looked like undertakers themselves in black suits, white shirts, and narrow black ties.

I felt rather chic in my new dress. I'd grown out of my black dress purchased for the last church memorial service a few years earlier. My mother had taken me to the mall where I had more choices. This time, the dress looked grown up — sleeveless and straight, showing off my body in a subtle way, one that didn't raise either of my parents' antennae. My shoes were ballet slipper style, soft black faux leather. I was not allowed black nylons.

I kept my pride to myself. It was a sin all on its own, and compounded with the solemn occasion would have been viewed as a horrific display of ungodliness, not to mention insensitivity and vanity, which is slightly different from pride.

The service was long, made longer by the lack of sound coming from the audience. Everyone was silent with tears, or their own feelings regarding the unjust tragedy of teenagers who ended their own lives. Of course that fact wasn't mentioned by the preacher or anyone who offered a eulogy. Tony's cousin hinted at it, but kept himself from stepping over the line, mentioning that it was impossible to comprehend how things could sometimes go wrong in life, before he quickly moved on to Tony's kind words for every living creature.

There were four hymns and three light-rock songs sung by everyone, as well as two solos accompanied by piano.

At the end, we were ushered out, row by row, starting from the front. The silence continued. Occasionally there were some whispers, but mostly everyone was eager to turn their backs to the coffin and escape the building. They wanted to reach the hall where tiny sandwiches and cookies were served. They could chase away their despair with a sweet high, drinking soda or coffee thick with sugar while the family stood in a line waiting to hear hundreds of people say the same thing over and over.

It must have been torture, listening to *so sorry* and *let me know if I can do anything* close to five hundred times.

I hung out with my friends and brothers. We talked quietly because even the building itself seemed to be closing us in, forcing words back into our mouths, muffling the sound, sucking out laughter before it could be heard.

I was taking a chocolate chip cookie off a large tray when I felt someone standing slightly behind me, too close, so close I smelled peppermint breath mints, a bit of perfume, and sweat. I moved toward the end of the table.

"I know who you are."

I turned.

The woman standing too close was Tony's mother. She looked at me, her lips withered and colorless, her face dominated by two rough red spots on her cheekbones. Her eyes were bleary but not particularly red from crying. They were dry.

For the second time, I reached out my hand as my father had instructed. "I'm so sorry for your loss."

I sounded phony, even in my own ears, but it was what we'd been taught. I could see the benefit of a canned statement rather than searching for something that tried too hard to be helpful and thought-provoking but might end up eliciting a shattering breakdown of the wall the family had put up around their feelings. Everyone appreciated the rituals.

"You broke his heart."

"We weren't in love."

She glared at me, then spit out the words — "He was."

That was not my fault and not something I could do anything about. I wasn't sure whether she was assuming it was my duty to love him back, or if she thought I could have had any control over making him fall out of love with me. Either way, she was wrong. I didn't think she'd agree, so I kept my mouth shut and gave her a tiny, hopefully sympathetic smile.

I wondered whether she knew about the fingernail clippings. Did she notice his shorn nails? Had she ever noticed their length?

"Aren't you going to say anything?" she said.

"He wrote nice poems."

She grabbed my arm just below the elbow. With her opposite hand, she closed her thumb and index finger around a piece of flesh on the inside of my upper arm. She tightened her fingers, hard.

"Ow!" I pulled my arm away and she let it go too fast. I stumbled to the side.

"You crushed his heart. You killed him."

"I don't think I did." I waited to see if she would mention the poems. It was possible he had others he'd never given me. Had she seen them? I held my breath as her eyes bored into mine. I felt her desire to punish me, to stir up something inside that would torment me. Maybe she wanted to be close to me in some weird way, knowing I was something her son craved and now she craved my presence in her life. That, or she wanted me to burn in hell.

"Don't get too cocky. The Lord does not discriminate when He hands out tragedy."

She was right about that, but again, I kept the thought to myself.

She turned and walked away, almost tripping in her rush

to get as far away from me as possible in the shortest amount of time.

I ate my cookie and walked slowly toward the back corner of the room. I wished I'd fought off her accusation, but there were so many people and my father's eye was always on me. No one would see my side. They would lash out at me for being heartless, arguing with a grieving mother.

I wondered again if she knew about the fingernails. It wasn't normal, giving those as a gift. Those dead pieces of his body disgusted me. He had some confusing twists inside his brain if he thought that would be a pleasant gift for a girl.

Blaming me wasn't fair. She didn't like that her son was dead. Why do people have to blame someone else when an event occurs that they don't like? It's almost as if they sort through the files of their memories, looking for something that removes the fault from them, and even more so, from the one who died.

As far as I was concerned, Tony's mother could only blame him. I suppose that was unbearable for her. Worse, maybe she secretly blamed herself and knew she might never escape her own wrath, not to mention god's.

56

Sydney

Before the door even closed behind Detective Joiner, everyone began scattering to their rooms. We were like a bunch of raccoons — black masks surrounding wide, startled eyes, running as fast as our little legs could carry us when someone shone a light on us.

I slipped away to the office. I shut the door and opened the shutters wide so I could enjoy the garden crowding up close and watch the cockatoos preen.

I launched Facebook and checked our page likes. They were up. I made some notes about the cadence of my posts for the rest of the week, and a note to think about the next demo and how I would make it significantly different from the last. I needed a longer runway this time so I could really start my non-stop virtual screaming and yelling to try generating a larger audience. I needed more than just a demo, but had no ideas about what that *more* might be.

From the corner of my eye, I saw what was at the top of the page. My note-taking and planning were deliberate avoidance.

Front and center on our Facebook page was my stunning photograph of the statue. It was getting more likes, more hearts, more wows.

Sometimes it seems that's all anyone does to communicate — emotes with cartoon icons. We're becoming mute, unable to articulate even the simplest thought. Why bother when it's so incredibly easy to find a tiny image that expresses our thoughts so precisely? If we can't express them with just one, we can add a string of adorable images — champagne glasses, a balloon, cake, flowers, confetti, a champagne bottle, then repeat.

Despite the foreshadowing of an inarticulate future, I was pleased with the likes. It's such an addictive force. Never having been on Facebook before I became the social media manager for TruthTeller, I hadn't realized the addictive quality of it. Posting something that gained a lot of positive attention was like being a virtual rock star. There was a flutter in my chest every time I observed more attention, new praise.

It was a game, like collecting chips or coins or whatever you will, winning at the contest of social recognition. I couldn't stop myself.

Before starting this job, I'd mostly used Twitter for watching what others had to say and occasionally as a rather public form of text messaging. This was much different. And I suppose, as the favorites and retweets piled up on Twitter, it would give the same adrenaline boost, but I'd never had many, preferring to stay in the shadows. Still, something about Facebook was more intimate. Maybe because people were coming to my page, paying attention to me, not just seeing me flow past on the river of thoughts.

The statue had moved to the top of the page again because Carmen had something else to say.

Carmen Dunn: *What's the word?*

To test the water, I posted the smiling yellow face wearing

sunglasses. One of the most inscrutable emojis available.

Carmen Dunn: *Well, where did he get the statue?*

Her chorus, Jane and Lara, immediately began cheering for the answer to the real-life mystery. This was going to get out of control quickly.

Despite Sean's despair over my exposure of his super-private personal statue, the love of his life, apparently, the one thing he wanted to protect, he never actually forced me to take down the post. He wavered, then backed off. Whether touching him had distracted him, or if he saw my point about being vulnerable, I wasn't sure.

The statue was getting more attention than the demo and more attention than any of the other things I'd posted, due to Carmen's persistence. Discussion of work-life balance and new models for living and working as a community had died. I imagined most people were so far from that, they felt they might as well be discussing science fiction. I'd have to give more thought to re-starting that topic and how to promote Sean's utopian vision as something relevant and real. Later.

Alex Teller: *Here comes the answer…*

I set the timer on my phone for three minutes. Floating bubbles in the comment thread indicated someone was typing, but then they popped like bubbles do and the screen remained static.

I put my hands on the keyboard. The timer went off.

Alex Teller: *It's not important. He just knows he's lucky to have it.*

Carmen Dunn: *Lucky?*

Alex Teller: *We all agree it's gorgeous. But he's the lucky one who discovered it, lucky that it belongs to him.*

Jane Horner: *Lucky he can afford it? LOL. I sure couldn't.*

Lara Merritt: *You don't know what it cost.*

Jane Horner: *I can guess. It's more than fifty bucks, so there you go. LOL.*

Their back and forth produced several more likes.

Carmen Dunn: *How is he lucky, Alex?*

I pushed away from the desk and walked out of the office. I needed to think this through. I'd thought my answer would satisfy her. She was after something. She was leading me into a trap, but I had no idea where the trap was placed or when the iron teeth would snap closed around my ankle.

It was fun playing with her, fun trying to guess what she might be after. But at the same time, I was closer than ever to the edge of risking my cushy job and luxurious temporary home. I couldn't figure out where the line was, when I would have gone too far and Sean would blow up once and for all.

He was always at the precipice, but he always stepped back.

The game was getting riskier. But what fun are games if there isn't a threat of danger? If you're playing poker for pieces of candy or even pennies, it's not nearly as exciting as playing for dollar bills, five-dollar bills, or stripping.

I made a latte and returned to the office. There was no lock on the door and when I was seated at the computer, my back was to the door. I wished I had a way of knowing if Tess came in. I tugged one of the chairs away from the conference table and placed it a few inches in front of the door. Opening the door would make a significant crash, especially if it was opened with force. Hopefully it wouldn't scratch the door, but I needed to concentrate. I didn't need her creeping into the room and startling me as I was typing, or coming in so stealthily that she was able to walk up behind me and watch what flowed out of my fingertips.

I sat down.

Alex Teller: *He discovered it. Isn't there a bit of luck in that?*

I sipped my latte and waited.

Carmen Dunn: *Luck? LUCK?!!*

What the hell did that mean? I'd already answered. I closed down Facebook. I knew what I wanted to say, and knew what I should say...but first, a shopping trip — to distract me, and to settle my other problem.

57

Alex had taken off shopping. She wouldn't say where, just a cryptic comment about interior decorating. Tess spent an hour doing yoga, then changed into jeans and a T-shirt. She went into the office and opened up her calendar and planning tools. She fiddled, adding new items and changing dates on her to-do list, re-mapping the product announcement schedule, and revising notes about press release plans. She was tempted to check Facebook, to see what Alex was up to there, but she resisted the impulse. It was better to wait for Alex's next report. She needed to demonstrate confidence. Delegate.

The doorbell rang. She glanced out the window. The patio wasn't visible from the office and the street was blocked by the lush clusters of plants and trees.

She waited, expecting Sean to appear from somewhere, usually quick to answer.

The bell rang again.

She went into the foyer and looked through the window to the right of the door.

One of the detectives stood on the porch. The man, Bender.

She opened the door.

"Tess! It's Tess, right?" He held out his hand.

Why the show of trying to remember her name? She

shook his hand. Despite the cool air, his skin was warm. He released her grip easily in a professional manner, but the look on his face contradicted his body language.

"I'd like to speak to Alexandra."

"She's not here."

He moved closer to the entrance. "Can you and I talk for a minute?"

"About?"

"Still some questions. You know how it is." He laughed.

It was too bad the cops in San Francisco weren't this diligent with an unexplained death. Sydney was a large city, probably not with the crime rate of San Francisco, but also, she guessed, a slightly smaller team of detectives to pursue it all. She forced the thought out of her head. It was a bad habit, thinking of that situation. She refused to allow it to continue. She was moving on.

"May I come in?" he said.

"I don't see why not." She stepped back and he moved into the foyer. He turned deliberately and looked up the curved staircase to the second floor landing. "Quite a place." He looked at her.

She nodded her head once.

"Where can we talk?"

She gestured toward the short hallway leading to the offices. As they entered, he closed the door behind him. They settled at the conference table. He smiled, professional or not? She couldn't get a read. Nice enough, friendly, the laid-back Aussie air, but something about it seemed put on.

"Why isn't Detective Martin with you?"

He gave her another slow, lazy smile. "Detective Martin is off the case."

"That was sudden."

"Not really."

"Does that mean you're wrapping things up?"

"Maybe."

They sat in silence for a moment.

"So you have more questions for me?" she said.

"We would have been done by now. But Miz Martin was wasting time. Chasing murder when it was obvious to me this is not a murder investigation. She wouldn't listen. So stubborn."

Tess waited. It seemed unprofessional for him to criticize a colleague to an outsider, but what did she know about cops, especially Australian cops.

"Typical...she got too emotional," he said.

"Emotional?"

"Yep."

"About what?"

"A dead woman, thinking it had to be murder. Needing to prove she was smarter than *moi*." He grinned. "Needing a big case. That, and getting all weepy about a woman her age who was found in such a pathetic state."

"She didn't strike me as a weepy person," Tess said.

"You all hide it. *Try* to hide it. Am I right?"

"Actually, I'm working, Detective. Do you have questions for me?"

"Just one."

They could have had this conversation on the front patio. Instead, he'd insulted his partner, veered close to denigrating her, and finished it off by disparaging women in general. She really did not like this guy. She was glad they were wrapping up.

"Two, if I think about it."

"Can we get on with it?"

"What's your rush? Do you always take this attitude with the authorities? Here I've given you good news — you all are off the hook as murder suspects, well, at least for the gal in your pool. Can't say about the guy next door. And you're getting all mouthy?"

"I have a lot of work to do." She was a visitor. She didn't know all their laws and customs. She'd better watch what she said. Still, she wanted to smack the guy. Even if he still had views from decades ago, didn't they have sensitivity training? Or did he think he could get away with it one on one? She wouldn't file a complaint, being a visitor.

"Such a busy girl."

She waited, keeping her expression neutral.

"Did you see the body before we arrived the morning of the first?"

"No."

He nodded. He pushed his chair away from the table and stood.

"That's it?"

"There was one other thing. Just talking as a human being here, not an officer of the law."

She stood and took a few steps away from the table, hoping to force him toward the door.

"That Alexandra." He smiled.

She felt a sigh rise through her chest.

"Quite a piece of work."

She stepped around him, reaching for the door handle.

He put his hand on her wrist. "Wait. I need to ask you something."

"Regarding the investigation?"

"I think she was coming on to me."

"Is this related to the investigation?"

"Oh, you mean she was coming on to me because she's hiding something? She wanted to divert me?"

"No. And no. She was not coming on to you."

"I pick up on things that aren't being said." He smiled.

He was still holding her wrist. She wanted to twist away but the presumed authority made her meek, uncertain. She hated herself for it. "Will you let go of my arm, please."

"If you promise not to open the door."

"You're making me uncomfortable."

He laughed and squeezed her arm several times, still not releasing his grip. "Women. You just don't know what' you want. I guess that's why you and your friends had to design some bullshit app to figure out your own minds."

"Please let go of me. I don't think this conversation is productive." She wanted to threaten to report him but she had no idea how things worked here. And she couldn't risk her visa status. Were the two even connected? She had no idea about that either, maybe he was just trying to scare her. "If there are any additional questions, I'd feel more comfortable talking to Detective Martin."

"I told you she's off the case." He narrowed his eyes. "And don't think you're going to tattle on me for asking a personal question. It's perfectly legit. God I'm so sick of this. Women want attention and then they get all twisted around and start crying about harassment. It's tiresome. My CO feels exactly the same way. Exactly."

She wasn't entirely sure what the CO felt the same way about, but it was a door slamming in her face. For a moment, she imagined the rush of air, the shock of thinking a solid wood door might actually make contact with her cartilage and bones.

"Your friend was definitely hitting on me. And I'm trying to scope out the situation. She laughed when I suggested she was getting it on with her mates. So tell me what the deal is, help me figure out if I should make a move."

"No."

"No? You're rather confident. For someone who still has a cloud over her. Just because the woman snuffed out her own life doesn't mean the murder investigation next door is over. Know what I mean? In fact, it's very much ongoing. So be a good sport and help me out. Or do you two also have something in play?" His eyes grew glassy and he moved his face close to hers.

She smelled his breath — not offensive, but stale, laced with coffee and possibly some kind of jam. Strawberry. "I don't know what the laws are here, but this conversation is inappropriate," she said. "If you don't have any more questions about the drowning, I need to get back to work."

He released her arm suddenly. "Tell Alexandra not to play hard to get." He held out a card. "Here's my number."

She kept her hands by her sides. "Tell her yourself. Why are you even talking to me?"

"As I *said*, I want to find out if she's available or just a tease. Didn't want to embarrass myself." He gave her a coy smile of his own.

"Too late."

He was still holding the card in her direction. "You gonna give this to her?"

"I said, no."

"Better watch that mouth." He let the card fall to the floor. He opened the door and walked out of the office. A moment later, she heard the front door open. There was no sound of it closing. She went into the foyer. The door stood open. The front walkway was empty. He moved fast.

58

I was getting more comfortable using Uber in Australia. I'm not sure why it had taken me so long to hook up with them. They'd served me well in San Francisco. Maybe it was riding on the left side of the road with a stranger at the wheel. Even with Tess, a fairly predictable driver, sitting on the side where I'd driven a car all my life and now being in that same seat without gas and brake and steering wheel was harrowing. Riding in the back seat with an empty front left seat and a total stranger, often an Australian man who was talking ninety miles a minute in a flow of words laced with incomprehensible slang, was too much culture shock all at once.

For a country that speaks the same language I do and has similar architecture, relatively similar climate to the west coast of the US, and the same style of clothing, along with familiar food, I felt a ridiculous amount of culture shock. Everything was just slightly different, and maybe that's what caused the problem. I'd expected the same rather than priming myself for minor shifts in every aspect of life. It made me feel as if the ground was undulating beneath my feat, making me slightly dizzy.

But if I wasn't going to remain trapped in a luxury home, enjoying free food and alcohol at the cost of sharing my every waking minute with other people, it was Uber or nothing. I suppose I could have bought a bicycle, but my range of travel would be limited. And a bicycle combined with that wrong side of the road thing could be deadly.

This time, as luck would have it, a female driver picked me up. She talked just as fast but with less slang. I was able to follow her conversation about why I was in Sydney and how long I planned to stay, sprinkled with helpful pointers to landmarks.

"Where are you off to?" This question came ten minutes into the ride, which was strange timing, but I suppose my pointer to the Chinatown area had given her enough info to get started, but leaving her curious all the time she was chattering away.

"Shopping."

"New clothes for winter?"

"No. A bit of decorating."

"Your friend's home is lovely. It's very sexy, from the outside."

"It is."

"I can't imagine it needs a lot of decorating."

"Not a lot. Just a few things to spiff up my bedroom."

"That's nice."

She didn't ask more.

She dropped me by Paddy's Market. It was a bazaar of sorts, housed inside a cavernous hall filled with booths selling high-end knives and glassware and trinkets and nice jewelry and chiropractic services, purses and toys, water filters and clothing, all jumbled together.

I entered the din and began making my way down the aisles. I moved quickly, sure of what I wanted. I'd come back another time to browse. There were a lot of things calling out to me — the things that call out saying, *you didn't know you need me or want me, but here I am.*

There were displays of bracelets and toe rings that called the loudest. Right away I saw that if the need arose for disguising my appearance while I was in Australia, this would be the place to find what I needed. No one would remember me in the throngs of people touching and talking and buying, nothing to make me stand out when so many were dragging huge shopping bags behind them, filled with an eclectic mix of purchases.

Finally I found what I was looking for — a large booth with racks displaying Persian rugs. A rolled up rug was the perfect place to conceal the telescope I'd stolen from John North. There was a slim chance that Sean would allow Detective Joiner to take a casual walk through the house without a search warrant. I didn't think he would. He resisted their very existence, but I'm always careful in these things, even if I'm risky in others.

I purchased a six-by-eight-foot rug — green with touches of black and cranberry on a creamy white background. The clerk wrapped it in brown paper. It made for a heavy, awkward load. I created a bit of a spectacle, jockeying for position among the surprisingly thick crowd of shoppers for a weekday in the middle of June. Kids were in school, presumably most people were working, but still the place was packed and I bumped the end of my rug against more than a few shoulders, getting peeved looks, but fortunately no over-reactions.

A new Uber driver was waiting when I reached the main exit. He was double parked. He made a move to get out of the car when he saw that I was his passenger, but I waved at him to pop the trunk. I stuffed the rug inside, slammed it closed, and climbed into the back seat.

At home, Tess was standing in the foyer. She looked lost. Her expression changed quickly when she saw my bundle.

"That's more than *a bit* of interior decorating."

I smiled.

"Why do you need a rug? The carpet is fantastic. So comfortable, and it gives the room an open look. You'll feel crowded with an area rug on top of carpet."

"I needed a change. More color."

She shrugged. "Can we talk?"

"Sure. Give me half an hour."

"Do you need help getting it up the stairs?"

"Nope."

She drifted away toward the kitchen. Before I'd made it up four steps, I heard the rather loud snap of the top coming off a wine bottle, surprising in the large house that usually blocked sound from traveling between rooms.

I put the rug down and walked up the rest of the way backwards, tugging it after me, which resulted in tearing the paper. At the top, I picked it up in my arms like a large dog and carried it to my room. Inside, I tore off the paper and took the rug into the closet.

I unrolled it, picked up John's telescope, and placed it near the edge of the rug. I hadn't used it since before Karen drowned, there was no time. And for now, it was best to keep it well-hidden. I rolled it up and pushed it into the space below the rack where my dresses were hanging. A rolled up carpet would pass any glance from a detective. Without a warrant, they wouldn't be unrolling it.

If Tess asked why I hadn't placed it on my floor, I'd tell

her she was right — the room looked better without it after all.

I changed into leggings and a long sweater. I took my laptop and my usual substitute ashtray in the form of a glass with a few inches of water to the balcony. I lit a cigarette, opened the laptop, and fired up Facebook.

There were a few more likes for the photo of Sean's statue. The post still sat at the top of the page.

Carmen's last comment asking about luck still waited for my reply. I could almost feel her staring at the screen, fingers hovering over the keypad on her phone, ready to smack me down again. As fun as it would be to get into that kind of contest, I knew what needed to be said to keep Sean from losing it entirely.

Alex Teller: *Send me a PM.*

As I expected, she replied immediately.

Carmen Dunn: *Isn't this outfit called TRUTH-teller? And I ask an honest question and you want to take the conversation private? What kind of truth is that?*

I stared at the screen. I dropped my half finished cigarette into the glass of ashy water.

Taking down the photo at this point would cause more problems. Then she'd really start in on the truth-telling angle. What was she after? I had the sense she wanted something from Sean.

Did he and Carmen know each other?

I closed the laptop and lit another cigarette. I'd have to talk to him before I answered.

59

When I went downstairs, Tess was in the living room, an icy bottle of Grey Goose bleeding onto a sandstone coaster on the coffee table. Beside it was a bowl of buttered popcorn.

Apparently the sound I'd heard of her opening a wine bottle had either been something else, or she'd inhaled the aroma and decided a glass of wine wasn't going to cut it for her. Nestled up close to the vodka were two shot glasses.

I settled beside her and pinched up a few fluffy pieces of popcorn. I put them in my mouth and let the salt and butter melt into me while she filled the shot glasses. She handed one to me.

"To survival." She drank hers in proper shot fashion.

I sipped mine and put down the glass. I ate another few pieces of popcorn. "Is our survival at risk?"

"Sometimes I just can't take it any more…when I have to deal with the kind of man who thinks he can push me around, who thinks women exist for nothing but sex."

"Doesn't sound extremely unusual."

"I'm sick of it."

"What happened?"

She refilled her shot glass. "I feel like I shouldn't be talking to you. I'm your boss. But living like this makes for muddy boundaries."

"It does."

"And we are friends, even if we have the boss-employee issue."

I smiled and sipped my vodka. With my other hand I grabbed some popcorn. Tess hadn't eaten a single piece. Maybe it was there for the sole purpose of luring me into a friendly conversation. Despite the uncertain and constantly evolving nature of our relationship, she knows me well.

"Detective Bender came by while you were gone."

"What for?"

She slammed back the second shot. "Detective Martin is off the case. According to him, he engineered her departure. It sounds like he basically sabotaged her career, and he was perfectly happy to brag about it. Now that she's gone, they're wrapping up. Murder is off the table."

"Sean will be giddy."

"It doesn't mean everything is over. There's still John."

I smiled. Things were moving in the right direction. Despite Detective Joiner's questions, investigation into his death had been less aggressive than the one for Karen. To the police, the circumstances were equally perplexing, but there was no obvious line of inquiry because of an apparent tie to the neighbors. I didn't think there would be any problems. There was no evidence of me being in his house the day he died. I imagined they were looking at his business relationships, searching for gambling and other illegal interests.

"I'm so pissed I can hardly think." She poured another shot. She took a small sip. Her face was pale but the tip of her nose was red, either from the vodka or her rage, it wasn't clear.

"Why?"

"Didn't you hear me? He got her removed from the case. He undermined her to their boss. He talks as if women are incapable of being police officers. And it sounds like she doesn't have a lot of options for recourse because their commanding officer is a jerk too. Of course Bender doesn't see it that way. He thinks his boss is another guy on the same team. Watching his back."

"It's not surprising, is it? I would think there are a higher percentage of cops drunk on macho ideas, who don't want women treading on their space."

"You should have been there. I can't explain how it was. He grabbed my wrist and wouldn't let go."

I sipped my vodka and watched her eyes as she stared past me, as if she expected him to walk through the front door.

She sighed. "I can't believe he got her removed."

"Well we didn't want her searching for signs of murder. She was making a big deal of everything, dragging it out, hunting for something that wasn't there."

"That's her job," Tess said.

"Yes, but aren't you glad it's done?"

She glared at me. "He thinks you were hitting on him. He wants you to call him." She laughed and took another sip of vodka.

I pulled the popcorn bowl closer and ate several pieces, one at a time, savoring each one, chewing it slowly.

"I refused to take his card and he just dropped it on the floor and walked out, knowing I'd have to pick it up. He didn't close the front door…"

"You sound really upset."

"I am. Maybe you had to be there. Doesn't it bug you that he's so smug, so puffed up with himself he thinks you were hitting on him? What a joke."

"Maybe I was."

She swallowed the rest of her shot. "That's not funny."

I shrugged.

"Were you?"

"No."

"That's what I mean. Full of himself. Assuming..." She studied my face. "Why did you say *maybe you were*? Don't you care that he just assumes that? Surely you don't mean..."

"I think it's interesting."

She glared at me. "He's an asshole. It's terrible that Detective Martin's career is damaged."

"I'm sure she can take care of herself."

"It's impossible to take care of yourself when the game is rigged against you. You know that."

I had my own way of taking care of myself, of course. Tess used to be pretty good at that, with the occasional slip-up. I understood why she was angry. I didn't like it that a woman was being systematically removed from a position of power. I hate it when a man believes he's born superior simply because he has testosterone instead of estrogen pumping through his system. I didn't like that Martin couldn't even count on her boss, although really, it's often not possible to count on anyone. You have to count on yourself.

But with all that, she was a cop. A good cop. I prefer cops who aren't as thorough, who take things at face value. Could I ever be pushed into helping a cop, getting rid of a man who was working diligently, and succeeding, at pulverizing her career into something limp and lifeless? I wasn't sure it would be worth it. There's always satisfaction in removing someone who tries to keep women in some sort of slightly sub-human category, a different species, an addendum to the male gender.

But he was a cop.

We drank several more shots in silence. I polished off the bowl of popcorn. She never even looked at it.

After a while, she leaned her head back on the couch and closed her eyes. I had a slight buzz. I was ready to do something more interesting than moping about the career of a cop I hardly knew. At the same time, I couldn't stop thinking about Bender.

If I did decide to get him out of Detective Martins' life, would that help her at all? She still had a boss who apparently didn't value female officers, who would just as soon have them off the force. The biggest question was — would I ever kill a cop? That would be sticking my neck out so far, anyone could chop off my head.

Cops are a brotherhood of protection. If you do anything to one of them, they swarm like wasps. Even when one dies accidentally, they turn into a mass of blue cohesiveness — us against the world. They act as if the death of a cop is an assault on every single one of them. They care more about a dead cop than they do about a dead citizen they're supposed to protect.

It's probably fear. Most things are. The animal instinct rising up under a threat. They know they have a higher than average chance of dying every single day of their lives. Death brings that fear right up to the center of their thoughts. If an accidental death in a motorcycle crash, or the common failure of the human body makes them huddle into a single loyal cell, a murdered cop drives them mad with rage and revenge.

They would never give up on a case like that. Never rule it

an accidental death. They would never stop asking questions that went far beyond invasive and aggressive. All rules against harassment would go out the window. They would do whatever it took to find the perpetrator and bring her to justice. I knew this in my bones.

Killing a cop could get a woman killed.

60

Everything was empty — the shot glasses, the popcorn bowl, and the bottle of vodka. The bottle hadn't been full when we started, but we'd definitely consumed more than is wise on a weekday afternoon.

Tess was resting her head on the back of the couch. Her neck was stretched out long and white and vulnerable. Her eyes remained closed. It looked as if she was asleep, but it was difficult to tell from her breathing — smooth and gentle, not the deep, gulping breaths the body sometimes adopts during sleep to prove to itself it's still alive and functioning correctly.

I took the remains of our drinking and rage into the kitchen, washed the glasses and bowl, and tossed the bottle into the recycling container. I went up to my room and took a nap.

When I woke, it was dark. Very dark. Late in the evening dark, pushing midnight dark. I suppose you can't actually tell by the quality of the darkness how late it is, but there's a certain feel. Maybe it's something in the body — the circadian rhythm. Or maybe it was simply the fact that I was very hungry and completely sober, which told me I'd been asleep for quite a long time.

Downstairs, the living room was empty. I wandered past the offices, workout room, and billiards room — all empty.

The kitchen lights were out except for three small lamps that descended from a stainless steel rod over the eating island. The counters and cooktop were spotless as always.

I walked toward the patio doors. The lights around the pool glowed. Sean was reclined on one of the lounge chairs. I opened the door a few inches. The waterfall was running, creating a lot of noise compared to the stillness surrounding the rest of the yard and the neighboring houses.

He was smoking a joint.

I opened the door and went out. "I'm going to make grilled cheese sandwiches. Want one?"

He didn't look at me. "Brilliant." He put the joint to his lips.

I'd expected him to be his more enthused self now that the investigation was over, but maybe Tess hadn't told him.

I went back inside and turned on the oven. I drank two glasses of water while I buttered bread and cut thin slices of cheese. I made four sandwiches. If Sean only wanted one, I was pretty sure I could eat three. I slid the sandwiches on a large plate, grabbed a few paper napkins, and stuffed them partway into the pocket of my jeans. I refilled my water glass and carried it and the sandwiches outside. I put the water on the ground, pulled up a chair, and sat beside Sean.

We demolished the sandwiches without talking. The waterfall continued rushing into the pool. After a while, the lights went dark from the lack of motion and I could no longer see the water. It was a shockingly pleasant sound, as long as I kept the idea of the pool it was spilling into out of my thoughts.

"Do you know someone named Carmen Dunn?" I said.

He didn't speak or turn to look at me. But I felt, even

from several feet away, that his shoulders had stiffened and the tendons in his neck were tight.

Several minutes passed.

"Since you didn't say *no*, I'll assume you do," I said.

"I was enjoying the quiet," he said. He picked up the joint out of the ashtray on his lap and re-lit it.

"I need to know how you know her. She's posting a lot of questions about the statue photograph on our Facebook page."

"You're not required to answer."

"These kinds of things can blow up on social media. You know that, right?"

"That's your job. Handle it."

"I feel I've been set up, not knowing that someone from your past was a potential stalker."

He inhaled smoke. The water splashed. He released a cloud of smoke. "That's your fault, for putting my private life out there."

"What's the deal with her and the statue?"

"I'm not going to discuss it."

"You have to."

"No, I don't."

I waited. With each puff of the joint, I wondered if he would offer it to me out of a sense of social obligation. After consuming all that vodka, I had no desire to alter my brain a second time that day, so I didn't mind what some might consider rudeness. Mostly, I was just curious, as usual, about polite behavior that's forced by upbringing and a desire to be liked, the mistaken belief that doing what other people want will get you that elusive *like*. A thumbs up.

When the joint was gone I stood and moved over to his

lounge chair. I sat at the foot and put my hand on his ankle. He looked startled, but said nothing. Maybe he thought I wanted him, maybe he wondered why I was suddenly excessively warm and touchy.

"You have to listen to me. This woman is accusing me of hiding the truth because I asked her to pose her questions about the statue in a private message. She's mocking the TruthTeller brand."

"Your fault."

"It doesn't matter whose fault it is. There's a problem."

"Still your fault. You deal with her."

"If I take down the picture of the statue, she'll escalate that accusation. And before you point out again that it's my fault, that doesn't matter right now. Do you want the brand to get negative attention?"

"Still your fault."

"So that's a *yes*? You're okay with the brand being viewed as a farce?"

He glared at me, his eyelids lowered in the stupor of someone who's high, but there was something tense and alert — panther-like, ready to pounce and rip out my liver. "Are you going to apologize for how you fucked this up?"

"No. I didn't fuck it up. I'm trying to get attention in a world where everyone is screaming at the top of their lungs. You can't just go out there with a clever little bit about understanding your subconscious. It won't work."

He moved his leg, trying to extract his ankle from the grip of my fingers.

I held on tight. "This Carmen woman has an agenda of some kind. I don't know what it is, but she asks pointed questions and I can't get a read on what she's after. There are two other women, who appear to be strangers to her, cheering her on."

He wriggled his shoulders and re-positioned himself so he was sitting up straighter. "What are their names?"

"Jane Horner and Lara Merritt."

"Don't know them."

"Like I said, pretty sure they just like the drama and are egging her on."

"I hate social media."

"You might as well say you hate cars. It's how the world is."

"People are shit."

"Maybe. Some of them. A lot of them. But Carmen, we're talking about Carmen. I need to know what your relationship is, or was, and why she's so fixated on the statue. Then I can deal with her."

"It's all in the past. I don't want to talk about her or even think about her."

"You don't have a choice."

"She's close to my ex. Okay? Are you happy? How is that going to help you deal with her?"

"Did she ever see the statue?"

"Yes."

"Did it belong to her? Did…"

"That's all I'm saying. Tell her to fuck off."

"You know I can't do that."

"Figure out how to get rid of her."

"Do you think she wants to get back at you for something?"

He turned his head to the side, staring into the darkness.

"Can you arrange to talk to her?"

"Don't want to."

He sounded like a child, refusing a serving of broccoli.

"Maybe you don't have a choice."

"There's always a choice." He reached forward and pried my fingers off his ankle. "For example, you had a choice about posting something very private and personal online. Without my permission."

"If you want to be private, social media is not going to work for this company. The whole purpose of the app is the most personal thing you can imagine. The questions it asks are beyond personal. And if you don't know, social media is heavily weighted toward photos. And video. If you think the statue is a problem, wait until I start recording our meals and scenes from the offices."

"I notice you're all about exposing me and keeping yourself in the background."

"You're the CEO. Supposedly the face of TruthTeller. And we need to tell a plausible version of the truth to Carmen. So who is she?"

He sighed and settled back into the chair. "She's my ex's sister, okay? She took it upon herself to punish me for my bad behavior. That's all you need to know."

"I just needed context."

Now, I could figure out a way to put Carmen on her back foot. So far, she had all the knowledge and I'd been forced into following her lead. That was no longer the case.

61

Sean was making dinner. A baked dinner, he called it. When Tess asked what a baked dinner was, he stared at her as if she were a four-year-old.

She'd watched as he peeled and cut up potatoes, sweet potatoes, and pumpkin. Now, he was arranging the potatoes and pumpkin around pork in a baking dish. When it was done, it would have a rich gravy and crisp pork fat, which he called *crackling*.

Tess sat at the bar. She was sipping a cup of peppermint tea, hoping it would stop the jitter of her nerves and settle her twitchy muscles. Even her bones hummed with desire.

Sean wore a baggy gray sweatshirt and jeans. His feet were bare, the shark tattoo crisp and colorful, prominent under the bright kitchen lights. His hair was tied back with a thin leather strap which gave him a wild outback appearance, at least in her mind. She had no idea how people dressed in the outback, but she imagined it was something like this.

It was the deft movement of his hands, the precision of his fingers as he handled the food, that was making her body respond without seeking any input from her mind. Simply thinking about why the movements of his hands aroused her, made her desire him more.

She was in an endless loop of desire and she couldn't figure out if her deprivation was making it more intense or if the intensity was specifically about Sean.

A small part of her loathed her lack of self control. And another, more significant part, didn't care at all. She wanted him so badly she was afraid she would slide off the chair, walk around the granite-topped island, and wrap her arms around him as he ran the knife through the last sweet potato.

The knife blade glittered. It cut through the root vegetables as if they were the consistency of butter. Yet another image that made her insides feel soft, collapsing into a pool of liquid.

If she was smart, she *would* slide off the stool.

Then, she would pick up her teacup and leave the room and not return until the meal was served. Maybe not return at all. She would go for a drive, do some shopping, and take herself out for dinner. She would follow dinner with a drink in a bar and meet someone with whom there were no sticky, tenacious fibers weaving their lives into an inescapable web.

God, this was torture. She took another sip of tea. The peppermint had done nothing to settle her body or her thoughts. All that talk about the calming effects of herbal tea was pure bullshit. She was sure of it. "Anything I can do to help?"

He laughed. "You've asked me that four times."

"I want to help."

"And I want you to watch." He grinned.

She felt as if she had a genuine fever. She put the back of her hand to her forehead. She swallowed the rest of the tea in a long gulp. It was lukewarm and it tasted more like a scented candle than something she was supposed to put inside her body. She pushed the cup and saucer away from her.

Would she be insane to flirt with him, to find out where

his head was at? Or maybe a better approach was directness. Flat out tell him she was interested and find out what his thoughts were.

"Do you want a glass of wine?" Sean pulled open the door of the fridge and took out a bottle of Chardonnay.

"Sure." It was a mistake, but not one she had the will to avoid.

He filled two glasses halfway and handed one to her. He held up his glass. "Cheers."

She said the same and took a sip. It was crisp and biting cold. The hot liquid of her body grew heavier, warmed by alcohol instead of being chilled by the temperature. She took a second sip. She slid off the chair. "I'm going outside for a bit."

"It's supposed to rain," he said.

His back was to her, which helped her stick to her resolve to remove herself before she made a complete mess of things.

"Even nicer," she said. "I'll sit on the patio."

"It's very seductive, isn't it?"

"What?" Her hand trembled. She put the fingertips of her other hand on the glass to steady it.

"Listening to the rain. I wonder why the sound feels so good?"

"I have no idea." She turned and walked quickly out of the room.

Outside, she pulled a chair from the table close to one of the lounges. She sat down and used the lounge as a footrest. Her legs were bare beneath a flowing black skirt. It wasn't helping — wearing a soft spandex and cotton skirt that moved around her legs, stroking her skin, making her aware of the warmth inside her body. Her toenails glistened burgundy. Had he noticed? She'd been told her feet were beautiful, and she agreed with the assessment. They were slim with well-defined arches. Her toes were long and evenly spaced. With polish on the nails, they looked elegant and full of life. She giggled. What an odd way to describe one's toes.

She closed her eyes and took a sip of wine.

That woman she'd met on the plane was half the problem. She'd gotten Tess's mind turning in a new direction — insisting that things didn't matter nearly as much as you thought they did. Or maybe it had started with Detective Gorman, realizing life just didn't go the way you wanted and it wasn't that big of a deal. You chose to be passionate about a dead man, wound up, obsessed, and tied to doing what was *right*. Or you put it behind you. And who defined right? Religion? Laws? Some vague concept of a conscience? Agreements from thousands of years ago about what was necessary for a civilized society?

And where did sleeping with a work colleague fit into that list of societal restraints? Was it morally wrong? Not really, unless there was an abuse of power.

Thinking about it made her head spin as if she were on her third glass of wine instead of barely halfway through her first. She took another sip.

Angela would say, *Go for it. Absolutely.* She'd make a game of it. She'd dress up in a fuck-me outfit from Victoria's Secret. Or maybe something more playful — fishnet stockings and high heels, blood-red lipstick and a hat, dressing as the quintessential femme fatale of a noir film.

She laughed. She hoped Sean hadn't looked out the window and seen her laughing madly to herself as mist began to fall across the yard with the soft touch of a lover caressing your skin. Maybe she was mad. Everything made her think of sex — her toenails, the lightly falling rain, her skirt...cutting up sweet potatoes, for God's sake.

She wasn't the type to wear some ridiculous outfit — armor to make herself feel less vulnerable. It wasn't necessary. Direct was best. And Sean wasn't the type either. She couldn't imagine him being enticed by a costume.

What turned him on? That wasn't something you discovered until you'd been with a man for a while. It was backwards, really. That would be useful information to have up front.

She finished the wine and put the glass on the patio floor. It made a bright, solid click. She was not going back into the house until dinner was ready. It would be a long time. The baked dinner took close to two hours in the oven. But watching the rain was pleasant, and she could succumb to its seductive presence and her desire without crossing any lines.

62

Friday morning I was on a roll. I got up at five, ran four miles, spent twenty-five minutes lifting weights, topped off with a few yoga poses to make sure my equilibrium was stable and my mind centered. Or at least that's what's supposed to happen with yoga. Ninety percent of the time my equilibrium is good. My mind is always flitting except when I'm running or smoking a cigarette. A strange contrast, but that's how it is. Yoga doesn't move the needle much, but it does feel good stretching out my muscles and tendons, and getting the blood into the tiny crevices it might have missed with more intense workouts.

I hadn't looked at Facebook since I'd talked to Sean. I was still mulling over my response to Carmen, trying to figure out the most effective way to put her on the defensive. Maybe the very act of not responding was doing that. Unless it was making her more aggressive. I didn't want to know. Not yet.

I showered and dressed in an outfit that turned out to be perfect for what the day held for me — a black dress, short but not too, black gladiator sandals, my hair flat-ironed until it looked like a sheet of metal.

I put on more makeup than I'd been wearing recently. I can't say why, I was just in the mood.

After a latte, three pieces of bacon, and a glass of tomato juice with lemon, I went into the office. It was only eight-twenty. I heard my roomies-slash-colleagues moving about in various parts of the house — water rushing through pipes, a door opening and closing, a few light coughs, but that was about it. Earlier I'd heard a splash in the swimming pool.

I adjusted the shutters and looked out at the damp yard, turned an extra brilliant shade of green by the mist that had drifted out of the sky all night. It never became a proper rainstorm, but the leaves dripped water and the soil was damp.

The doorbell rang.

I walked into the foyer and opened the door.

Detective Bender stood just past the threshold.

"Hi there." He moved closer. "Just the person I wanted to see."

I smiled.

"You feel the same?"

I shrugged.

"You looked happy to see me."

"Did I?"

He nodded. "Can I come in?"

"Tess said the case was closed."

"Did she? What else did Tess say?"

"Just that." I smiled in a more friendly, inviting manner.

"Well can I come in? There might be one or two open items."

I stepped away from the door and made a sweeping gesture toward the foyer.

He stepped inside. His gaze darted around the entryway and up the staircase. "Where can we talk?"

By now, they knew the layout of the first floor. I suppose it was polite, not wanting to assume access to a particular area, but it seemed put on for some reason. Maybe it was the suggestion we needed privacy, as if Gavin, Sean, Tess and I weren't discussing their questions behind their backs. Did they really believe we didn't compare notes?

"My office," I said.

"Your office? I thought it was shared? The two girls."

"It is."

He gave me a condescending smile. I turned to go into my office. He followed and closed the door. He sat on the couch. I sat at the desk and turned the chair to face him.

"Isn't this cozy." He grinned.

I smiled and tipped my head to the side, feeling my hair slip over my arm. I watched him follow the movement of my hair across my skin. "So what can I do for you?"

I thought he might fall off the couch. He quickly regained his composure. Sort of.

"Do you always get this dolled up to work from home?" He put air quotes around *work* and *home*. He gave me a knowing smile, although I wasn't sure what he thought he knew.

"So you have more questions? Before the final closure?" I said.

"You make it sound like closing a coffin," he said.

I shivered for his benefit. He liked that.

"What did Tess tell you?"

"She said Detective Martin was off the case. And now that you're in charge, it's no longer a murder investigation. You knew from the start it wasn't murder, didn't you?" I smiled.

"So you've been talking to your roommates." Again, the air quotes.

"Why do you do that, the air quotes regarding my roommates? We're colleagues, you know."

"There's something else in the atmosphere," he said.

"Maybe it's inside your own head, not the atmosphere." I used my own set of air quotes.

His face reddened slightly. He glanced toward the window, studying the plants outside, although there wasn't much worth studying for more than a moment. He couldn't see the activity of the birds from his position. He needed to catch his breath, I suppose.

"I have good instincts," he said.

"I can imagine."

"That's how I knew right off it was a suicide. Martin doesn't have those instincts. She lets her feelings cloud everything. You can't be a detective and allow feelings to dictate your inquiry choices. Not gonna work."

I nodded, looking thoughtful. What I was thoughtful about was that he was more of a sleaze than I'd realized. Between the things Tess had told me and his behavior now, I wondered how he'd kept his job. I suppose if his boss was the same type he could get away with anything. Men working in male-dominated institutions have done just that, for centuries. It's easy to get lulled into thinking the world has changed. In some places it has, but I wonder if even that isn't a facade. A thin facade that cracks easily.

"Instincts are critical. Feelings have nothing to do with anything. All this bullshit you see on TV where cops get all emotional for the victim, pursuing justice on behalf of the victim? It doesn't work that way. It's an intellectual game and if you become a crusader, it doesn't end well. Detective Martin is on her way to a breakdown."

I nodded, trying to look solemn and sympathetic for the poor, helpless woman in the grip of her sad, uncontrollable feelings. In my experience, men have just as many uncontrollable feelings. Those feelings tend more toward rage, but they're equally, and often more, uncontrollable. "So, your questions for me?"

"Mostly for my own satisfaction. Not required for declaring the death a suicide."

So much for not being driven by feelings. Did he not recognize that satisfaction was a feeling, something that can drive you in the wrong direction as easily as sadness or a pursuit of justice? I wanted to laugh, but managed to maintain my look of solemnity.

"The fact that the death took place in Mr. Farmer's pool has significance."

"I thought the significance was that Karen's house doesn't have a pool."

"Also the nudity."

I nodded.

"It must strike you as having some meaning," he said.

"I guess so."

"Or, maybe it wasn't murder per se. An accident. Some cops like to call accidents murder. I'm not one of them."

I waited, holding his gaze.

He crossed his arms over his narrow chest, gripping his biceps as if he wanted to reassure himself they were still there. "Let's consider this scenario...Your roommate has a thing with this gal. They do it by the pool. She gets clingy..."

"Did the autopsy show she'd had sex?"

He laughed. "What do you know about the morbid details of autopsies, sweetheart?"

"Just asking."

"So, the two of them go for a swim. Or, maybe they argue and it gets physical. She ends up in the pool. She's drunk. Maybe he's in the pool with her. Maybe the struggle all takes place in the pool. And next thing he knows, she's not breathing."

"Wow. I never thought of that." I kept my lips parted, shocked and awed by his clever insight, trying hard not to let my mouth twitch into a smile that might get out of control.

"However it played out, I get how he might have done what he had to do. I don't think that's murder in the same sense as lying in wait. A fight goes wrong, gets ugly. It's not murder. It's a fight, an accident. Going to bed, leaving her for someone else to find…I get that."

I crossed my legs and flung my hair over my shoulder.

He put his ankle on his opposite knee and leaned back as far as the couch would allow. He put his hands behind his head, clasping his fingers, spreading his elbows out to the side. "I respect the fact that you kept your suspicion to yourself. Him being your boss — you can't turn on him, no matter how much Miz Martin pressed you about what time you woke. It's perfectly logical that their fight woke you. Maybe you even saw it."

"No."

"Or heard it."

"No."

He smiled. "You seem like a gal who's sure about her place in the world."

"Knows her place?"

He laughed. "Yes, my initial instincts are always correct."

"That's impressive."

"You're an asset to his company. He's lucky to have you. Eye candy for the boys. I don't have a problem with women working for the police, as eye candy. But most gals won't put up with that. They want to be in charge. They want to be just like the guys. It's kind of sad. I'm sure a feminine gal like you agrees with me."

"I never thought about it that way."

He took that as agreement. "So there's nothing going on here? No romance between you and the CEO? Or the geek?"

I shook my head.

"Huh. I would have said otherwise."

I smiled.

"Not to overstep…I shouldn't do this on the job…but here we are, like it's fate. And the case is closed."

There was nothing fateful about it, but it was clear by now that he lived in a world he'd created inside his own head, and there was no way to pierce those walls with even the sharpest needle of reality.

"How about getting a drink sometime? You and me?"

"Sure."

He lowered his arms and uncrossed his leg. "Great. I guess my instincts aren't perfect. I did think you were with one of those two guys, or both. And maybe even the other gal." He winked.

"Nope."

"So a drink." He stood and reached into his pocket and pulled out a card. "Here's my info."

"I don't have a card, but you know where I live."

He laughed.

"Why don't we set a date now?" I said.

"Tonight?"

"How about tomorrow?" I said.

"Sure. You're the boss."

"I'm thinking…" I smiled.

"Yes?" He ran his finger down my arm, lifting a few strands of hair off my skin.

I shivered. "I was thinking — with your job, your reputation — maybe we shouldn't meet in Sydney."

He tilted his head and looked past me, obviously thinking of this for the first time.

"We could meet in Cronulla. I read about a fun bar right by the beach."

He nodded. "A bit of a drive for you."

"No worries. I love the train."

"Good idea." He walked to the door. "Looking forward to it."

"Me too."

He left the office and thumped across the foyer. He opened the front door and closed it loudly. The confident sounds suggested victory.

63

I ran upstairs and watched from the sitting area window as Bender got into his car. After turning on the engine and looking at his phone while the car idled, he pulled away from the curb. I returned to the first floor and made another latte. Tess was in the pool, swimming laps, moving so fast it seemed she was racing with a phantom as it glided effortlessly through the water beside her.

I returned to the office and shut the door.

I sipped my latte and opened Facebook.

There were no new comments from Carmen. That in itself was a victory. There were a few more page likes, the statue had acquired several more hearts, and some new comments had been added to the discussion of work-life balance. None of them were meaningful. Five additional people had watched the replay of the demo.

I needed to kick this page into turbo mode. The go-around with Carmen had slowed me down. I was letting her control the agenda. That side trip needed to end.

I returned to her last comment, before she'd gone off the rails accusing TruthTeller of being untruthful — *Luck? LUCK?!!*

In the light of my new information, I interpreted this to mean she felt Sean didn't deserve luck, therefore anything good in his life was not the result of luck, however that's defined. She believed he didn't deserve the statue. In fact, I guessed it had likely belonged to both him and his ex. Maybe it was a gift from Carmen. There were many possibilities. I hadn't considered any of that and sort of wished I'd asked Sean. But getting the information I did had taken considerable effort, and for now, he wasn't like to provide any more. It would have to be enough, so I shoved down my curiosity.

I posted a few quotes about finding your passion in life and added my thumb to the new comments. I went outside and snapped some photos — a bird of paradise blossom, a magpie strutting across the lawn, and a young, fragile snail with a nearly transparent shell. I returned to the office and posted all three, adding comments to each.

Returning to Carmen's snarky — *Luck?* — I hit reply.

Alex Teller: *We're all lucky in our own way.*

Her response was immediate, as if she'd known what I was going to say.

Carmen Dunn: *What's luck got to do with it?*

Alex Teller: *You don't believe in luck?*

Carmen Dunn: *Lucky belongs to those who are born lucky.*

Alex Teller: *Fair enough.*

Carmen Dunn: *Why are you posting all the updates on this page, if it's Sean's company?*

Alex Teller: *I'm in charge of social media.*

Carmen Dunn: *So even that's a misrepresentation — you only talk to us because you're paid.*

Alex Teller: *Lots of people do social media as a job.*

As we furiously typed our messages at each other, Jane and Lara weighed in on every line Carmen posted, adding thumbs and hearts and faces with open mouths — her own personal Greek chorus.

Carmen Dunn: *If this app is so special, he should be here talking about it.*

Alex Teller: *He will.*

Carmen Dunn: *When?*

Alex Teller: *When the timing is right.*

Carmen Dunn: *Dodging the truth again?*

Alex Teller: *Seriously. He's busy with the product right now. It's revolutionary. That sort of innovation doesn't happen without a lot of hard work.*

Carmen Dunn: *I'm sure.*

Carmen Dunn: *"TruthTeller". Makes me want to laugh and puke at the same time.*

Jane and Lara immediately added yellow faces with open mouths.

Alex Teller: *That's harsh.*

Carmen Dunn: *Truth is important to me — it's not a sales pitch.*

Alex Teller: *We all tell the truth when it's convenient, and avoid it when it's not.*

I clicked a winking face into its own comment box. I hit reply again.

Alex Teller: *That's why we need an app like TruthTeller, don't we, Carmen?*

No more comments appeared.

I'd finally shut her down. For now. I wasn't sure how good it was for our brand that this string of comments was out there, but from my perspective, it mostly made her look like a troll. I thought I came across as a friendly, charming, easy-going, truth-telling person.

I spent some time on Twitter and prepared a new report for Tess. I glossed over most of the action so far, focusing on the demo results, and then outlined my plan for the next two weeks.

When I returned to Facebook, my comment was the last one. It had twenty-seven likes, but nothing from Jane or Lara. I was rather surprised. Maybe this had worked in our favor after all. Carmen truly did come across like a troll and people were defending me with thumbs if not with their words. Of course, some people will click *like* for anything, so I couldn't read too much into it.

Since it was almost lunchtime, I decided to take myself out. I needed time to think about my plan for Bender. I also needed to establish a visible habit for my roommates, letting them know I would be going out more often, whenever I pleased. And I needed a quiet lunch without being required to navigate my way around Sean.

64

I changed out of the black dress and sandals. Although it was a fortuitous outfit for Bender's surprise visit and request for a date, I had serious shopping to do.

Most of the time, I'm not one of those women who likes to dress up for shopping, looking the part of the fashionista. I don't put on an appearance to attract the attention of aloof, beautifully dressed and made up clerks in an effort to demand they take me seriously as I'm trying on clothes or browsing the makeup counter. There are other ways to ensure people take you seriously. Neither do I go out looking as if I'm dressed to clean the bathroom.

I wore jeans and a tight black T-shirt and black leather jacket. I put on flat black ankle boots and grabbed an oversized black bag. The only things I put inside the bag were my wallet and phone, sunglasses and a floppy hat that folded easily into a small bundle. There was plenty of room left over to conceal my smaller purchases.

I ordered an Uber. While I waited, I scrolled through my phone looking for a restaurant. I found a place called Appetito in The Rocks. I'd do a few errands first, eat, and then head to that massive hall with its eclectic booths and offer of near anonymity.

It wasn't clear when the decision to kill Bender had solidified in my thoughts. Killing a cop is a huge risk, so I think my cautious side was pushing it away for quite a while. That, and the fact I wasn't overly passionate about trying to improve a cop's career growth. On top of all this, there was no guarantee any effort from me would change Detective Martin's situation at all. It sounded as though she would still have a boss working around the clock to keep her down. But maybe without a man prepared to spend the rest of his life belittling and badmouthing and booby-trapping every woman he encountered, she'd have a chance.

Martin was a nice enough person. Serious and dedicated. Relatively smart. I liked those things about her. Doing my part to make sure a woman is treated with respect and allowed to work on an equal footing carried more weight than her job description.

The other benefit was that maybe, without Bender, the police would back off from looking into John's death. They'd be too busy chasing madly after a cop killer they'd never find, if I was meticulous.

I'm good at what I do, but this required extra planning.

My first stop was the bank. I took out a thousand dollars. Killing is expensive, and doing it in a foreign country, to a cop, even more so.

Next, I went into an alley and put on the sunglasses and hat.

I arranged a new Uber for the forty minute drive to Cronulla, an upscale coastal town south of Sydney. When the driver let me off, I walked two blocks and entered the lobby of one of a handful of hotels — a high rise with half the rooms looking toward the water.

I booked a room for the following night, placing cash on the counter. The clerk scooped it up but he still wanted ID. I asked to see his manager.

A guy in a dark jacket came out of the office behind the front desk and walked around to where I stood. Pleased that I'd lucked out with a male manager, I sidled up to him and murmured in a low voice that it was my husband's fortieth birthday. My husband was a very crafty, curious guy and I couldn't have my name in the computer. I wouldn't put it past my husband to call every nice hotel in New South Wales, trying to find out whether I'd planned anything fun for him. I smiled eagerly.

The manager said it was against all the rules and he could get in trouble and my husband sounded rather controlling and how did I put up with that and all kinds of other hesitations. Finally, I reminded him what a fantastic hotel it was and how impressive it was that he was in such an important position at such a young age.

Five minutes later, I had the access card to a room on the seventh floor and was on my way out to the valet parking area, waiting for an Uber back to the city.

Lunch was the best Spaghetti Carbonara I'd ever eaten. I had a martini with my pasta which was very nice after so many nights of beer and wine. For a guy with all that money, it was surprising that Sean didn't suggest eating out more often. A nice restaurant can still provide a chummy, team-building experience. Sometimes it's even more fun — experimenting with new foods, sharing different tastes. Maybe he'd planned it and the constant distraction of the police kept it from ever being implemented.

Inside the building housing Paddy's Market with its cavernous ceilings and rows of booths and stands, crowds of people streamed past the displays, some hardly even glancing to the side, as if they were on an afternoon walk rather than a shopping expedition. I moved into the flow.

After less than two hours walking up and down the aisles I had everything — a new dress, a lightweight winter coat, and inexpensive but nice-looking high heeled ankle boots. The coat was white — striking and likely to make the temporary hair color I was planning memorable. I'd chosen a moderate heel height since Bender only had a few inches on me. I also had new lingerie and martini glasses.

On the way back to Sean's, I stopped for garbage bags, cleaning supplies, and duct tape. Everything fit into my oversized bag.

Next, I asked to be dropped at the mall where I had the coat, shoes, and glasses packaged and gift wrapped in three separate boxes with large white bows. If I ran into any of my roommates, I could explain I was shipping a few things to the states for a friend's birthday.

Another Uber driver pulled up to the curb outside the mall. She offered to stash my things in the trunk, but I assured her I was fine with the packages near my feet. I liked having them close by where I could feel prepared while I worked through my mental list for each step of the process.

Two big pieces were missing from my plan. First, I needed a way to get Bender to suggest a night in the hotel without sending him a text message or calling. I couldn't have any electronic contact with him. I'd have to rely on my manipulation in the moment.

If he didn't respond according to my expectations, I'd have to forego the entire thing, which was a waste of money. Besides, once I get my head set on a course of action, I'm driven to see it through. Changing plans now was becoming less acceptable with every minute that passed.

The other missing piece was something to immobilize him. Alcohol wasn't enough. Sure, most people get rather limp and their bodies are easy to control after a lot of drinking. But in some men, that phase is often very close to the vomit phase. And in a number of men, it doesn't go that way at all. It has the opposite effect.

Alcohol fires them up. It gets their blood pumping faster and wakens their rage. Controlling them becomes next to impossible. I could see Bender falling into that category.

65

My return to the house couldn't have worked out more perfectly to solidify myself as a woman getting out and about. If any of my roommates saw me leaving to meet Bender the next day, it would be less noteworthy.

As I closed the door behind me, Gavin appeared, coming from the office area.

"I was looking for you." He took a few steps closer. He leaned in as if about to kiss me, then moved back. He reached out and let his fingers slide along the silky, flat-ironed sheets of my hair.

I held up my packages. "Shopping."

"Can I help you carry them up?"

"I got it." I leaned toward him and kissed his jaw.

He looked relieved.

"You were gone quite a while."

"Lots of things I needed. And I had a nice lunch."

He nodded. "I was thinking — you and I should go out."

"Like a date?"

He smirked. "No need for a definition. Hiking, or something."

"That would be great."

As I turned to go up the stairs, Sean appeared on the landing. "A little early for Christmas, isn't it?" He took a few steps down.

I smiled up at him. "Birthday gifts."

"Ah. Very good. I love birthdays." He walked down the stairs. "Everything going smoothly on Facebook?"

"Yes."

"Good. No problems?"

"Not any more."

He looked like he wanted to hug me. He turned and headed toward the offices, following closely after Gavin.

I hurried up the stairs, unlocked my door, and stashed my supplies in the closet. I made a note in my phone that I'd have to take a trip out to dispose of the wrapping paper and boxes the following week.

I went out onto my balcony and smoked a cigarette. I leaned on the railing. Normally I sat in the chair, well back from the edge so only a small sliver of water was in my line of sight. It felt very bold, leaning over that dark pool. I closed my eyes and recalled seeing Karen floating there. She had indeed wanted something or she wouldn't have come to Sean's house. My guess, knowing the inclinations of her ex-husband, was she was looking for sex. A crude and sad effort to attract Sean's attention. It was understandable. What woman wouldn't be drawn to him?

I stretched my left arm overhead, then moved my cigarette to that hand and stretched the other arm.

Despite all the walking, my muscles felt hungry, as if I hadn't moved all day. I couldn't imagine sitting down and gluing my hand onto the mouse, spending the afternoon immobilized in front of the computer screen. I'd grab a glass of water and go for a walk. It was breezy and cool with a clear sky, the kind of crisp blue that makes you wonder why human beings ever spend a single daylight hour indoors.

At the end of Sean's front walk, I turned left and headed toward the harbor. Two blocks over was a tiny park shared by seven or eight homes situated around a cul de sac. From the edge of the park there was a partial view of Sydney Harbor.

I stood for a while and looked out at the distant water — so much deeper, vastly more dangerous, but mostly unreal and therefore unthreatening from that distance. It was pretty to look at, and I felt secure with trees and rocks and hundreds of houses between me and the water.

I still couldn't decide whether I would ask Gavin to teach me to swim. I knew I should learn, I knew I'd feel stronger. I knew it would give me one more way that I'd never be threatened by someone I didn't know. But each time the thought arose, it was immediately followed by a quick succession of images filling my mind.

Those images flipped past like a booklet with line drawings that becomes animated by the moving pages — I saw myself stepping into the pool, I felt the water creeping up my body as I walked down the stairs, I heard Gavin telling me to recline in the water and let it hold me, to put my face in while water lapped around my ears, filling my head.

Those images and sounds made my breath stop. I felt I was choking. I was overcome with the urge to suck in as much air as I could, letting it out in a rush, breathing until I was close to hyperventilating.

I turned away and walked quickly out of the park. I walked another six blocks before heading back. When I reached the end of Sean's street, Elizabeth came to mind. There was no sign of her in the yard. I wondered how she'd take to my ringing her doorbell. She'd seemed eager to talk to me, but ambivalent about whether or not she wanted to blurt out all of her thoughts, first speaking freely and then holding back. Eager to be friendly, afraid of saying too much.

If Sean's information was correct and she was selling weed, her caution made sense. There was no reason for him to make up a story like that, but it seemed so odd — a woman alone in that enormous house, running an edibles business. It made me want to laugh. Was she doing it for the money? She hadn't mentioned a husband. Only her son, the business partner. I tried to remember whether I'd seen a wedding ring on her finger, but I couldn't recall anything about her hands.

I approached her house and stopped in front of the iron gate.

What would be my rationale for ringing her bell? I could tell her the investigation into Karen's death was closed. She'd like that, relieved to know the cops would be spending less time in the neighborhood...

If she did sell edibles, she might be able to help me out. Weed doesn't have the power of a roofie, not even close. It doesn't provide the guaranteed result — complete unconsciousness — but it would help get me where I needed to go.

I unlatched the gate and walked to the porch. It was crowded with ceramic pots glazed in gorgeous glistening colors — rust and dark blue and teal and yellow. They were filled with unusual plants. I didn't know any of their names. One looked like a cross between a large red artichoke and a sea anemone. The bottom petals spread out flat like the outer leaves of an artichoke and the round cluster in the center had individual tube-like pieces. I touched it, surprised by its strength.

I stepped up to the door and rang the bell.

Elizabeth answered a moment later. Her feet were bare and she wore a sea green unitard. Her hair was woven into a tight braid and her face, free of makeup, was damp and shiny. I glanced at her hand. A silver band on the middle finger of her left hand. Three rings with tiny blue and red and green stones on the ring finger of her right.

"Perfect timing," she said. "I just finished yoga. Come in."

She offered me a chair at a table in an octagonal alcove that was lined with floor to ceiling windows. The sun streamed in, making it feel like a summer afternoon. I took off my jacket while she boiled water for tea. I wondered if it would be cannabis tea.

"Cinnamon okay?" she said.

I nodded. I hate cinnamon anything, but I had more important things to address, I wasn't going to waste energy and effort on the flavor of tea.

She moved around the kitchen, chattering about her yoga routine and her plans for the garden. Watching her and listening to her talk was jarring. Her voice had the slight breathiness of age, and the skin of her arms and ankles and feet was thin and papery, but her movements were like those of a woman my age. Maybe it was the yoga. Maybe it was the result of consuming some of her own edibles.

She put the cups of steaming cinnamon on the table. The vapor filled my nostrils with a smell that made me think of burned leaves, a thick sweetness that carried the suggestion of something rotting.

"Thanks." I touched the saucer. "I only stopped by to tell you they decided Karen's death was suicide." As soon as I said it, I wasn't sure at all that was the decision. I suppose it was what they were saying, but based on Bender's comments, there was still quite a bit of doubt. I didn't believe any of his speculations about Sean, which was another reason to be rid of him. Sean didn't need that hanging out there for an indefinite length of time, knowing they might change their minds and follow up on Bender's crazy, self-serving story. Given my cushy life right now, Sean's interests were my interests.

"I'm glad to hear that." Elizabeth picked up her cup and took a sip of tea.

I let mine continue cooling. I studied her face.

"And?" she said.

I gave her a confused look.

"Why else did you stop by?"

"Just that."

"I don't think so."

I smiled. "Are you a psychic?"

"No. But I can feel something else. There's a tension about you."

"No tension."

"You want something."

"You're very perceptive. It feels like mind reading."

She laughed. "Just age. When you've been around enough people for enough years, you start to sense when they want to speak and they're not. You sense when they're angry, upset…"

"Okay."

"And I watch people. I have to be careful, with my business. Not as much as I used to, things have relaxed. But still."

"Your edibles?"

"I wondered whether Sean told you. When I saw you lingering around the gate…If you were just coming up here to tell me about the cops…well, you wouldn't have hesitated."

I tried not to inhale the scent of the tea as I forced my fingers to grip the thin handle and raise the cup to my lips. I took a tiny sip.

"Why did you say cinnamon was okay if you don't like it?"

I put down the cup.

"You don't strike me as the type to favor politeness over your own wishes," she said.

"I honestly don't know. It just seemed easier."

"Let me make you another cup."

"No thanks." I pushed the cup and saucer away from me. The cup was pure white with a thin black line around the rim, mirrored on the saucer. Very nice and fitted to my taste. I wished it could have been filled with something I liked.

"So why are you here?"

"As a customer."

She smiled. "Sean likes to smoke. But women tend to favor edibles. Maybe they're more health conscious."

"Not all women."

"This is true." She pushed out her chair. "I'll show you what I have."

She took me to the second floor and down to the end of a long, narrow hall. The doors lining the hallway were closed, making it almost as dark as evening. Because of this, I expected the rooms to be dark — an illogical assumption. She opened the door into a large corner room with two bay windows. It was filled with light, but no direct sun. The walls were painted pale pink and lined with glossy white bookcases between the windows. Like a bona fide shop, the cases were filled with oils and lotions and edible products. In one corner was a shoulder-height refrigerator unit with a glass door.

Her supply was astonishing — everything from tea to hard candies. She had a limited amount of baked goods, telling me she preferred to make those to order, and that she could get me a banana bread or brownies or cookies that afternoon.

I settled on something I'd never seen before — large green olives infused with cannabis. It was perfect for me. Rather than trying to persuade Bender to eat candy or a cookie, I would enhance the martini I'd planned for him. Although, another unknown — not everyone likes olives. He seemed more like a maraschino cherry guy.

Elizabeth told me she'd been in business for twelve years. She'd done very well, after her husband died leaving her with nothing but a house that had been too large even for two, and a pile of debt.

She was very invested in a neighborhood that remained stable, filled with people she knew and trusted. It was why she'd desperately hoped Karen would return to the house across the street. A neighborhood with people who didn't interfere. Pleasant people. Open-minded people.

A neighborhood without the constant presence of the police.

66

The front door opened before I could touch the handle. Sean stood just inside, hands in his pockets. "You need to get all that stuff about the statue off the Facebook page."

"Why? Did something happen?"

"You bet something happened. You pissed her off."

"Did she write something else?"

"No, but I read your exchange with her. She will."

"Are you going to let me in?"

He moved away from the door. I walked into the house, pressing my hand against my jacket pocket to hold the cannabis-infused olives in place. I hoped the jar wasn't bulging out terribly. Not that he would mind, or care. But it was just better to keep that purchase to myself.

"I'll watch while you do it," he said.

"We already had this conversation."

"And I made a mistake, letting it stay. I don't want her commenting on the statue. She's taking over our profile. She's going to blow up over this. I can feel it." He pulled out the chair in front of the desk in his office and I sat down.

"I think it would be better if you talked to her," I said.

"Not possible. We don't need personal stuff all over the internet. You need to figure out another way to get people excited. The app should be enough. It's revolutionary. There's nothing else like it on the market."

"Selling an app, selling any product is not revolutionary. It's boring."

"This will practically sell itself."

"She's not going to stop making comments. If I take it down, she'll get more riled up, based on what I've seen from her so far." I woke the computer. The browser was already open to Facebook. "If you're so upset, you could have done this yourself. It's not complicated."

"I know that. I want you to do it. You're responsible. It's your job. And I want you to think about the problems you've caused. I want you to think about all the positive fans that are now going to have a bad taste in their mouths."

He sounded like my father. He acted as if I were a defiant child in need of punishment.

"I didn't cause any problems. I had no way of knowing someone from your past would start attacking you over a piece of art." I pushed myself away from the desk and looked up at him. "I think you aren't really sure. Otherwise you would have done it yourself. I think you just want me to convince you it will all work out."

He looked at me, his eyes burning with something. Rage? Fear?

I pushed the chair farther away from the desk. "Did Tess tell you they're done looking into Karen's death?"

"Yes."

"So that's a relief."

"We aren't done with the police," he said. "They'll be back to talk about John. Always sniffing around."

"But not as much. Since he didn't die on your property."

"You're changing the subject. How are you going to fix this? How are you going to get rid of her?"

"There isn't any way to be rid of her. It's best to ignore her. She'll flame out."

"I never wanted my company to be the kind that fires people, but I should terminate you for this."

"But you don't want to." I smiled. "And you know it's not really my fault. It's yours, for having some woman in your past who wants to bring you down. The photo of the statue isn't the problem."

He clenched and unclenched his fists, his shoulders pulled up toward his ears.

I stood and pushed the chair under the desk. "You wouldn't really fire me."

He stopped the flexing of his fists and pinched the bridge of his nose between his thumb and index finger. He stared past me, breathing hard. After a minute, he let go of his nose. "I don't know how to deal with you. Yes, I often think the company would be better off without you. But Tess…" He folded his arms across his chest. He walked to the couch and collapsed onto it. "I may have baggage, but you provoked her. You invited this by putting up something personal."

"I had no way of knowing it would cause a problem."

"Even if you had known, I wonder if you would have done it anyway. You seem to like stirring the pot."

I walked to the couch. I sat beside him and put my hand on his leg.

"What are you doing?" he said.

"Trying to talk to you. In some ways, this might not be so bad. Let her spin out of control. She already has two cheerleaders reacting to every word she types. It could be one of those things that gets us attention, if there's a huge drama. You know they say there's no such thing as bad PR."

He pushed my hand off his leg. "I don't subscribe to that belief. Maybe Americans see things that way, but Australia is different."

"You're trying to market a global product, other countries besides Australia are important."

"I don't *want* this exploding. She could really damage me."

"How?"

"I just can't believe this is happening. I can't believe she found me. I can't believe…"

"Okay. There's a lot of things you can't believe. But this is reality. You can either let it ride or kill the post. If I delete it, I have no doubt she'll make an even bigger deal out of it. The only other solution would be to delete the page entirely. And then what? We already had a demo. We have followers and fans. We'd have to change the product name. And she knows you well enough…she can easily find us again."

He stood and went to the windows. It seemed as if he was trying to run away from me — first sinking into the couch, now escaping to the windows. I crossed my legs and waited for him to say something.

"Do you want to sabotage this venture?" he said.

"Why would you say that?"

"Because of what you did. Why can't you see how invasive it was? How it brought her out of the shadows? It's the statue that got her riled up. Not me. She never tried to contact me before you put up that picture." He turned and adjusted the shutters. He looked out at the yard. His shoulders were curved toward his chest again. He still looked like he wanted to punch me, or someone, or maybe the window, shoving his fist through the glass.

I walked toward him. His perspective was completely

distorted. He was so upset about whatever Carmen might say to him, or do on the Facebook page, he was letting her have all the power. He needed to let go and let her do whatever she wanted. It could definitely turn out to be something positive for the company. It wasn't as if she was the person he'd broken up with. What could she possibly do to damage the app? He would cause more damage trying to hide something at this point. Why couldn't he see that?

I moved up until I was a few feet behind him. Maybe the guy was just horny. He was so wound up — about everything. He lived like a monk in that room — nearly empty except for the statue. He never went out. The only thing he did was swim laps in that rather small pool which I don't think was enough to get rid of all that energy.

I put my hand on his neck, feeling his hair across the back of my hand, the warmth of his skin. I slid my hand up his scalp.

I heard a quick intake of breath and then he lurched away from me, turning and stumbling toward the desk. His upper thigh slammed into the corner and he groaned, but it was a sound of pleasure. "You need to leave."

I smiled.

"Now."

"Are you sure?"

He closed his eyes. "There's something deeply wrong with you."

I waited. His eyes remained closed.

"Please leave me alone."

"If that's what you want."

I turned and walked slowly out of his office. I didn't look back to see whether he opened his eyes.

67

The room was pitch black when Sean woke. At night, he kept the shutters tightly closed. There was no nightlight in the bathroom. He hardly ever woke before the alarm so there was no need. On the rare occasions when he did wake, he liked the comfort of total darkness.

Now, he wasn't sure what had caused him to rise up out of his dream so fast his head spun as if he'd had too much to drink. Something was different, the temperature seemed warmer than it should be at this hour of the night. Although rarely being awake at this hour didn't make him an expert on that point. He turned on his side.

There was no way to know the time. His phone was stored in a drawer in the closet, the charging cord threaded out through the narrow space he left, not closing the drawer fully. Even that tiny flash when a silent text appeared on the screen felt like an intrusion. Absurd as the possibility might be, he didn't like the inaudible hum of electronic devices disturbing his sleep, altering his brain waves. He loved technology, loved what it could do for a human being, and loved its potential for correcting the world's ills, but he didn't like the grip it had on a person's life.

The natural world and human interaction were important. Critical. Life-giving.

When Tess told him they would be marketing the app

primarily on social media, he'd had huge doubts. She was so sure of herself, and he'd hired her for that confidence. He didn't doubt that was the way most people marketed their ideas now, and he was absolutely certain that social media was the only sure way to reach the vast majority of people. But still, it irked him.

Alex's insistence that he needed to expose his personal side, her push to do something attention-getting, made him even more uncomfortable. And now look what had happened. He had no idea how to fix it, and he knew she didn't either.

The way she'd touched him, suggesting she wanted to fuck was unbearably disturbing. He couldn't decide whether she was manipulating him or wanted to start something. He wasn't even sure she liked him and at the same time, he was disgusted with himself for thinking in those terms. He was already off balance, unsure whether he could be alone with her. Now…

Had there been a dream about Facebook, or the statue? Carmen? Was that what had woken him at an hour he couldn't identify? It might be just a few minutes before midnight. It was equally possible it was close to dawn.

Why did the room feel so warm? He threw off the duvet. He moved his pillows, shoving one to the side and pulling one with a cooler case beneath his head.

The air, silent and heavy, seemed to move stealthily around him.

He sat up suddenly. Was there someone in the room? He might have heard a subtle intake of breath. Or was he still half dreaming, imagining the statue had come to life? It was human-sized, and so life-like. In the semi-darkness of pre-dawn, he'd often marveled at how real it looked. A woman standing there, wanting him, stretching languidly, looking pliable despite being carved out of oak.

The darkness appeared softer now and he thought he could just make out the shape of the figure. Maybe his eyes had adjusted, lying here utterly sightless for several minutes. Had the statue moved closer to the bed? He couldn't be sure. No, he was sure. It hadn't moved and of course it hadn't come to life. What was the matter with him?

His dreams must have been tangled and confused. And in this half-waking-half-sleeping state, his mind was drifting to all sorts of fantasies and odd arrangements of reality and imagination and desire.

He heard another breath. This time he was certain. He moved to the side of the bed, feeling around for the light switch. It was just out of reach.

"Is someone there?"

He heard breathing, definitely breathing. He felt a gentle movement, a shadowy figure took a step away from the wall opposite his bed.

Suddenly, he knew. "What the fuck is your problem?" His voice was rough and hard, despite having been asleep. "Don't you have any boundaries at *all*?" He crashed out of bed and slammed his fist on the light switch. The overhead light came on and he rolled back onto the bed to cover himself with the sheet. He wasn't modest but neither did he like that nutter coming into his room every time she felt like it.

He looked up, squinting in the bright overhead light.

It was Tess. She stood a few feet from the foot of his bed. She wore skimpy black underpants and nothing else. Her dark, almost black hair covered the fronts of her shoulders leaving a small piece of pale skin exposed on either side. Her breasts made him gasp and he felt a surge of desire flood his body. "I thought you were Alex."

She continued studying him, slowly moving closer to the bed. She stepped to the side to avoid the footboard, brushing her fingertips across the twisted duvet.

"What are you doing?"

She smiled. "Waiting."

"Why do women do this? I don't get it."

"Women?"

"You. Karen. Standing there half naked."

He shouldn't have said it, but the thought rushed through his mind and it came out before he realized the pitfall. Trying to determine why Tess, specifically, was standing half naked in his room was too unsettling. He couldn't think. Now it was too late.

"Karen?"

"Never mind."

"Was Karen here?"

"I said never mind. Why are you doing this?"

"Don't men like women who take the initiative?" She moved closer.

"Men aren't a monolithic beast," he said. "We like different things."

"I know. But in general."

"No. Not in general. We're individuals. With different desires. Different…everything."

She looked sad, but continued moving toward him. "There's something wrong with our business model. We're more creative living like this, more connected to each other as friends, but we can't be celibate." She sat on the side of the bed. She put her hand on the sheet, her fingers probing for his shin. When she found it, she held on, like Alex had done earlier.

"Don't do this. I can't."

"No strings."

"I can't do this. I've taken a vow."

She smiled. "A vow? How quaint."

"I'm serious. No sex. You need to leave."

"Are you rejecting me?"

"No, I'm rejecting sex. I can't."

She laughed. "Who does that?" She moved her hand up his leg, scooting along the bed so her reach was farther.

"Please."

"I'm not looking for a relationship. Not at all. I don't think that would be good for the company. But we're adults. With needs."

He couldn't take his eyes off her breasts, her crossed legs. He groaned. "Please go." He moved his leg away from her. He pulled his knees up to his chest. "I'm serious. I can't do this."

"Because you were expecting Alex?"

"No! I wasn't expecting anyone. She comes into my room all the time…"

Tess raised her eyebrows slightly.

"I assumed…" He couldn't stop looking. Now that she was so close, he could almost touch her breasts. But he refused. He was stronger than that.

She moved her hand. "I thought it was a good idea. We like each other, we respect each other. We can…"

"No. I'm sorry. Please go."

She looked at him with such longing he thought he might

collapse, but he managed to keep the thought from revealing itself on his face. She stood and walked to the door. She picked up a terrycloth robe from the floor and wrapped it around her. "The business is doomed if we don't change," she said.

"You can go out any time you'd like. Meet other people. Have relationships."

"Can I? That hasn't been my impression."

"I'm not keeping you a prisoner."

"I know. But there's an inertia."

"It was the police. All the suspicion. We can live normal lives, now that they're gone."

"It wasn't them." She opened the door and went out.

He slid under the sheet. His skin had the consistency of a steamed dumpling. He felt sick with desire and a lost chance. He'd always moved relentlessly forward in his life, never spending much time second-guessing or indulging regrets. Now, he wished he could re-wind the clock.

68

No one noticed me leaving to catch my Uber. Since I'd be arriving back at Sean's house well after two in the morning, although hopefully not so far after that the sky would be growing light, neither did I expect to be seen then. But after Tess caught me leaving Gavin's room, I was reminded that the potential was always there. I was sure I had it all worked out, I just needed to stay alert.

The driver let me out two blocks from the hotel and I went to the room I'd booked earlier. First, I dyed my hair a brilliant copper color. Before I took a shower to rinse the excess, I scrubbed the bathroom, making sure every droplet of red was gone, as if I were cleaning up blood.

After my shower, I put on my new outfit — a tight dress with a white and black geometric design and the black high-heeled ankle boots. I used a curling iron to create piles of tendrils and coils in my hair. I did my makeup, applying a primer followed by foundation and powder that made my skin as pale as I could. I used various shades of green shadow around my eyes, including a dark green eyeliner circling my entire eye.

I put on the white coat and went down the back stairs and out into an alley, avoiding the lobby and any possible attention from the front desk or the concierge.

I was only five minutes late meeting Bender at the place I'd suggested.

He was shocked by my appearance. He couldn't stop staring at my hair. He kept asking if I felt okay because I looked like I was going to pass out. The one thing he didn't do was ask why I'd made such dramatic changes. I think the red hair was too exciting for him. The very act of dying it suggested I was teasing. He liked that.

I ordered a glass of white wine. He asked for a whisky and soda. I put my hand on his arm. "I have a reputation for mixing incredible martinis. The best you've ever tasted. I thought we could have one...later." I smiled. "So maybe just wine for now?"

He changed his order.

With only one or two prompts to get him going, he talked about being a detective, about growing up watching American movies set during Prohibition and how he longed to be like the detectives in those shows. He talked about his skill at sailing and surfing, and described his fifteen-foot sailboat with precise detail — about as much attention to detail as I'd put into adjusting the appearance of my face.

We talked for nearly an hour, through three glasses of wine, for him. I made my first last through his second and third. Mostly he talked, I listened and smiled. I was surprised by his lengthy life story. I'd expected him to want to make an immediate trip to a hotel room.

"You've made this quite pleasant," he said.

"How is that?"

"I know you and your housemates are all a bunch of fucking liars." He laughed. "Don't think you've fooled someone with my years on the force, with my instincts."

I smiled and took a tiny sip of wine. "How do you know when someone's lying?" He clearly didn't realize the dramatization of a lie going on right in front of him.

"The minute I saw all of you. Four hot people living together, but *Oh no, Detective Bender, no one is banging anyone. We're all colleagues. We're professionals. We respect each other.*" He laughed, a loud rough sound like a cough.

"It's the truth."

He held up his hand in a slicing gesture, as if slitting his throat, or mine. "Like I said, I get it. Sean was negligent. There are things to cover up. She came on to him, but it wasn't his fault she drowned. Just…"

"Negligence," I said.

"Exactly."

"The failure to take proper care," I said.

He gave me an odd look. "What are you, a fucking dictionary?"

"Just making conversation."

"I don't mind looking the other way. Especially once he let me know there was a perk like you." He put his hand on my leg.

I tried to keep my voice level, curious and not at all disturbed. "Sean said that?"

He grinned.

Was it severely twisted or an outright lie? Sean had his quirks, but still… Most likely, it was Bender's imagination, so proud of himself for how well he'd done getting rid of Detective Martin, so caught up in his own story of the events.

"I mean…" he sipped his wine, "…it was clear that you were available to all of them. Sooo…"

When the server came by and offered another round of

drinks, I put my hand on Bender's wrist and looked up at the server. "I think we're ready to go." I turned to Bender and offered him an inviting smile.

He pulled out his wallet and handed over his credit card.

Without any direct conversation about where we were headed, I steered him toward the hotel where I'd booked my own room. It's a small town, the hotel was a block and a half from the bar. It was the obvious choice.

"You are one classy lady," he said.

"Why is that?"

"You make it easy. You don't play games and give me all kinds of grief about the situation here. In fact, I think you're as hot for me as I am for you."

"Was there doubt?"

He leaned over and bit my earlobe.

"Do you mind asking for a room on the top floor?" I said.

"What's it matter?"

"It's just a thing I have. I like to be on top."

He nearly ran to the desk and a few minutes later he returned, ushering me toward the elevators.

The rest was routine, and not as difficult as I'd expected. Once we were in the room, I opened the sliding door and stepped onto the balcony, looking out at the glistening dark water in the distance. I urged him to come out and enjoy the cool evening air and the view. He moved up next to me and kissed me. I leaned against the railing.

After a few minutes, I told him I needed to run back to the car for my bag. He didn't wonder about the car, too busy being annoyed that I was leaving, even if only for a few minutes. I told him I had vodka and glasses and everything, even the most fantastic olives I'd ever tasted. I'd make us killer martinis and we could really get the party going.

When I returned to the room after stopping for a bucket of ice, he laughed at my large bag. "You gals sure need a lot of stuff."

I smiled. I pulled out the glasses, a bottle of vodka, vermouth, and Elizabeth's olives.

We stood on the balcony again, his hand creeping up the back of my leg, and sipped martinis. He wasn't thrilled with the olives — considered them unnecessary decoration. I was forced to show him the beauty of olives by holding each one gently in my mouth and feeding it into his. Then, he chewed quickly, making sharp, tiny movements with his jaw, eager for the next. He ended up eating his three large olives as well as the three from my drink.

According to Elizabeth, three of those extra large olives had enough cannabis to ignite two people. She advised martinis with a single olive, two at best, and only for someone who regularly ingested edibles and was used to the different effect compared with smoke.

She was telling the truth. Between olives and kisses to prolong the moments, he was feeling a major buzz. He slumped against the railing, working overtime to keep his head from lolling to the side.

"That was one helluva martini." His words were thick and incomplete, as if several whole olives remained inside his mouth and his tongue was trying to work its way around them.

I eased him onto one of the balcony chairs and suggested he take a little rest while I changed into something a bit more fun.

"I don't feel so good," he said.

"You'll be fine. Just take it easy."

"Did you put…" He let his head fall back against the railing.

I moved to the doorway and leaned against the frame. Waiting. I longed for a cigarette, but I couldn't risk pulling him out of the unconscious state overtaking his brain.

Finally, his elbow slid off the arm of the chair. His shoulder slumped low, dragging his head with it. I was surprised he didn't slide completely off the chair.

Time was tight.

I went into the bathroom. I opened my second bottle of dye and transformed my hair back to a nondescript brown. I scrubbed my face free of makeup. While the color set, I cleaned the bathroom, washed the glasses, and stashed vodka, olives, and everything else back into my gym bag.

Every three or four minutes, I checked on Bender.

I showered and rinsed my hair. I blew it dry on the hot setting. I dressed in jeans, a blue T-shirt, and a white hoodie. I pulled up the hood and left it sitting loosely around my hair, a few strands showing at the front, latte brown against the white fabric. I put on socks and running shoes and stuffed a cleaning rag in my back pocket.

After a last sweep of the room, I returned to the balcony.

The most difficult part was ahead of me. In comparison, feeding him the olives in such a seductive, gag-inducing way, getting him to drink the martini at all, and guiding him to this hotel where the balconies were free of modern safety measures, had been easy. Choosing the hotel where someone had recently fallen from the tenth floor would help divert attention from a dead cop to the tragedy itself.

By leaning his torso over the railing, then squatting and heaving his body up as if I were doing squats in a barbell cage, I managed to pitch him over the edge.

I barely registered the unpleasant sound of his body hitting pavement. I had to move fast, foregoing the temptation to look down and see how quickly a crowd gathered at this hour. I wiped the railing and chair where he'd been seated and the handle of the sliding door. I used the rag to press down on the handle of the exterior door. I stepped into the hallway. It was empty. I slung the strap of my gym bag over my shoulder and walked quickly to the stairwell. I trotted down the steps.

On the first floor, I pulled off the hoodie and shook out my hair. I opened the door and walked through the lobby as slowly as I could. It was nearly empty, the desk clerk and any guests who had been getting into or emerging from elevators were now out in the street looking at the hideous sight of a man's body smashed on the pavement. I turned away from the stream of blood running from his head.

Continuing my casual pace, I walked five blocks to a coffee shop with live evening music where I put in the order for an Uber. I scooped my fingers through my hair, tousling it so I looked like I'd just finished a caffeinated evening of serious conversation and good music. I smiled at nothing in particular.

It was one-forty-three when the Uber dropped me at Sean's, much better timing than I'd expected. The house was dark. Inside, it was silent. Still, my heart rate maintained the accelerated rhythm it had kept up during the walk through the lobby and the entire forty minute car ride. It didn't settle until I was in my bedroom, the door locked, and my gym bag in the closet. I'd have to get rid of things the following day. Being back in the house as soon as possible, anticipating being seen by a roommate, was a higher priority.

Hopefully the loads of cannabis in Bender's blood wouldn't be too much hindrance from a ruling of suicide.

69

The following morning I woke burning with energy and ready for something new, such as learning to swim.

Before I broached that topic, I needed to enjoy a cheerful breakfast with my housemates and find out whether Tess had indulged in any more midnight drinks or whether anyone else had noticed my absence. I took a shower and put my wet hair in a ponytail. I dressed in spandex Capri pants, a long T-shirt, and walked quietly down the stairs.

No one else was up.

I made scrambled eggs with cheese and tomatoes and jalapeños. I fried pork sausages, turning them dark brown with crispy skin, aiming to fill the house with an enticing aroma, drawing the others down to the kitchen. The espresso machine was ready to start brewing. Champagne flutes were filled with orange juice, waiting to be topped with champagne for a proper Sunday morning brunch. Toast was being kept warm in the oven.

As predicted, they all arrived in the kitchen within fifteen minutes of starting the sausages.

When they were all seated and their bellies halfway to being satisfied, I launched a conversation about favorite weekend activities. Nothing emerged regarding the previous evening. Despite the desire for all of us to escape the hothouse, we rarely took that initiative. I couldn't figure out whether it was Sean's personality that seemed to hold us in thrall, not wanting to miss a moment, even though many of those moments were empty, or a deep, barely acknowledged sense that we were stagnant. Maybe we felt compelled to stay in the house because we knew we ought to be working overtime, even though we were not.

Sean mentioned the rugby game he and Gavin had watched the night before. Their team lost, which sent them to bed early. Tess looked distant, managing to smile vaguely without making eye contact. If she'd seen me, her eyes would have been boring into mine.

I cleaned up the kitchen and the others drifted away to find a movie or something else on TV to pass the time.

The doorbell rang while I was cleaning out the espresso machine. I took a deep breath. No one would come to inform us of Bender's death this quickly.

I went to the front door.

Detective Joiner stood on the patio. She smiled. "May I come in?"

I tried to keep my shoulders from rising and the sound of my deep sigh inaudible.

She walked into the foyer and looked up the spiral staircase. People often did. I suppose because it was so elegant, and rather unusual. But since all our visitors had been detectives, maybe it was their habit to look at anything for possible insight and evidence. For me, the feature of the entryway was the glass enclosed pond surrounded by plants, home to several water turtles. Once a week someone came to clean the pond, trim the plants, and make sure there were plenty of snails and water insects for the turtles.

"Are your housemates here?"

I nodded.

"I'd like to talk to all of you."

I escorted her to the living room, taking slow, careful breaths as I walked. The request was odd, but it didn't mean it was related to Bender. My mind was filled with an image of his pulverized body, but that image wouldn't be consuming Detective Joiner. There was no image, for her. I had to keep my perspective. Even if she already knew, it was unlikely that was the reason for her visit.

Tess, Gavin, and I sat on the couch, Sean sat on the floor, leaning against an armchair while Joiner took a seat across from us.

"I wanted to let you know the status of our investigations."

The plural was concerning. Didn't she know we'd already been informed Karen's case was closed? Hadn't she talked to Bender? Or was that his bullshit, targeted at me rather than a truthful update? For all I knew, the removal of Martin wasn't the truth either.

"We've reached a wall in our inquiry into John North's death."

It seemed we held our collective breaths, but maybe it was only me.

"Because we found nothing in his finances or during interviews with neighbors and acquaintances to offer a line for further inquiry, we developed a theory of a hired killer."

This felt a little close for comfort.

"A hit man?" Gavin said.

The room was quiet for a moment.

"Something like that. Yes," Detective Joiner said.

This was one time when I appreciated the pervasive

gender bias toward men in certain roles. I smiled inside, but kept my face like a sheet of opaque glass.

"The theory we've developed is that Mrs. North, for a reason we haven't determined, hired someone to kill her husband. It fits with the lack of physical evidence."

We waited. I was pleased that my colleagues and roommates were equally cautious about expressing their reactions. It wouldn't matter, they had nothing to say that would damage me, but still, I was pleased.

"We'll continue to pursue that theory. And we believe it explains her suicide. It doesn't entirely explain her nudity and her choice of your pool, but in the bigger picture, those items are less important. We learned that Mrs. North didn't know how to swim. That might point to an accident, but then, there were no abrasions on the body to suggest any kind of accidental fall into the pool." She gripped the arms of the chair and pushed herself forward. "So…"

"Does this mean we don't need to expect any more detectives knocking on the door?" Sean said.

"We have no further questions at this time. Unless…"

It felt as if all of us sucked in air and held it.

She stood. "Unless any of you recall Mrs. North saying something that might give additional weight to this theory?" She looked from face to face, deliberately moving her head a few fractions of an inch to take in each one of us individually.

We shook our heads simultaneously.

"Thank you for your time." She nodded once, turned, and walked to the front door. A moment later, it opened and closed softly.

People are horrified by suicide. For a good reason, I think.

The will to survive is supposed to be the strongest drive of all — superseding safety, food, comfort, sex, companionship, and the search for meaning. It's the reason I fight against water. That rush of liquid swallowing my breath, threatening to suck it away forever, is instinctive. I don't have to think about thrashing my way to the surface. I didn't have to think about twisting away from my father's hands as they tried to hold me under the waters of baptism — my body took control.

It's the same when a car pulls out in front of you, your foot flies to the brake of its own volition, pressing down with all the force available in your body.

It happens when you're alone on a dark street and you hear footsteps that grow more rapid behind you. Grabbing for the railing is instinctive when you're on top of a tall building. Gripping the handlebar when you're pitching forward in a roller coaster car is an independent action of your will, driven by the animal brain's scream for survival, even when the threat isn't actual death, just a message to the central nervous system that it's more within the realm of possibility than it was a moment earlier.

As a collective group of beings, we can't get our heads around a person's decision to override those instinctive responses. We can't comprehend nothingness. We can't imagine the unknown being more welcome than the known. Even the worst pessimist among us has logical thoughts suggesting a situation that's horrid at any given moment has the potential to improve. Even if the odds are small, the *potential* remains.

It's the reason people can't comprehend suicide bombers. The willingness to override the drive to live is impossible to understand on its own. Secretly, we marvel at the kind of belief that is so intense it trusts there is indeed something fascinating and satisfying and better on the other side. Something so wonderful, it must be had right now.

No one in my church youth group could understand why Tony took his life. His mother thought she knew, but that wasn't all of it. Millions, probably billions of hearts are broken every year. Most go on to glue the pieces back together. The majority even manage to do it seamlessly, leaving no evidence of the damage. Only a few decide that a shattered heart should stop beating. There were other things, a different genetic makeup, that caused Tony to take that step. It wasn't because I told him to stop sending me poems. Or that I said I'd never love him.

None of us knew why Karen ended her life. There was still a fair amount of murkiness around it, the slim possibility that she'd stumbled and fallen. But as Detective Joiner pointed out, there were no abrasions on her hands or knees to prove that conclusion.

Did she do it simply because Sean didn't come out and affirm her desirability? It seems unlikely. The theory of a hired killer and later remorse was as good as any. But still, her decision was difficult to grasp.

If the theory was correct, she'd gone to a lot of trouble and expense to be rid of her ex-husband. She must have been certain of what she wanted. Why the sudden remorse?

Possibly Detective Martin might think Bender had felt extreme remorse for trying to sabotage her career. Perhaps not. She knew his type, and remorse wasn't high on his list of qualities.

Surely the police force was huddled in a corner discussing

various causes, just as the Pure Truth Tabernacle kids did after Tony's death. They must wonder why a tough guy would do something so weak. They would wonder why someone so in love with his job would decide to quit for eternity.

Of course there would be questions into whether Bender's death was truly suicide. They'd interview his friends and colleagues. They'd go over the room with tweezers, and blood- and semen-revealing lights. They'd comb the carpet and bed for skin cells and hairs. They'd scour his home for a note, or anything suggesting despair. Maybe other misdeeds, not the kind that were overlooked by the hierarchy, but drugs or prostitution or taking bribes would be considered and investigated. They would take a long time to swallow the idea of suicide.

Eventually, I was confident, they would.

70

A moment after the front door closed, ushering Detective Joiner out of their lives, Tess turned toward Sean. She kept her gaze steady until he became aware of her focused attention and turned to meet her eyes. "I need to talk to you for a few minutes," she said. "My office?"

He nodded.

She stood and walked to the foyer. Gavin and Alex remained on the couch, as silent as they'd been during the detective's wrap-up. Hopefully it was truly a wrap-up. It sounded like a wrap-up. Although she was starting to feel that an awful lot of people died under somewhat suspicious circumstances and nothing was ever resolved. The answers remained elusive. It was like life itself — so many things left unresolved at the end of every day, every year, and at the end of your life. She thought of her father's sudden departure from the world. A car crashing, metal tearing, then silence.

TV and movies and novels gave the impression every unnatural death was explainable. Maybe that was the attraction to those kinds of stories — not the fantasy of perfectly administered justice, but the simple knowledge of what the hell happened.

She stepped into the office and turned.

"Why don't we go out for another mimosa, or even better, a Bloody Mary?" Sean said.

She nodded.

Twenty minutes later they were seated in a dark pub. Blood red drinks glistening with ice cubes sat on the narrow oak table between them. If she sat facing him straight on and he did the same, their knees would touch. Acutely aware of this, both of them were angled sideways on their respective benches.

"I wanted to clear the air," she said.

"Please don't think…"

"I'm not looking for an explanation," she said.

"I'm sorry I…"

"Or an apology. Let me finish."

He nodded, his eyes wide and the pupils somewhat small despite the dim light.

"I had a bit too much scotch Friday night. You drink very nice scotch, by the way." She smiled. "But that's not an excuse, just part of the picture. I was in a *whatever* frame of mind. Like I told you, we do need more balance. I'm all for the work-play team-building concept, but it's claustrophobic. We have to get out."

"You can, any time."

"Yes. And I realize that's on me. But I think some structure to mealtimes would help. When someone starts making dinner, it's hard for the others to leave. There's a sense of obligation."

"I don't see how."

"You've been more than generous with us, Sean. This house is spectacular. And we have every comfort we could want. And I think with that comes a subtle pressure that we should enjoy it as much as possible — that there's no need to join a gym or go to a bar or out to eat, to meet other people, when everything is right here. Even friendship, and potentially, sex."

"So?"

"My point is, autonomy needs to be emphasized more. I think an assigned night for each of us to cook, with the expectation that on other evenings, we'll go our separate ways, will help."

He nodded.

"Also, I don't want any weirdness between us. I drank a bit more than normal, I wanted to fuck. No strings. That was all. You didn't want to, end of story."

"I didn't mean to hurt your feelings. Or insult you. You're a gorgeous woman."

She didn't smile or respond. That wasn't the point and he wasn't getting it. "No hurt feelings. No imagined insult. I wanted something, you didn't."

"I took a vow."

"I'm not looking for an explanation."

"But I want you to understand."

"It's not necessary."

He put his hands on the table, palms flat, fingers spread. His hands were as beautiful as the rest of him. How would those hands feel on her body? Were they warm? Cool? She ran her fingertips over the edge of the wood. It was slightly warm. Did he feel that?

"Look at me, Tess."

She lifted her head.

"I want to tell you. I need to tell you."

"I don't think you do."

"It's important to me."

"Why?"

"Because it will make it more real. It's all been inside my head. And now…"

"What's different now?"

He pulled his hands off the table. He gestured to the side, pointing at nothing, simply moving his hands as if he needed to do something physical. "Everything that happened…the police thinking I had something to do with Karen's death. I didn't."

Tess sipped her drink and let her gaze wander away from his face. He was too intense for her to keep looking at his eyes, so full of whatever was roiling inside his head.

"Yes, I saw her outside. But I didn't talk to her. I saw her standing there, holding the scotch bottle. That's all. She wasn't even near the pool. She walked to the lounge chair and nearly collapsed onto it. I figured she'd pass out, or get cold and go home."

Tess turned back to him. So that's what he'd meant. Women showing up naked. If he hadn't tried to hide that from the detectives, he probably would have saved all of them a lot of headaches.

"It wasn't my fault," he said. "I know when to take responsibility, and I know how far my responsibility goes. Her being in my backyard was her choice. And taking off her clothes. And drowning herself. All of that was her choice. It had nothing to do with me. I never suggested, by anything I did, that I was interested."

"Is that why she killed herself here? To get back at you?" Tess felt like laughing — how dramatic. How demeaning. She restrained the laugh.

"That was suggested."

She took a sip of her drink.

"I made a vow. Because I did feel responsible, another time."

"For what?"

"I was in a relationship. It was pretty intense, but I wasn't sure about things. I thought I was in love, maybe. But I wasn't a hundred percent sure."

She gave him a small, hopefully encouraging smile, although she wasn't sure she wanted to encourage him. Sex with him was one thing. Intimacy rising out of shared hurts from the past was something much more threatening to their working relationship. Didn't he see that?

"My first company was in talks for a possible acquisition. I knew there would be a lot of money. Head-turning money. Personality-altering money. And I wasn't sure how she, Terri, would change, with that much money. We hadn't been together that long. And I wasn't sure I was ready to share that with her. I think that was the main thing. It was my company. My work. My vision. I don't mean to sound full of myself, but..."

"You don't."

"Good, because it's the simple truth. I just wasn't sure about her, or us. So I broke up with her."

"A few weeks later, she went climbing with her sister on some mountain in Nepal. She wasn't prepared for it physically. She had a bad fall and died."

"How terrible. But that's not your fault."

"In a way, it was. She wouldn't have gone if I wasn't so selfish."

"But you weren't sure."

"The head-turning, life-changing money turned *my* head. I was greedy. I doubted my feelings for her because I let the money be more important than she was."

"I don't think…"

"I know it's the truth. I searched my own mind. It's how the idea for the app started — being brutally honest with my own thoughts."

She put the straw in her mouth and sipped out a steady stream of vodka and tomato juice. There was something more. She felt it coming.

"Terri was pregnant."

"Oh. How sad."

"She told me after I ended it. But she was upset. Screaming. She told me in a rage, and swore I'd never get to hold my child, I'd never even see it."

"Oh. Oh, wow…"

"Yeah."

"But still, what happened wasn't your fault."

"After she died, I felt the world was out of balance. I felt I'd contributed to her death, and the child's. I had the idea to take this vow, to avoid sex, the drive to procreate, for two years."

"But you're not procreating." She laughed, hoping it didn't sound insensitive. But really…

"That's why we have the drive. I feel there's a balance that needs to be restored."

"If you say so."

"I do. I really believe this. And I feel good about it. I know it's the right thing. For me."

She was glad he added that last part.

"Anyway, I wanted you to know. I wasn't rejecting you."

"I didn't feel rejected." It was the truth. She honestly hadn't felt it. Her reaction was more shock at the unexpected.

Thinking about how he was — so in tune with the natural world, so concerned about the preservation of the planet, his devotion to the Great Barrier Reef and his concern for its future, she understood. He was a very spiritually-minded person. It made a little bit of sense. But a vow? It wouldn't accomplish anything. It wouldn't save the woman he'd loved or their child. His vow was as effective as people who believed that shouting out their point of view on Twitter would persuade others to change. Again, she wanted to laugh, and resisted.

71

The four of us were sitting on the patio finishing a platter of baby back ribs marinated overnight and barbecued by Gavin. Tess had made a huge bowl of German potato salad. Gavin had also grilled artichoke hearts, eggplant, and peppers.

Gavin and Sean were drinking beer, Tess and I were drinking a Zinfandel-Cab blend. It was rich and dark and made the amazing food taste even better.

I couldn't get my head around the beer. Beer comes across like a flavor that wants to stand on its own, dominating the meal. Like a pompous man who takes over the conversation and turns everything in his direction, beer shoves the subtlety of other tastes into a dark corner. Like a police officer who thinks men are the only half of the species that possess good investigative instincts.

Over the course of the past few days, Gavin and Tess had both poked around on the Facebook page. They wanted to see the ongoing results of the live demo, but they'd been sidetracked by Carmen Dunn and her effort to undermine the TruthTeller brand. We'd discussed it over dinner, but Sean hadn't participated much. We hadn't come to a conclusion.

Finally, we agreed there was no conclusion to be had. Every possible course of action had the potential to make things worse.

"Who knows what a vengeful woman will do," Tess said.

She nibbled on a rib that had only a few pieces of meat clinging to the bone, making it seem as if she were considering the pleasure Carmen might have of gnawing on the bones of TruthTeller.

No one looked at me when she said it. Why would they?

I smiled and settled back in my chair. I took a sip of wine. Who knew indeed.

Bender surely did, if there was any consciousness beyond the grave. We'd heard a news report covering his fall from the tenth floor. Suicide was mentioned. Homicide was alluded to. No one was interviewed for the story, which made it seem as if they weren't treating it as something important. The focus was the horrific nature of the fall and the inadequate height of the railings on those hotel balconies.

After another bottle of wine and vanilla ice cream bars encased in chocolate, Sean said he was going to bed. A few minutes later, Tess did the same.

Gavin and I sat in silence. Soon, the lights by the pool went out and we drank in the surrounding darkness.

I finished the last of my wine. "Will you teach me to swim?"

"Sure."

He didn't say anything more. I wondered what he thought of the sudden request, but I liked that he didn't push for details. He thought I'd forgotten, and forgiven Sean for throwing me into the water, but I hadn't. I didn't like Sean knowing I had a weak spot he could exploit. Maybe learning to swim would give me the upper hand with him.

Who knows what a vengeful woman will do.

A Note to Readers

Thanks for reading. I hope you liked reading about Alexandra as much as I enjoy writing her stories.

I'm passionate about fiction that explores the shadows of suburban life and the dark corners of the human mind. To me, the human psyche is, as they say in Star Trek — the final frontier — a place we'll never fully understand. I'm fascinated by characters who are damaged, neurotic, and obsessed.

I love to stay in touch with readers. Visit me at my website: CathrynGrant.com

To find out when the next Alexandra Mallory novel is available you can sign up for my new book mailing list here: CathrynGrant.com/contact.

As a thank you for signing up, you'll receive a free Alexandra short story — *Death Valley*.

www.ingramcontent.com/pod-product-compliance
Lightning Source LLC
Chambersburg PA
CBHW021130260626
47169CB00005B/1545